WAISTCOATS & WEAPONRY

WAISTCOATS & WEAPONRY

FINISHING SCHOOL ✳ BOOK THE THIRD

GAIL CARRIGER

www.atombooks.net

ATOM

First published in the United States in 2014 by Little, Brown and Company
First published in Great Britain in 2014 by Atom

A CIP catalogue record for this book
is available from the British Library.

ISBN 978-1-907411-61-8

Typeset in Goudy by M Rules
Printed and bound in Great Britain by
Clays Ltd, St Ives plc

Papers used by Atom are from well-managed forests
and other responsible sources.

MIX
Paper from
responsible sources
FSC www.fsc.org   FSC® C104740

Atom
An imprint of
Little, Brown Book Group
100 Victoria Embankment
London EC4Y 0DY

An Hachette UK Company
www.hachette.co.uk

www.atombooks.net

For Rhonda:
She glittered.

SESSION 1

Beware Vampires Wearing Flowerpots

'Funambulist,' said Sophronia Temminnick, quite suddenly.

'Sophronia, such language!' Dimity Plumleigh-Teignmott reprimanded.

'Pardon?' said Agatha Woosmoss.

Sidheag Maccon, the final member of Sophronia's group, muttered, 'Bless you.'

'I wasn't sneezing, nor being indelicate, thank you all very much. I was thinking out loud.'

'As if thinking out loud weren't *decidedly* indelicate.' Dimity was not to be swayed out of disapproval when she felt it might exercise her creativity.

'*Funambulist*. Do you think that's what Professor Braithwope was, you know, *professionally*, before he became a vampire? A tightrope walker in a carnival?'

'I suppose it's possible,' said Dimity, mollified.

With which, the four girls all returned to staring over the railing of the squeak deck. They were, theoretically, in class with some ten fellow pupils and Professor Braithwope. It was their vampire teacher's custom of late to administer decidedly oddball lessons. Which is to say, more oddball than an ordinary lesson with a vampire in a floating dirigible espionage school.

It was a drizzly January evening, 1853, the sun recently set, and Professor Braithwope was currently twirling back and forth along the thin plank that stretched from the forward-most squeak deck's railing to the pilot's bubble. He was leagues up in the air.

Sophronia had watched the professor run that particular plank with deadly grace the very first day she came aboard Mademoiselle Geraldine's Finishing Academy for Young Ladies of Quality. She'd never anticipated watching him *dance* along it. Admittedly, he danced with no less grace than he ran, performing some sedate quadrille with an imaginary partner. However, he was doing so while balancing a flowerpot on his head, one that contained Sister Mattie's prize foxglove. Before his troubles, Professor Braithwope would never leave his room without a top hat occupying that sacred spot on his glossy brown coiffure. But for months his behaviour had become increasingly erratic; witness the fact that he also wore an old-fashioned black satin cape with a high collar and scarlet lining. His fangs were extended, causing him to lisp slightly, and he punctuated his quadrille with a maniacal laugh that, if inscribed for posterity, might have been written as 'Mua ha ha'.

'Should one of us go after him?' Sophronia worried that he

would fall to his doom. Plummeting to the moor would snap his tether to the dirigible, and it was tether-snap that had caused his madness in the first place.

'Why?' Preshea turned to her. 'Are you some kind of tightrope walker yourself?'

Since the dratted Monique had matriculated on to a new life as drone to Westminster vampire hive, Miss Preshea Buss had taken over all residual nastiness. She netted herself a group of stylish associates from among the new debuts, too young to know better.

Sophronia ignored Preshea and looked at Dimity. 'What do you think?'

Professor Braithwope pirouetted. Far below, the wet grasses and prickly gorse slid by, partly visible through the mist.

'Perhaps someone should go for matron?' suggested Dimity.

'Or Lady Linette?' said Agatha.

'Is it all that different from any of our other lessons with the idiot?' asked Preshea. She and the rest of the class enjoyed the fact that their hours spent with Professor Braithwope had turned into a free-for-all with little guidance or actual work.

'He's not usually this bad.' Sophronia didn't wish to be thought a goody-goody, especially not at a school of espionage, but she wanted their old mercurial professor back: the one who taught them to manipulate vampire politics; to use fashion to confuse and kill; to interact with government, high society and curling tongs. This new vampire was bonkers, in a flowerpot-wearing way, and not at all useful. She understood why the school kept him on. Since he was tethered here, he must stay on board and couldn't be retired groundside. So far, he didn't *seem* dangerous to anyone but himself, but it was difficult to forget that he was a crazy immortal and they all were, in the end, food.

Sophronia's green eyes narrowed. Perhaps he was being used as a new kind of lesson: how to deal with a risky vampire in a powerful position.

Professor Braithwope whirled to face the sea of staring faces: a dozen bright, pretty young ladies, confused, amused and concerned by his quadrille. 'Ah, class! There you are, whot. Now remember, no matter how high, there is always time for frivolity or politics, whot?'

Sophronia perked up. Were they about to *learn* something?

'Speech,' encouraged Preshea.

'We are all Queen Victoria's subjects, vampire or werewolf. We owe her allegiance. Only in England do we have a voice, a vote and a snack. We help build the Empire, we keep our noble island strong.'

Sophronia frowned. This was not new information. This was simply the progressive party stance.

'We have been members since King Henry's day. Or should I say night? My, but he was *fat*. And no pickle should relish that sandwich!' He finished there, arms wide.

The young ladies all clapped politely.

'Now, who would like to dance? One of you must be willing to trip the light mahogany? Miss Temminnick? You would not deny me a dance, whot?'

Sophronia adjusted her skirts. This might be the only way to get him back on to the squeak deck.

'Now, Sophronia,' warned Dimity, 'don't do anything hasty.'

She was one of the few who knew that Sophronia felt guilty over their teacher's insane condition.

Sophronia levered herself on to the railing and from there, the plank. It was just as narrow and as slippery as she expected. Her wide, heavy dress – held out with multiple petticoats – acted as ballast. She inched towards the vampire, not looking down.

At one point she slipped slightly and wobbled, arms pin-wheeling.

Behind her, all the gathered young ladies gasped.

Dimity let out a small shriek.

Sophronia heard Agatha say, 'I can't watch. Tell me when it's over.'

'Sophronia!' said Preshea. 'Come back here this instant. What are you doing? What if you fall? Can you imagine the scandal? This is ridiculous. Agatha, go fetch Lady Linette. Sophronia's going to get all of us into trouble. Really, Sophronia, why must you always spoil everyone's fun?'

Sophronia moved closer to Professor Braithwope.

'Ah, Miss Temminnick, how kind of you to join me. Would you care to dance?'

'No, thank you, Professor.' She struggled to guide his fantasy back to safety. 'But perhaps you could fetch me a little punch? I'm parched.'

'Punch is it, whot?' The vampire tapped her lightly on the chin with his closed fist. 'Mua ha ha! Aren't I droll? Of course, my dear girl, of course. But would you like blood punch or brain punch?' He paused, shook his head, and then said in a small voice, 'Oh, wait, where ... Miss Temminnick! What are you doing here? Whot whot?'

'You invited me, sir.'

'I did? Why would I do that? What are you doing at a Buckingham Palace supernatural reception? You aren't even out yet. Plus, I'm tolerably certain you aren't a supernatural. You aren't high enough rank, either. Although I suppose we are both tolerably high up, whot.'

'You were going to fetch me some punch, sir?'

'Was I?' He lowered his voice to a whisper. 'I don't think Queen Victoria likes punch. In fact, I know she doesn't. Would a glass of resin do? For the wood. A nice sealant. Necessary in weather like this. They're collecting crystals, did you know? Pretty round ones, crystals to rule the world. Then there are mechanicals to think about. I don't trust them, do you? No, exactly! Not with punch, at any rate.'

Sophronia remembered Westminster Hive. 'Do any vampires trust mechanicals?'

'No. Nor do our brother werewolves. Why should they, whot? I mean to say, why should we? I am a vampire, am I not?'

'Yes, Professor, have been for hundreds of years.'

'That long? Miss Temminnick, you should come with me.' With that, Professor Braithwope picked Sophronia up bodily under one arm and carried her *away* from the squeak deck towards the pilot's bubble, mincing along the plank.

The pilot's bubble was the size of two very large bathtubs, one overturned on top of the other. It was supported from below by scaffolding but was otherwise far from the safety of the airship.

Professor Braithwope set her down on top of the bubble on a flat area big enough for two.

'Now what, sir?' Sophronia asked politely.

'Miss Temminnick, what are you doing on top of the pilot's bubble?'

'You just put me here, sir.'

'Oh, yes. Now, would you like to dance?'

'If you insist. There doesn't seem to be a great deal of space.'

'It is quite the rout, whot? I've never known Buckingham to be so crowded. Usually, the queen is more selective. Why, I believe there are even clavigers present. I mean, drones are one thing, but clavigers are little more than prison wardens! Not to worry, little bite, I'll do most of the work.' He began a gentle waltz on top of the bubble. He was inhumanly strong and unbelievably well balanced. Sophronia trusted in his ability to hold her up and hoped he wouldn't suddenly forget about her, or think she was a hat and try to wear her instead of the flowerpot.

'Professor Braithwope, really!' came an autocratic voice from the squeak deck.

Agatha had returned with Lady Linette.

'Put Miss Temminnick down and come back here this instant. Shameful behaviour, sir.'

The vampire looked like a crestfallen schoolboy and stopped waltzing. Mademoiselle Geraldine was the official headmistress, but everyone knew Lady Linette held the real power. Accordingly, the vampire let Sophronia go, turned, and dashed back along the beam.

Sophronia slipped on the bubble roof. Her feet went out from under her, and she slid over the side. Her petticoats bunched and snagged on a loose nail, but not enough to do more than slow her fall.

Several of the watching young ladies screamed in horror.

Fortunately, Sophronia was accustomed to gallivanting about the hull of the ship. Her instincts kicked in. Instead of grappling for purchase, she reached one hand over to the opposite wrist. Pointing that wrist up, she ejected her hurlie. The hurlie looked a bit like a turtle one wore as a bracelet, but when it was deployed, two grappling hooks sprang out from underneath. The hurlie arced up and over the bubble, taking hold on the other side. It trailed a rope, so Sophronia fell only that distance before her left arm was fairly jerked out of its socket. She got her right hand around the rope to relieve the strain and found herself dangling like a fish at the end of a line.

'Miss Temminnick,' she heard Lady Linette cry, 'report your condition.'

'Sophronia,' shrieked Dimity, 'are you all right? Oh, dear, oh, dear.'

Shocked and winded, Sophronia needed a moment before she could answer either.

'Professor Braithwope, go after her!' Lady Linette ordered.

'Dear Madam,' protested the vampire, 'must protect the other young ladies from an equally dire fate.' With which there came the sound of splintering wood.

Sophronia twirled sedately at the end of her rope, eventually able to witness the vampire destroying his former dancing beam with his bare hands.

'Professor, stop that immediately!' instructed Lady Linette.

'Sophronia, are you well? Oh, please answer.' Dimity again.

Sophronia mustered enough breath to yell back, 'I'm perfectly fine. However, it appears I am now stranded.' She couldn't see any way to climb up to the deck or down along the bubble's scaffolding to return to the ship. Fortunately, the pilot's bubble remained in place, although it did sway a bit more without the added stabilisation of the beam.

'Miss Temminnick,' said Lady Linette. 'Where did you get that ingenious hook thing?'

'A friend,' replied Sophronia.

'Unregistered gadgetry is not allowed on school grounds, young lady. Although I find myself pleased you had this particular one to hand. Or to wrist, I should say.'

Sophronia, still spinning serenely through space, replied with, 'I do apologise, Lady Linette, but might we discuss this later? Perhaps now we should solve my immediate predicament?'

'Of course, dear,' yelled her teacher, and then, distracted, 'No, Professor Braithwope, not the soldier mechanicals. Bad vampire!'

'Lady Linette?' hollered Sophronia, feeling neglected.

'Yes, dear. If you could climb up to the underside of the pilot's bubble? You'll find a hatch to get inside just there. We'll use capsule pipeline eggs to communicate with you once you're safe. I'll send Professor Lefoux. She's better at these sorts of engineering difficulties.'

How, wondered Sophronia, *is my dangling off the bubble an engineering difficulty?* She said, 'Very good, thank you.'

She spun around enough to see back up to the squeak deck, in time to witness Lady Linette dash after the mincing Professor Braithwope. 'Now, now, Professor, please!' He was still wearing his potted plant.

She saw Sister Mattie's round, drab form appear and heard that teacher say, 'My dears, have you seen my prize foxglove? Oh, no, Professor, really? I spent weeks on that one!' She bounced up and down, attempting to extract the plant from Professor Braithwope's head.

The assembled young ladies, with the exception of Dimity, Agatha and Sidheag, found the spectacle of Sophronia dangling no longer to their taste and turned to follow the high jinks of their teachers.

'Sophronia,' came Dimity's voice, 'will you be all right?' Her face was wrinkled with genuine worry.

'Can we help in any way?' Agatha wanted to know. She, too, worried, but was less aggressive about it.

'Want some company?' said Sidheag. She rarely worried about anything and had complete confidence in Sophronia's ability to extract herself from any predicament.

'Oh, dear me, no,' replied Sophronia, as if she had a mild case of the sniffles and they had called round to enquire after her health. 'Thank you for your concern, but don't linger on my account.'

'Well . . . ' Dimity was hesitant. 'If you're certain?'

'I'll see you at tea,' said Sophronia, sounding more confident than she felt.

'Either that or we shall come back up here in an hour and toss crumpets to you.'

'Oh, how thoughtful, tossed crumpets. Thank you, Sidheag.'

'Can't have you starving as you dangle.'

'No, I suppose not.'

'Bye for now.' Agatha turned reluctantly away.

Dimity said, lingering, 'Are you *quite* certain?'

'Quite.'

'Carry on, then, Sophronia,' said Sidheag with a grin, before marching off. Her tall, bony form somehow transmitted sarcastic humour even across all the empty space that separated them.

Sophronia was left suspended and alone.

Despite her wrenched shoulder, Sophronia managed to climb up the rope hand over hand – she had indecently large arm muscles for a young lady of quality. By dint of some fancy footwork and the tension from her hurlie, she wiggled around the outside of the bubble to the hatch. It was difficult to open, as if it had not been used in a long time. It was also narrow. Her skirts were so wide she stoppered up the opening like a wine cork. She had to ease herself back out and shed two petticoats, utilising a one-handed unlacing technique. They fluttered to the moor, doomed to cause confusion to a small herd of shaggy ponies that roamed there. She was resigned to the loss. Espionage, Sophronia had learned, was tough on petticoats. After that she squeezed through, finding herself, with a good deal of relief, inside the pilot's bubble.

Sophronia didn't know what she'd expected. Some wizened man who spent his days cooped up in a bathtub? But the bubble was not designed for human occupation at all.

The front had three small portholes, through which, on a rare clear day, all of Dartmoor would be laid out like a tablecloth. Tonight the view was nothing but dark drizzle.

The whole forward half of the bubble was filled with

engorged mechanical. Had it been human, it would have been one of those gentlemen who partook too freely of the pudding course and too little of daily exercise. Most mechanicals were human sized and mimicked the shape of a lady's dress – which is to say smaller on the top, wider on the bottom. Or perhaps it was ladies' fashion that imitated the shape of mechanicals? Skirts were getting so ridiculously wide, one was hard pressed to walk down a hallway without knocking things over. Mechanicals were more reasonably sized … except this one. This one could give Preshea in her most fashionable ballgown stiff competition. Its lower extremities formed a pile of machinery, not hidden under a respectable carapace but exposed and horribly functional. Perched on top of this was a normal mechanical brain, facing forward. It boasted multiple arms, like a spider. Occasionally, it reached out one claw-like appendage and pulled a lever or twiddled a switch.

'Pardon me for introducing myself, Mr Mechanical. I'm Miss Temminnick. Are you equipped with verbal protocols?'

The pilot ignored her. Perhaps it did not have the ability to see that a wayward pupil had climbed into its domain. Lacking options, Sophronia explored. There wasn't much: a few ropes, a cornucopia of tools and that squatting mechanical. She brushed off her skirts and sat down atop a tall leather hatbox thing. She ran an assessment of her physical condition, finding herself basically unharmed, simply sore. She considered how to retrieve her grappling hook, still embedded on the outside of the bubble. Her only option might be to climb back out, using one of the ropes as a safety line.

A whooshing noise interrupted her thoughts. An egg-shaped pod spat out of a tube and skidded along a specially designed trough. One of the mechanical's arms came crashing down and cracked the egg open.

Sophronia jumped and squeaked at the suddenness of it.

The mechanical reached out with yet another of its appendages and unrolled the paper within. The paper was perforated with small holes of variable location. This the mechanical rested on a reader that looked like the voice coil of a standard mechanical – music box technology.

Another arm turned a crank and the paper fed through. Sophronia supposed this would normally issue a set of protocols to the mechanical on how to pilot the ship, but in this case it caused the tinny voice of an underused vocal-quadringer to read instructions.

'Rope ladder stashed below Pirandellope Probe, near feeding tube for capsule pipeline.'

Sophronia knew the instructions were for her. Somehow, even though the sound was mechanised and lacked emphasis, the message conveyed Professor Lefoux's special brand of French disinterest.

On Fans and Flirting

'That's it?' Sidheag was disappointed in Sophronia's desultory description of the pilot's bubble.

'When did you get interested in technology?' replied Sophronia.

'It's not that; I was hoping that after we left, you would fall to your doom. Something exciting for once.'

'Thank you kindly, Lady Kingair. The fact that I was initially dropped overboard by a vampire wasn't exciting enough for you?'

'Not with you, Sophronia, it wasn't.' Sidheag passed over the buttered pikelets without having to be asked.

'I spoil you, that's the problem.' Sophronia, secretly flattered, deposited a pikelet on to her plate.

Sidheag's masculine face lit up with a grin.

Teatime conversation flowed smoothly among the members of their little band. Over a year and a half's association and Sophronia would have described the other three as *confidantes extraordinaire.* The best part being that she knew they felt the same way about her. Each had her own set of abilities. Sidheag had stoic strength. Dimity a guileless craftiness. Agatha ... well, perhaps Agatha was a bit of a wet blanket. She was loyal to a fault and she did try. She tried too hard sometimes.

As if to illustrate this, the chubby redhead looked suddenly panicked and began to pat her person and rifle through her reticule. 'What class do we have after tea?' she asked, voice wobbling.

Dimity looked up from applying strawberry jam to her pikelet. 'Captain Niall. It's Thursday, we always have him on Thursdays, unless the moon is full. Really, Agatha dear, how could you forget? It's *Captain Niall!*'

Agatha was relieved. 'Oh, that's all right. Unless ... we weren't meant to bring anything, were we? Scissors, or paperweights, or wheat paste, or ... ?'

'No,' Sidheag answered. She was *always* prepared for Captain Niall's classes. They were her favourite, and not only because he was a proper bit of sweetmeat. Sidheag liked weapons training. She was Scottish, after all. 'We're moving on from deadly library supplies to something else this evening. He didn't say what.' She tugged on her earlobe, uncomfortable. Sophronia wasn't certain if that was because she didn't know what was going on or because of Captain Niall. Sophronia suspected Sidheag of harbouring a good deal of romantic interest in their werewolf professor. Of course, half the young ladies of Mademoiselle Geraldine's tendered feelings in his direction. Captain Niall was quite dashing. Sidheag, either because she was embarrassed to acknowledge any emotion or because she was disgusted with herself for belonging to a popular movement, had yet to confess said interest.

Sophronia, as a result, rather enjoyed teasing her on the subject. 'Didn't say? Not even to you? But I thought you two were so close.'

Sidheag walked right into her trap. 'Not that close! He doesn't share lesson plans with me.'

'Well, then, does he share something else?'

Dimity was feeling equally mischievous. 'Dead rabbits, perhaps? Laying his kill at your feet.'

'What?' Sidheag was genuinely confused.

Dimity was not to be turned aside. 'As if we didn't see you nuzzling up to the lovely captain regularly.'

Sidheag objected to this unwarranted accusation. 'Nuzzling! He's ten times my age!'

Dimity waved an airy hand. 'Immortals usually are, and he certainly still cuts a fine figure.'

Sophronia nudged Sidheag's shoulder. 'And you know werewolves. I mean to say, *you* know them.' They so rarely got to rib Sidheag.

The Scottish girl actually blushed.

Mindful of her chamber-mate's finer feelings, Agatha returned them to the subject of preparing for class. 'Well, thank goodness it's him. I was sure we had Lady Linette, and I've misplaced my chewing tobacco for card rooms and informant recruiting.'

'Again? Really, Agatha.' Sidheag was unsympathetic.

'To be fair, yesterday it was the lip tint. If you only kept your side of the room cleaner.'

'You can't blame me for your absent-mindedness.'

'Yes, I can.' Agatha only really had any gumption with Sidheag. Which was funny, because Sidheag was so gruff and Agatha so timid. But after months of their living together, Agatha had learned to stick up for herself. Sidheag was a big softy underneath her grumbling. It came, they all suspected, from being raised by werewolves. As Dimity said, 'Sidheag surely does grumpy old man very well for a sixteen-year-old girl.'

'Are you four going to sit there gossiping all night?' Preshea was standing above them, looking down her nose. A rare opportunity for the girl, as she was quite short.

The dining room was empty. Somehow, they had missed the mass exodus. The maid mechanicals were beginning to clear the tea tables.

'Oh, I see, you're waiting to gather up the extra pikelets, so Agatha can have a snack later.' Preshea had a very clipped way of talking, as though each word were murdered just after being spoken.

At the dig over her portly frame, Agatha teared up.

Dimity gasped and put her hand to her lips.

Sophronia was so perturbed by the direct nature of the attack that she lacked a ready rebuttal.

Sidheag, on the other hand, simply threw her mostly uneaten pikelet at Preshea.

'Lady Kingair,' said Preshea, shocked, 'this is a new gown!'

'Well, you shouldn't go around being nasty when the rest of us are armed with nibbly bits, should you?' Sidheag was unperturbed by the smear of jam that now decorated Preshea's décolletage.

Preshea flounced off, still in possession of verbal superiority. After all, they ought to have responded with wit, not flying pancakes. But Agatha looked cheered by Sidheag's pikelet defence.

Dimity sniffed. 'That girl is like walking, talking indigestion. Sophronia, can't we *do* something about her?'

Sophronia frowned. 'I don't know if it's worth the risk. They've been watching me closely since the Westminster Hive incident.'

'Please?' Dimity gave her big hazel-eyed look of appeal.

'I'll think about it. Now come on; we're late, and the staircase won't wait.'

They abandoned the last of the pikelets uneaten and trooped down after the rest of the pupils towards the midship deck. Before they could catch the other young ladies, however, they were waylaid.

'Lady Kingair, a moment of your time, please?'

Professor Lefoux was the most fearsome teacher at the school. Her subjects included deadly gadgetry, high-impact weaponry and infiltrating academia. Even Sophronia was equal parts terrified and impressed by her visage, attitude and abilities. However, she was not the type of teacher to accost one in the hallways, nor intercept a pupil when she was already late for class.

Sidheag, controlling her surprise, faced the austere lady. They were almost of a height. Professor Lefoux was the only person at the school next to whom Sidheag's governess-like attire seemed soft and approachable.

The professor, Sophronia always felt, looked as if she had

been sticking her head out the side of a very fast carriage. All her hair was pulled back from her unlined face, making her seem stretched.

'Yes, Professor, how may I help you?' Even Sidheag knew when to be polite.

'You have received' – Professor Lefoux paused, distressed, if such a thing were to be thought possible – 'a *pigeon*.'

The girls gasped. Pigeons were for emergency use only.

Sidheag blanched. 'Has someone died? Is it Gramps? Has he been challenged?'

Professor Lefoux glanced at the other three girls, who nudged up to their friend sympathetically. 'It is a private matter. This way, please. *Alone*, young lady.' She turned and strode down the hallway, expecting Sidheag to follow.

Dimity gave the taller girl's arm a reassuring squeeze. 'Good luck.'

The three watched until Sidheag was out of sight round a bend in the passageway.

'What do you think could possibly require such extreme measures?' wondered Dimity.

Agatha and Sophronia looked at each other.

'Problems with the pack,' said Sophronia, 'has to be. Only a crisis in the supernatural community warrants *the pigeon*.'

Agatha nodded, upset. They all knew how devoted Sidheag was to her pack of werewolf uncles. Plus, crises in the supernatural community rarely stayed localised.

They proceeded to their next lesson minus one companion, and a great deal more sombre as a result.

*

Captain Niall's classes took place groundside, on the moor proper. Like all werewolves, he was unable to float. His classes also involved all the pupils at the school together, some thirty-eight or so, fewer than when Sophronia had first arrived. Many of the older girls had gone out into society, and Mademoiselle Geraldine's hadn't taken on an equivalent number of debuts.

The school sank as far as it safely could, the propeller whirling to steady the airship against the winds, and the staircase folded down. The deployment crank was manned by a couple of sooties up from engineering. One of them – a tall, good-looking young man with ebony skin and a quick white smile – issued Sophronia a private wink. She should, of course, have been shocked by such forwardness from an underling, but Soap was one of Sophronia's best friends and favourite people in the world. So she winked back – when she knew none of the teachers were watching, of course.

Once the staircase settled, partly sunk into the green grasses, the young ladies trooped down.

Captain Niall was waiting for them. Their werewolf teacher was a truly handsome beast, if one overlooked the fact that his top hat was tied neatly under his chin, he wore no shoes, and his carefully buttoned greatcoat did not quite conceal that the rest of him was indecently bare. For some of the young ladies, not overlooking these facts actually increased the man's appeal.

'Good evening, ladies,' said Captain Niall in his velvet voice. 'And how are we tonight?' The girls chorused polite replies, some of them blushing; the youngest ones – not yet trained in the correct method – curtsied too deeply. Sophronia was pleased to note that her curtsy was nearly perfect.

'Follow me, if you would?'

Captain Niall led them down the hill to a small stream. He produced a leather case from the depths of his greatcoat. About the size of a lady's jewellery case, it looked particularly dainty in his large hands. Despite his size, Captain Niall had a harmless, floppy demeanour. Most people forgot that he was, in actuality, a supernatural creature who could decapitate the average ruffian as easily as peeling an orange, and probably faster.

'Now, on to this month's weapon.'

What weapon is so tiny thirty-eight of them fit into such a small case? Sophronia wondered.

With a flourish, the werewolf flipped the lid, displaying the contents. The case was full of fans – clunky and not very pretty fans, at that.

'Ladies, please form a queue. One each.'

The girls lined up by age and each received a fan. Sophronia was startled by how heavy hers was. Close examination showed that the fan's leaves were fabric but its ribs and guards were metal, the tips razor sharp. *A fan that is also a weapon, ingenious!*

Captain Niall began to demonstrate movements. Many of the techniques were similar to those of the letter opener, in whose deadly application they'd already received much instruction. He expanded on their existing repertoire, with butterfly-like movements. There were sharp, quick slashes designed to surprise. There was no stabbing with the fan; the idea was to disarm and disable, not kill. It was amusing to see a werewolf waving a fan about like some imitation of an exotic dancer in the music halls.

The girls practised with leather guards over their fans, for safety. This also kept Dimity from fainting. Over a year and a half of training to be an intelligencer and Dimity still fainted at the sight of blood. Poor thing, she wasn't meant for this lifestyle.

Sophronia adored the bladed fan the moment she took it through the first pass. As a result, she tried extra hard to master the movements. Captain Niall was impressed. After an hour's work, he summoned her forward.

'Miss Temminnick, Miss Buss? You're both looking well. How about a small duel?' The teacher's mellow brown eyes shone with anticipated glee.

Sophronia had never before faced Preshea one-to-one, but she was game. Particularly after Preshea's dig against Agatha.

Preshea gave her a nasty smile, tucked a stray lock of glossy black hair behind one perfect, shell-like ear, and took up the guard position. Or at least Sophronia assumed it was guard position – hard to tell in skirts. One of the advantages of being a fighting female: legs were, for all practical purposes, invisible.

Their movements were cautious and clumsy at first, nothing like Captain Niall's speedy grace. Preshea mostly attacked and Sophronia mostly defended.

Captain Niall shouted instructions, which Sophronia – at least – tried to obey.

'Miss Temminnick, try the treble clef defence. Miss Buss, the *fleur de lys* attack. Well done! And now, Miss Temminnick, the pirouette. Oh, look, ladies, she's already doing it.'

The girls crowded around, fascinated.

Captain Niall switched from instruction to commentary.

'Now Miss Temminnick has taken up the Valkyrie flip. Note the curves of her movements? And a very nice snap of the wrist there from Miss Buss.'

Sophronia caught the flicker of the werewolf's hands as he gestured for the other pupils to collectively do something, but her attention was taken up with Preshea.

The ground beneath her feet became uneven and squishy. Captain Niall was using the crowd to herd the two fighters on to the bank of the stream.

Sophronia had barely a moment to realise this, for several things happened in quick succession.

Preshea stripped the leather guard off her fan. With a yell of triumph she cut in, slicing at Sophronia's unprotected face.

Sophronia reeled, raising her free hand in defence. Her pagoda sleeve fell away, exposing the undersleeve. Preshea's fan sliced easily through the muslin and into the flesh below Sophronia's left elbow. A few of the younger girls shrieked. There was a thump and skirts rustled. Dimity had fainted.

Captain Niall cried halt, but Preshea was out for more blood. A look came into her beautiful eyes that was more common during poison class. Captain Niall would have intervened, but Sophronia met his eyes briefly and shook her head. She did not strip the guard off her own fan, but she did switch from defence to attack. Also, she began to employ not only the slashing letter-opener technique Captain Niall had taught her but some of the dirty fighting she'd learned from Soap.

She commenced a flurry of quick nips and twists, half-*fleur* attacks designed to alarm but not injure. Preshea was forced to guard, not realising that Sophronia's real intent was to edge about so that she was uphill from her opponent. Soon Sophronia was pressing Preshea back, closer to the stream.

With her injured arm, Sophronia reached for her chatelaine and the small bottle of perfume dangling there, the one they were instructed to carry at all times. She used to stock rose oil, but an incident during her debut had left her with a marked preference for lemon-infused tinctures in a metal flask with snap-top lid.

With Preshea distracted by the wickedly darting fan, Sophronia poured out a quantity of the perfumed alcohol with, and into, her free hand. Then she flicked the liquid into Preshea's eyes.

The girl squealed and stumbled back, straight into the stream, landing on her bottom with a splash. Her beautiful skirts poufed out around her before sagging as they absorbed the muddy water. The skirts – a rich purple colour, in a modern petal cut – looked remarkably like a water lily before they deflated. Afterwards, the dress looked more like a wrinkled old prune.

There was a round of giggles and some gloved applause from their fellow pupils.

Being a true gentleman, Captain Niall went into the stream to offer Preshea a hand up.

'Now, Miss Buss, bloodthirstiness is all well and good, but you ought to have stopped the moment you bloodied Miss Temminnick. First blood always ends a duel.'

Preshea pouted prettily and offered no excuse, although she eagerly accepted his assistance.

The werewolf turned to Sophronia. 'Miss Temminnick, commendable defence. You are to be applauded for not buckling under the pain. Now let Lady Kingair see to your injury. Lady Kingair?'

Of course, Captain Niall would suppose that Sidheag had knowledge of wounds, being the child of a werewolf pack. But Sidheag was not there.

Captain Niall's boyish face looked older when he frowned. 'Where is Lady Kingair? It's not like her to miss my class. Miss Woosmoss?'

Agatha looked panicked by the direct attention of the teacher.

'Called away by Professor Lefoux,' said Sophronia, gritting her teeth at the pain, which, now that she'd stopped running about with a fan, was quite intense. 'She had a pigeon.'

Captain Niall continued to frown. 'A *pigeon*? We shall see about that. Miss Woosmoss, perhaps you would wrap Miss Temminnick's arm? I think you are not the type to faint.'

Agatha nodded, coloured, and shook her head, trying to respond to both statements without actually saying anything.

'Good girl.'

Sophronia, feeling weak, sat down abruptly on the mossy bank, despite the inevitable damage to her own skirts. Oh, well, her dress was probably ruined anyway; blood was near to impossible to get out of silk.

Agatha squeaked and ran over to her.

Rather callously, Captain Niall continued with class. 'Ladies! What did we learn from Miss Temminnick's tactics?'

'She used the terrain to her advantage,' said one.

'Exactly so, obstacles are not always a detriment. What else?'

'Uh, sir,' came a timid voice. 'It's Dimity, sir. She's fainted.'

Captain Niall, well used to Dimity, since his classes were the ones most likely to produce blood, said only, 'Apply the smelling salts to the silly chit, do.'

He turned back to Sophronia. 'The arm?'

'I'll do,' said Sophronia, although the pain was, if possible, more intense under Agatha's ministrations. The redhead had dipped her handkerchief into the stream and was patting clumsily at the gash.

Sophronia realised why the werewolf was keeping his distance and acting so uncaring. She explained in a low voice to Agatha, 'He won't come and check. My blood probably smells too tasty.'

Agatha blanched and looked with wide eyes at their teacher, whose general attitude and demeanour were not significantly different from normal. He was very good at putting on a front. They had learned from Sidheag that this was also a sign of age in werewolves.

Sophronia said to Agatha, 'Why not apply some of my lemon tincture? Sister Mattie always says alcohol helps clean cuts, and the lemon scent will hide the smell of my blood.'

Agatha reached for the little bottle hanging from Sophronia's waist. Since she hadn't recapped it during the fight, most of it had sloshed out, but there was enough left to pour over the wound. Agatha then wrapped Sophronia's arm with her handkerchief.

'All good, Captain Niall,' said Sophronia as Agatha helped her to stand.

The werewolf sniffed and then raised both eyebrows.

'Goodness, I can't even smell ... Miss Woosmoss, what did you do?'

Agatha said tremulously, 'Sophronia's idea, sir. We used her perfume to clean the wound and modify the scent.'

Captain Niall came over. 'Remarkable.' He turned back to the other girls. 'Now, who would like to duel next? Keeping the leather guards on this time, please.'

Sophronia retreated up the bank to sit next to Dimity, who was coming round.

'What did I miss?' Dimity sat up, patting at her bonnet to check the straw for injury.

'Oh, nothing much, I dumped Preshea in the river.' Sophronia gestured to where Preshea stood, bedraggled and shivering in a shawl, surrounded by solicitous girls.

'Oh, bother. That's your best so far.'

Sophronia grinned. 'You know, I might agree with you there.' She looked down at the fan she still held in her good hand. 'I believe I may have to get myself one of these. Do you think they are available on Bond Street or will I have to special order?'

'You will have to order several in different colours to match all your outfits,' said Dimity with conviction. She was always serious about the fashionable side of matters deadly.

Sophronia groaned. 'How will I get Mumsy to outlay? There's Ephraim's engagement ball coming up. She's bound to hold that against me for funding reasons. You've no idea how lucky you are to have only one sibling. Being an intelligencer is rather an expensive undertaking.'

Dimity smiled. 'How about getting a patron? Lady Linette did just instruct us to start considering our options.'

Sophronia grimaced; there were no good options. Everything meant lack of independence. 'Quality marriage or patronage.'

'You have to pay back the school somehow.'

'I'm not ready to marry yet.'

That, Dimity didn't understand. 'Not even Felix Mersey – rich and handsome?'

Sophronia replied, her tone wistful, 'Oh, no, Dimity, you know I couldn't. Sidheag would never forgive me.'

'Why? Oh, because his father is a Pickleman?'

'Sidheag has a supernatural's mistrust of Picklemen.'

Dimity said, 'I'm not deeply keen on them myself.'

Sophronia arched an eyebrow in agreement.

Dimity sighed. 'So no marriage; then what are your plans for patronage after we leave?'

'I hadn't really thought about it. Lord Akeldama seems nice enough – I'm not sure I want to be a vampire's drone, though. Do you think he'd take me on under indenture without a feeding plan?'

Dimity returned to the immediate necessity. 'Regardless, he wants you, so ask him for a fan.'

'What a shocking suggestion.'

'You're keeping what he's sent so far. How is a fan any worse?'

Sophronia paused to consider the odd Lord Akeldama. During a Westminster Hive infiltration, when she and Sidheag had rescued Dimity, Sophronia had met and formulated a strange friendship with the dandy vampire. Seemingly without the ordinary formalities, he had taken her under his wing. He occasionally sent her small goodies of a fashionable, deadly or silly persuasion – often all three. If Sophronia wasn't convinced of the vampire's romantic disinterest, she might have thought them courting gifts. The presents were so lovely she couldn't help but keep them, even though by all standards of decency she ought to have sent them right back to London. Sophronia suspected that actually requesting something specific, like a bladed fan, might be considered presumptuous, or worse, open her up to indenture and contractual obligation. Patronage was a sticky business, especially for a female intelligencer. If only Professor Braithwope were more mentally present. He was the one to ask.

Perhaps she would work on Mumsy first for the necessary, or see if she could get a message to Vieve at Bunson's. Vieve was Professor Lefoux's niece, now under cover of moustache at the local boys' school. A great inventor and friend, she might choose to make a bladed fan as a challenge, or take umbrage with the request, as it had been made before.

Sophronia switched topics. 'Whatever else is the case, I need to pay closer attention to Soap's lessons in dirty fighting. Flicking perfume in the face was his idea.'

'What?'

'Oh, you missed that bit. I slung scent in Preshea's eyes.'

'Jolly good.'

'Soap taught me the technique.'

'Your sootie beau? Of course he would teach you such a thing.'

'He's not my beau!'

'Whatever you say.'

Agatha came wandering over. 'What's going on now?'

'Sophronia's muttering about visiting her sootie beau for more lessons in ungentlewomanly conduct.'

'Oh, dear me, no. Sophronia, I don't think it wise to encourage him.' Agatha paled, making her freckles pop out under the moonlight.

Sophronia blushed. 'Not that kind of thing. I mean dirty fighting.'

Agatha pursed her lips. 'Of course you do.'

Sophronia turned away to watch the other girls fight. She had no way to defend herself on this particular subject. Sometimes she was horribly afraid her friends knew more than she did about her relationship with Soap. Ask her to learn a new weapon and she was ready and able, but learning how to cope with boys and affection still seemed elusive.

Mercifully, Captain Niall left them to recover while the rest of the class practised fanning. An hour or so later, he shuffled them all back up the staircase. Sophronia, Agatha and Dimity were the last up, only to find that Sidheag was waiting patiently at the top.

She was wearing an expression of such unhappiness, they all knew instantly that something was horribly wrong.

SESSION 3

MISSING SIDHEAGS AND MISAPPLIED SEDUCTION

gatha ran the last few steps to the Scottish girl and placed an arm about her waist, squeezing her close. The redhead's round face was puckered in concern.

Sidheag certainly looked in need of that supporting arm. For the first time, Sophronia thought of her friend as willowy and frail, rather than tall and gawky.

'My dear, what has happened?' Dimity demanded, bracing herself as if against a physical blow, her tiny fists clenched.

'Who needs to be killed?' Sophronia asked, trying to lighten the mood but also feeling quite murderous at the very idea that anyone might cause her unflappable friend such pain.

Sidheag dismissed both their offers of support and Agatha's arm. 'I can't ... it's not ... I just ...' Her amber eyes caught the moonlight as she looked past them. 'Captain Niall, please wait! Could you spare a moment to talk? Please?'

The werewolf was preparing to retreat behind a whortle-berry bush to change forms and dash off into the night hunting rabbits, or something equally small and fuzzy.

Instead, he approached the base of the staircase, shading his eyes against the glare of the well-lit ship. He sniffed, not in hauteur, but like an animal tasting the air.

'Lady Kingair, what's wrong?' He sniffed again. His voice changed, becoming rough and gravelly. 'What has happened?'

Sidheag moved away from her friends. 'I must talk to the captain. Only he can help.'

They let her go, reluctantly.

Sidheag stumbled as she climbed down, falling the last few steps.

Captain Niall caught her easily, supernatural strength barely troubled by her weight.

Once in his arms, she folded in on herself, broken.

The werewolf said something to her, so low the girls watching could not hear. Then he set her back on her feet. They were matched in height. Lady Linette would say that they'd dance well together. Except that Sidheag was a terrible dancer.

Sidheag raised her head, saying something soft in reply. Captain Niall responded with a gentle squeeze to the arm. Overcome once more, Sidheag crumpled, shoulders heaving. The werewolf whisked her off, his supernatural speed used in sympathy for once, into the darkness of the moor and away from prying eyes.

Sophronia, Dimity and Agatha were left once again with-out their friend, alone at the top of the stairs. At least

Sidheag's behaviour had not been observed. The shame of it, to show weakness and then affection, with a teacher!

Dimity's hand was pressed to her mouth, her eyes widened against sympathetic tears. Agatha looked almost as shaky as Sidheag, so that Sophronia slipped an arm about her waist. They stood like that for a long time until a polite cough caught Sophronia's attention.

'Miss, we need to crank up the stair.'

Sophronia turned to find Soap, standing shipside.

He looked about to crack one of his customary cheeky smiles. But the moment he saw her expression, he schooled his own and flitted over to join them. 'What in all aether's happened? Sophronia, are you hurt?' Usually he was punctiliously formal. They must look truly upset for him to call Sophronia by name.

'We don't know.' A great deal of frustration coloured Sophronia's voice.

Soap's eyes bored into hers, as if they were alone. 'Not you?' His gaze flicked to her bandaged arm.

Sophronia shook her head. 'No, I'm well. Just a little scrape with a fan. It's Sidheag.'

Dimity tugged at her sleeve. 'I'm sure this is a private matter! Hush.'

'Soap is her friend, too.'

Dimity bit her lip, uncomfortable with sharing anything that had so traumatised Sidheag with an underling, or a boy, or an outsider. Despite Soap's ongoing friendship with Sophronia, Dimity was too much a lady not to see him as all three, all the time.

Dimity hissed, 'Sidheag is *Lady Kingair*. I know that mostly we forget she's all over titled, being Scottish and such, but still, should Lady Kingair *be* friends with a sootie?'

'Oh, Dimity, don't be so snobbish. Sidheag can choose her own friends. And he might know something.'

Soap was clearly chuffed at Sophronia's ready defence. Still, he responded to the meat of the matter. 'Know something? About Lady Kingair? Not recently. Why, is she unwell?'

Sophronia shook her head helplessly. 'Something has gone pear-shaped. She received a pigeon and now she's gone off into the moor with Captain Niall.'

'And she was crying. Sidheag. I shouldn't have thought it possible,' whispered Agatha.

Soap considered. 'Pigeon, huh? I'll see what I can dig up. And now, before we all get into trouble, would you mind backing away from the stair, please? We have orders.'

Much sobered, the three made their way at a run to their next lesson. They had Lady Linette, and even with an emotional crisis of epic proportions, it wasn't done to be late to a lesson with Lady Linette. They couldn't even claim fashion as an excuse – Lady Linette forgave tardiness on account of style. But all three of them had grass stains on their gowns, and Sophronia's sleeve was ripped and bloody. They were certain to get into trouble.

'Girls, why are you so very late?' Lady Linette's blonde curls were perfectly arranged to spill over one shoulder in a style ill-suited to a woman of her years. She wore too much face paint and a dress overly poufy and of that exact shade of pale green that became no one. But Lady Linette overdressed *with purpose*. She was actually prettier and younger underneath, and would be quite the thing if she dressed her age, gave up rinsing her hair and forayed into jewel-toned fabrics. For a reason Sophronia had yet to fathom, Lady Linette did not. She kept up the facade, and the girls, who had now mostly worked out that it was one, kept it with her. This, too, was part of their training.

Lady Linette's anger, however, was not faked. She turned it on Sophronia. 'Explain yourself, young lady.'

'Stairway wasn't working well. It started to go up while we were still on it, caused quite a ruckus. You might want to have it checked next time you have a mechanic in.'

'Oh, indeed?'

Sophronia knew that the sooties would back her up in her fib, so long as she could get to them first. *I guess I'm visiting the sooties this evening.*

Lady Linette probably knew it, too, for she didn't pursue the reprimand. 'I suppose that explains your abysmal attire as well?'

All three girls nodded.

'Well, don't let it happen again. You should have allowed time to change. You're old enough not to be overset by misbehaving stairways.'

They all bobbed simultaneous perfect curtsies and chorused in unison, 'Yes, Lady Linette.'

'Or misbehaving vampires?' muttered Sophronia, under her breath.

Lady Linette flicked a curl at her. 'Now that you have reminded me, Miss Temminnick, please stay after class. I must have a chat with you about that thing on your wrist.'

In the time it took Lady Linette to say it, Sophronia had unbuckled the hurlie behind her back and passed it surreptitiously to Dimity.

'Of course, Lady Linette.'

Lady Linette gestured for them to sit. In her classroom, seats were made up of plush ottomans and sofas. They resided alongside velvet curtains and gold brocade-covered tables. The room had a definite boudoir-of-ill-repute feeling.

As it turned out, this was well suited to their lesson.

Sophronia and Dimity took a vacant love seat at the front, Sophronia dislodging a large, fluffy cat with a scrunched-up face. The cat gave her a disgusted look. Or seemed to; it was hard to tell with that face.

Agatha scuttled to the back, sitting alone on a hassock, as if she were truly in trouble. She slouched and stared at her feet, until Lady Linette reprimanded her and then began the lesson.

'Ladies, it has been decided that you are now old enough for lessons in the fine art of seduction. And so we will begin with multidirectional flirting. Few of you will have the opportunity to practise on boys for a good while yet, since we are no longer keeping company with Bunson's.' She turned suddenly to Sophronia and Dimity. 'Except you ladies, of course. I understand Miss Temminnick's brother has recently acquired a fiancée? And that you two have leave to attend his engagement masquerade?'

They nodded.

'Well, pay close attention, then, masquerade balls are ideal practise grounds.' She turned back and began instruction.

'She's still angry about it,' hissed Dimity to Sophronia.

They had gone behind Lady Linette's back to the head-mistress with their absence request. Mademoiselle Geraldine would grant permission purely on the grounds of marriage prospects, despite the fact that neither girl was officially *out*. Lady Linette would have thwarted the whole thing; it wasn't done to take off in the middle of session. But Mademoiselle Geraldine agreed with Sophronia that engagement balls were mandatory when one was related to the groom – it was the family's only opportunity for ostentatious show. Dimity had taken more effort. Finally, they had hit upon the fact that Dimity's birthday was around the same time. Mademoiselle Geraldine had proved amenable, and Lady Linette had been forced to make a show of following the headmistress's orders.

'Seduction in its purest form is a never-ending acquisition of knowledge about another individual. Every male is a new challenge, every occasion warrants a different approach. Take the greatest of care when applying these techniques, for they can be more dangerous than actual weaponry.'

The girls all straightened. Lady Linette's lessons were always interesting, but seduction was supposed to be the best. What young lady didn't want to know how to manipulate a man? This was what finishing school was all about!

'You already have eyelash fluttering and flirting with fan and parasol, now let us consider holding a man's gaze with intent and purpose. This can be perceived as a bold stance, an outright challenge or an unspoken offer. Let me demonstrate.' Lady Linette came before each of them and with a few micro-movements of lashes and lids demonstrated the differences among the three gazes. Each girl tried each gaze in return, feeling awkward, and then practised on a partner for several minutes, feeling even more awkward. Periodically, fits of giggles interrupted the concentrated staring.

Eventually Dimity said, 'Lady Linette, I don't mean to be ignorant, but what, exactly, is the *unspoken offer*? I mean to say, how do I know if I don't know, as it were?'

'Ah, yes, seduction. Have you read some of those horrid Gothics floating about? Oh, now, don't be coy, I've seen copies of *The Monk* passing from hand to hand. It's not forbidden, not at *this* school. Such an offer can encompass all things that men, as a general rule, require of women – from a kiss on the hand to one on the neck to the lips and beyond.'

Dimity's eyes went owlish. 'There's a *beyond*?'

'Don't interrupt, Miss Plumleigh-Teignmott. Where was I? Oh, yes. Then there is touching. A man may try to put his hands anywhere upon you, if you let him. A gentleman, of course, will ask first, but he will still try.'

'Anywhere?' squeaked Dimity.

'Anywhere,' said Lady Linette darkly.

'Oh, my.'

Sophronia giggled at Dimity's awe. She herself was equipped with older brothers, several of whom attended university. Even before finishing school she had enjoyed eavesdropping on her family. As a result of indiscreet conversations between said brothers, she was rather more familiar with the intentions of young gentlemen than she ought to be. Apparently, gentlemen not only liked to kiss and touch women everywhere, they did that and more, on a regular basis, and mostly not with ladies at all, but with women of less genteel breeding. Some gentlemen, her brothers had whispered, even did it with each other.

'Is that what the longing look is offering?' Dimity wanted to know.

'Generally speaking, yes. It is an invitation.'

'Oh, dear, rather powerful, isn't it?'

Sophronia suspected Dimity would never look a man in the face again, for fear of issuing invitations.

'This is why you must master the differences among the three, not to mention the nature and length of the look itself. Facial expressions, my dears, can be thought of as part of one's toilette. In fact, clothing can also transmit messages. Tight stays, for example, offer up to the gentleman the slenderness of one's waist. Wouldn't he like to put his hands about it? A low décolletage suggests that he might like to touch, just there.'

All the girls gasped. A few who were wearing dresses with low necklines surreptitiously tried to tug them up.

Sophronia found herself thinking of Felix Mersey. The young viscount had taken rather a shine to her, almost a year ago now, and they maintained a cautiously civil correspondence. The kind of correspondence no parent would sniff at. Although Sophronia's mother might have had the vapours if she'd known her daughter was receiving missives from a duke's son. Vapours of joy, mind you. Once or twice Sophronia had, rather desperately, searched between Felix's brief lines of courteous discourse for something more. But Lord Mersey either hadn't it in him to pen words of love, or had lost his taste for Sophronia after her Westminster Hive infiltration. In which case, his letters were mere formality from a gentleman who would not be so rude as to break off a courtship via the written word. Sophronia suspected the latter. After all, it would shake any gentleman's regard to find the object of his affection dressed as a male dandy and cavorting about with a chimney sweep.

Not that Sophronia was at all sure she wanted such attentions from Lord Mersey. His father was a Pickleman. She had come to like some of the supernatural set, all of whom, she knew in her heart, the Picklemen would happily see dead. As much as she admired Felix's slouch and overconfident flirtations, how could she reconcile his politics with her dislike of his father's secret society?

Nevertheless, Sophronia found herself daydreaming about the upcoming masquerade. She'd written to Felix of the momentous occasion, more for something to say than in the hope that anything should come of it. But, of course, he'd managed to wangle himself an invitation – after all, he was training to be an evil genius and his father *was* a duke. *If I wear a low-cut gown,* she wondered, *will Felix want to touch my décolletage? And do I want to lure him in because I think I may have lost him? Or do I want him for himself? He does have very nice eyes. And his waistcoat is always well fitted.*

Sophronia cocked her head, considering. *And would I want him to kiss me and more?* Her pulse raced and she had to consciously slow her breathing so Lady Linette would not notice. *It's amazing that there are such possibilities inherent in just a longing look. Men really are weak-willed.*

Lady Linette stopped the looks and returned to instruction. 'What were we discussing?'

'Um, touching,' said Preshea, in an unusually meek tone.

'Oh, yes. He may also wish to *kiss* there.'

'What, the *décolletage*?' Dimity squeaked.

'Quite often.'

Sophronia, thinking of her brothers' lewd talk, asked, 'And elsewhere?'

Lady Linette smiled. 'Well, yes, the very best ones like to kiss all over.'

Most of the girls inhaled in shock, and then began asking questions all at once. What did it feel like? Was it nice or was it damp? After touching and kissing, what happened? And could this really all start with simply staring directly into a man's face at a ball?

Agatha looked as if she would like to faint. Dimity's cheeks were rosy with embarrassment, but she was utterly enthralled. Sophronia hated to admit it, but so was she.

Lady Linette held up a hand as the wave of curiosity crashed over her. Had she been a more sensitive individual, like Sister Mattie, she might have been embarrassed by the unladylike enthusiasm. But Lady Linette was an expert in manipulation, and if knowledge of connubial relations would arm her girls better in how to infiltrate society, then she would deliver unto them the necessary.

'Calm down, ladies, do. Let us practise a few more initial seduction techniques, and discuss more on the consequences later. We are all a little overwrought at the moment. Suffice it to say that you must remember all the rules of polite society. No more than two dances with the same gentleman. No longer than the space of a dance and a half hour in one man's company. Do not walk out with a male alone, especially not to the conservatory, unless you are related. The goal is always to keep yourself safe from ruin or accusations thereof. After you have mastered the initial looks, we will move on to the seduction itself, and the boundaries that you must keep in place to protect your reputation. I will discuss how to employ canoodles and of which variety, without being caught. We may even study some light anatomy. Anything more than that, I hope you all understand, is reserved for the marriage bed. It is your mother's responsibility to explain such details of that situation to you as she sees fit.'

An audible sigh of disappointment met this statement.

The girls then spent a most enjoyable hour practising longing looks without any true understanding of what might result. It wasn't all that different from the entirety of their education at the academy. In a strange way, it was like practising to kill someone with a bladed fan when one had yet to experience any actual act of assassination. Sophronia found herself more worried about how to respond to an imagined Felix kiss – the amount of pressure, what if there was excess saliva, where to put one's hands? – than she was about dealing out death. Although the concerns were oddly similar – amount of pressure, what if there was excess blood, how to keep one's gloves clean?

Of course, Sophronia had kissed Soap. Or more precisely, Soap had kissed her. Which had managed to be both comforting and unsettling. She didn't like to think about her friend in *that* way. Although, when she let herself, Sophronia was all too apt to ruminate upon Soap's kiss. It had been a very nice kiss. And she hadn't worried about pressure or saliva or her hands; Soap had taken care of all of it. He was like that. Felix would be different. So very publicly suitable, a duke's son, yet so very politically unsuitable, *that* duke's son. Sophronia admitted to titillation; Felix was a challenge.

Sophronia shook off thoughts of both boys, which wasn't easy when practising seduction. Thinking of Soap, she found, turned her longing gaze into one of frustration and puzzlement. And thinking of Felix made Dimity, her partner, come over very fidgety.

'Sophronia, don't look at me like that!'

'Like what?'

'All wistful, it makes me uncomfortable.'

'Isn't that the point?'

'I don't know, is it? Lady Linette, please come assess Sophronia's look. I think she's executing it wrong.'

Lady Linette duly came over and Sophronia duly looked at her and thought of Felix.

Lady Linette blinked back at her, impassive. 'No, I think that is rather good. Perhaps a bit too much of an offer, Miss Temminnick. Can you tone it down slightly?'

Sophronia tried to think of both Felix and Soap at once.

'Oh, dear me, no, dear. No. Better the first time. Keep practising.'

Sophronia tried again.

Preshea said, 'Ooooh, Sophronia, who are you thinking about?' Exchanging smug glances with a few of her cronies, she added, 'I wager we can guess.'

When Sophronia did not answer, Preshea added, 'And how

is our dear Lord Mersey?' There was an edge of bitterness to the sly question. She had rather fancied the young viscount for herself. Miss Preshea Buss was so pretty, she resented that he seemed so concentrated on plain, brown Sophronia.

Sophronia replied, blandly, 'He's well, thank you for asking. Should I tender your regards?' The implication being, of course, that she had the right of correspondence when Preshea did not.

Preshea tossed her glossy black curls. 'No, thank you. Besides, you'll see him before another letter gets through.'

'Indeed I will, at my brother's soiree.' Sophronia's tone was deceptively mild. 'With ample time for conversation, as he has already requested the dinner dance.'

At which every girl in the room glanced at her with envy. Sophronia hadn't meant to antagonise the whole class. She'd only meant to use the social cachet to quiet Preshea.

'Ladies, a little less gossip, a little more longing looks!' reprimanded their teacher. 'Sophronia, you might consider your choice of escort with better care in the future. Lord Mersey is not on the agenda for a marriage of infiltration, and Picklemen do not make good patrons.' Sophronia was duly chastised.

The others got back to it, giggling softly among themselves.

Dimity asked Sophronia, 'Did he really ask you for the dinner?'

'No, but he will.'

'Are you sure? I thought you were afraid you'd lost him.'

Sophronia fanned out her gloved hands in a gesture of dismissal. 'Perhaps, but not to Preshea, I haven't! Besides, he's still interested enough to come to my family's masquerade.

Although that could be because as a gentleman he can only politely break off with me in person.'

Dimity nodded her understanding. 'If you learn these seduction lessons well, you might be able to keep him. Despite Lady Linette's opinion, I think he's a delicious prospect. For fun, if nothing else. I should like to see you try.'

Sophronia firmed up her spine. 'You're right! Let's practise.'

They tried diligently for the next twenty minutes. Sophronia wished for Sidheag. She was very good on the subject of understanding the male psyche, having grown up in a werewolf pack, all of them soldiers, not to mention visits with the rest of the regiment regularly. Her knowledge was far more complete than Sophronia's bits of gleaned gossip from indiscreet brothers.

At the end of the lesson, Dimity and Agatha scuttled off, eager to return to their private chambers, hoping that Sidheag would be waiting there, pigeon crisis averted. Dimity carried Sophronia's hurlie safely stashed in her reticule, out of Lady Linette's clutches.

That good lady rarely forgot anything. 'Well, Miss Temminnick, give it to me.'

'Lady Linette?'

'The unregistered wrist claw thing you used to save yourself earlier this evening.'

Sophronia pulled back her sleeves, showing the bandage on one side and the complete absence of the hurlie on the other. 'I'm afraid I lost it in that very scrabble. You see, I had to leave it behind, hooked on, in order to get through the hatch.'

Lady Linette was sceptical.

Sophronia stood quietly, no elaboration that might give away the lie, no excess blinking that might betray a direct falsehood. She was applying, with great expertise, every one of the lessons that Lady Linette herself had taught her.

'Sometimes, Miss Temminnick, I worry that we are training you *too* well.'

'Is that possible, Lady Linette?'

'I don't know. I suppose in the end it will ride on where your loyalties lie.'

'I suppose it will.'

'Where *do* they lie, Miss Temminnick? You are what, sixteen now? Old enough to marry. Old enough to leave this school, should your parents wish it.'

'I haven't learned everything yet.'

'Nor have you finished properly. That is not the point.'

'What is the point?'

'You are old enough to know your own mind. Whose patronage will you undertake? Queen and country, supernatural, Picklemen? Will you follow your training in the pursuit of our ends, or those of your beau?'

'And what of my own wishes?'

Lady Linette was not so foolish as to answer that. 'Or the vampire who sends you gifts?'

'Reading my mail, Lady Linette? How gauche. I guess the answer to your question is, I don't know yet.' Sophronia felt emboldened. 'I like this school but not the potentate, although working for queen and country seems no bad thing.'

'The one is tied to the other, I'm afraid.' Lady Linette seemed genuinely contrite, either because of the potentate himself – who did have a regrettable personality – or the fact that Queen Victoria's government had so fully integrated the supernatural element.

'That is the difficulty, isn't it? Right now my vampire friend's gifts, I must own, are attractive. Although not my vampire friend himself,' Sophronia replied.

Lady Linette was looking at Sophronia with more respect than she had ever shown before. 'He is not so bad a choice. We would be sad to lose you, but he could absolutely afford your indenture. Although he is a vampire; he might want something extra for it.'

Sophronia felt almost like an equal. What, she wondered, had just happened in that class to cause this shift in her own social standing with her teacher? Whatever it was, she hoped to capitalise on it. She rather enjoyed the novelty of garnering respect from an adult. So she accessed her training and responded as it dictated.

'When I have made up my mind, Lady Linette, you'll be the first to know.' *Well, after Dimity, Agatha, Sidheag and Soap. And Bumbersnoot. Bumbersnoot will have to be included in any of my future plans.*

'Very considered response, Miss Temminnick. A word of warning: you can't change him, Miss Temminnick.'

'Who? My vampire friend or my Pickleman beau?'

'Yes.' Then, in one of her rapid switches of topic, designed – they had all learned – to unsettle an opponent, Lady Linette said, 'Where is Lady Kingair, Miss Temminnick?'

'Unwell,' said Sophronia, instinctually covering for her friend's absence.

'Oh, indeed, and what form of illness has afflicted her? She's customarily so hardy.'

When fibbing, always stick as close to the truth as possible. 'Of the sentimental variety. She had a letter that quite overset her.'

Lady Linette's expression changed. So much so that Sophronia wondered if she knew the contents of Sidheag's letter. Had she intercepted a private pigeon before it reached its intended target? Highly illegal, of course, worse than reading Lord Akeldama's notes, but Lady Linette was an intelligencer. She did more illegal things before tea each day than most people did in a lifetime.

The teacher said, 'Understandable sentiment, I suppose. But I expect to see her at supper, otherwise I will send Matron. Perhaps she is in need of laudanum to settle her nerves.'

'Very good, Lady Linette. I will let her know.'

With which Sophronia escaped, gliding down the passageway as quickly as her skirts would allow.

Sidheag had not returned, not that they could conceive of a way for her to do so without being found out. The school was, after all, floating mid-air and very high up. In deference to the presence of Preshea; her new chamber-mate, Frenetta; and a gaggle of other girls, the three friends retreated to Sophronia and Dimity's room. Bumbersnoot was delighted to see them. The little mechanimal trundled about tooting smoke out of his ears and puffing steam from below his carapace. His tail tick-tocked back and forth and Agatha, despite Sophronia's admonishments not to spoil him, fed the metal dog torn scraps of a brown paper bag that had once held sweets.

'What will we do if she is out all night, alone, with a were-wolf?' Dimity was upset by the very idea.

'He's a teacher, surely that counts for something?' protested Agatha.

'He's not a relative. If word gets out, her reputation will be in ruins.' Dimity was probably correct in this assumption. 'Didn't we just learn that a young lady should never be alone with a gentleman for any length of time? Do the other teachers know she is with him?'

Sophronia said, 'I don't think so. Lady Linette just asked me where she was.'

Dimity swallowed. 'That is *not* good.'

'Worse, she only has until supper to reappear. Matron's coming by to check.'

'Then what will we do? Pillows in the bed won't work on Matron. None of us look enough like Sidheag to pull a wig-and-switch, either.' Dimity wasn't the best intelligencer, but some of the training had stuck.

Sophronia was out of options. 'We have to hope she returns in time. Nothing else for it.' She sat down on her bed with a thump.

Dimity said out loud what they had all three been secretly wondering: 'Do you think Lord Maccon has been successfully challenged?' It was a most delicate way of putting it. Lord Maccon was Sidheag's great-great-great-grandfather, in truth the only father she had. He was also Alpha of the Kingair pack, and Alphas had to fight for their position constantly. He was supposed to be the second-most-powerful werewolf in all of Britain, but new werewolves did happen, and loners, those unattached to a pack like Captain Niall, could be strong. If one had challenged Lord Maccon and won, it meant the Laird of Kingair was dead.

Sophronia said, 'I don't like to think it, but it would explain Sidheag's behaviour.'

Agatha, who knew Sidheag better than anyone, began to cry.

'Hush, now, we don't *know* that's what happened,' Sophronia tutted at her. 'It could just be war. Queen Victoria is always sending her werewolves to fight on the front lines somewhere foreign.'

Bumbersnoot butted up against one of Agatha's slippered feet, his tail wagging a little less, his floppy leather ears wiggling sympathetically.

Agatha blubbered, 'But she does love him so. I know she talks gruff, but he's her one and only gramps. If he's been hurt or killed . . . ' Great fat tears trickled down her round, freckled face.

'Now, now, Agatha, where's your handkerchief? You'll come over all blotchy, and Professor Lefoux will notice in our next class. Can't have that.' Sophronia bustled about collecting one of her spares.

Agatha tried to recover her emotions. She was terrified of Professor Lefoux. Professor Lefoux had no respect for finer feelings, even when they were being applied with purpose. Gadgets, felt Professor Lefoux, solved any problem.

Agatha disposed of one damp handkerchief, and by the time she'd finished with another, her sobs had subsided.

'Good girl,' said Sophronia.

Dimity said, 'Sophronia's right. We don't know the real truth of any of it.'

Sophronia added, 'If Sidheag doesn't return, our only hope is that Soap has uncovered something of merit.'

Dimity and Agatha looked uncomfortable. They knew it meant Sophronia was sneaking out later that night on one of her clandestine visits to engineering. They also knew it meant Sophronia had no means of protecting Sidheag's reputation, because if she had, she would be doing that instead.

Matron would come and Sidheag would not be there.

So it turned out to be.

SESSION 4

THE UNCLEANLINESS OF SOAP

While they nibbled a meal of baked cod, boiled aitchbone of beef, carrots, turnips and suet dumplings, Sophronia thought hard on which would be worse for Sidheag: being found missing on her own or having it known she was alone with a werewolf. After munching for a while in silence, Sophronia whispered, 'We must try to hold off saying anything to anyone until tomorrow. Let me have a confab with Soap, see what he's turned up. We can decide who to tell what before breakfast.'

Dimity blanched. 'By which time Sidheag will have been out with *him* all night.'

Agatha added, looking down the table at Preshea, 'And if anyone but us finds out, her reputation really will be in tatters.'

'Can't be helped. At least we know Sidheag can handle a werewolf no matter his mood or form.'

Dimity put down the roll she was buttering. 'Good thing we have Mademoiselle Geraldine after cards tonight.'

The other two nodded.

The headmistress was part of their training at the academy. She was kept in complete ignorance as to the clandestine nature of the lessons, so when they had a class with her it was *real* finishing. Mademoiselle Geraldine instructed them on manners, social niceties, tables of precedence, tea-sipping and the like. Any espionage techniques were assigned to them before they met with the headmistress, usually by Lady Linette. Luckily, tonight they already had instructions, so all Sophronia, Dimity and Agatha had to do was avoid answering any uncomfortable questions as to their friend's whereabouts during the course of the meal.

They managed all the way through to the sweets course, orange pudding with Naples biscuits and sherry. Then, by dint of running a boisterous and absorbing game of speculation after the pudding, they avoided any kind of private conference during cards.

They dawdled as much as possible while the mechanicals cleaned up, so that they had to glide with extreme rapidity on to Mademoiselle Geraldine's class, on the far side of the airship. They utilised some of the lesser-known passageways, disturbing more than one servant mechanical. If she had known what was really going on, Lady Linette might indeed feel that she had trained her pupils too well. Or she might be proud. In any event, she couldn't be too worried about Sidheag or they never would have got away with it.

Safely ensconced with Mademoiselle Geraldine, who was

instructing them in how to flirt at a hunting party, tweed jodhpurs notwithstanding, they made it through to bedtime unencumbered.

By the time Lady Linette came around to check that lights were out at two in the morning, they were all three solidly asleep.

Sidheag's bed was empty.

After Lady Linette closed the door to their parlour, Sophronia was out of bed with a glass to the jamb so quickly she managed to catch Lady Linette saying to Sister Mattie in the hall, 'Unfortunately, Sister, I believe we have one missing – Lady Kingair. It's going to be messy if we've misplaced an aristocrat. Even if she is Scottish.'

Sister Mattie, who had been checking on the debuts, said something sympathetic in a low tone. They moved down the hallway, out of eavesdropping range.

Sophronia's nightgown was so voluminous she could pull it on over her preferred after-hours attire – a pair of her brother's old breeches, with a corset under a gentleman's shirt and a waistcoat over the top. Sophronia didn't like to dress as a boy, not the way her friend Vieve did, but it was awfully practical for climbing. She scooped up Bumbersnoot, dressed in his frilly reticule disguise, and slung him over one shoulder. Bumbersnoot usually came with her to engineering. He liked to eat fallen bits of coal, and Sophronia thought it only right he go down to the boiler room and visit the mechanical gods. As Dimity had once said, 'I wonder if engineering, for Bumbersnoot, is like church. Or am I being apocryphal?'

Sophronia was on her own. Dimity, after a few ill-fated

jaunts, had elected to leave that dirty, smelly, greasy place to Sophronia and Sidheag. It was too rough for a *real* lady, she claimed. Dimity wanted to be a lady rather more than she wanted to be an intelligencer. She liked the idea of practising charitable works on the sooties, but gave that up in favour of filching nibbles at tea and sending them down with Sophronia to the unfortunates, as she called them, with her regards. Thus she did not risk smudges on her gown or crude language in her delicate ear.

Agatha simply hadn't that much of an interest in anything covert. Also, given the option between sleep and pretty much anything else, Agatha would *always* rather sleep.

The hallway outside was dark. The teachers turned off the gas after inspections. Sophronia, hurlie on one wrist and an even more illegal gadget, the obstructor, on the other, navigated with ease. The hurlie handled climbing and swinging from balcony to balcony, and the obstructor froze into six-second stillness any mechanical before it could raise the alarm. As a result, Sophronia was in engineering in under a quarter of an hour. She considered timing herself with a pocket watch next jaunt – how fast could she get around an airship if she really tried? When Professor Braithwope fell, Sophronia had risked life and limb swinging at speed, but that was almost a year ago, and she was better with the hurlie now. She could probably do it safer and faster. She flinched, thinking about that incident. *Poor old Professor Braithwope*.

Soap was waiting for her behind their customary coal pile. Sophronia was a lot less conspicuous fraternising with sooties dressed as a boy than when she'd first come down, stirring up dust in full skirts and a silly hat. She settled on the coal pile next to Soap's lanky frame.

'What ho, miss?'

'Good evening, Soap, any word on Sidheag's pigeon?' There was no point in shilly-shallying about with pleasantries. Sophronia and Soap were close enough to have done away with social niceties a long time ago. Besides, he was common born and didn't care for such folderol. Sensible man, Soap.

'I didn't get a peek at the message itself – either Sidheag still has it with her or they burned it right quick. But I did overhear a few things while tinkering with a dodgy boiler in Lady Linette's parlour. The human staff sure gossip.' Soap's dark eyes were grave, but he managed to exude warmth and welcome.

Sophronia relaxed into the comfort of his familiar affection. 'Go on.'

He leaned in towards her, unconsciously intimate. 'Well, miss, it sure seems to be a matter of pack. Things are unsettled in Kingair.'

Sophronia shifted; he was a little too close, not preserving the space most gentlemen leave in the presence of a lady. 'So we gathered. Is Lord Maccon dead?'

Ever attuned to her moods, Soap registered her discomfort and slumped back into the coal pile, as if it were an armchair. This instantly reassured her. 'No truck on anyone dying. So I think we're safe in assuming it's no challenge. But it does seem like to be concerning Lord Maccon.'

Sophronia frowned – if he wasn't dead, what could possibly be the problem? 'How do you mean?'

'Word is that he's maybe losing control.'

'Of his clavigers?' This time she leaned in to the conversation, struggling to make herself heard against a new din in the boiler room.

'No, of his pack.'

Sophronia thought back to everything Sidheag had told her about the Kingair werewolves. 'Lord Maccon? He's supposed to be the strongest Alpha in England, with the exception of the dewan.'

Soap smiled as though they were in on a joke together. 'And some would say even the queen's werewolf would lose three out of five challenges. It seems that it's not Lord Maccon's strength in question, it's the behaviour of the rest of the Kingair pack.'

'They *are* Scottish.'

'It's worse than that, miss.'

Sophronia cracked a small joke. 'Is there something worse than being Scottish?'

Soap declined to play. 'Being a sootie, and having the wrong colour skin to boot?'

In his eyes was something like the longing look they had practised in class earlier that evening. Sophronia didn't like it coming from Soap, and she didn't know how to defuse it. Lady Linette hadn't taught them that tactic yet. She hadn't told them what to do when one was on the *receiving* end of unwanted longing. *Perhaps that's something I should ask about next class.*

'Behaviour of the pack? Aren't they all instinctually bound to follow him until another challenges and wins? I do wish Professor Braithwope were available to consult. I suppose Professor Lefoux might have some insight.'

But strangely enough, Soap had further to offer on the subject. 'It's not that simple, miss. Beta supports, Gamma objects, loners challenge, and the others fall about the scale. Alpha is not an easy position to hold. I wouldn't want it.'

'Soap, how is it you suddenly know so much about werewolves?'

Soap shrugged. 'I take an interest. Not all sudden, you just never asked. I've been thinking ... if I went out for anything long term, claviger might be it. I'd sooner indenture to a pack than bind to a hive.'

Sophronia had never even considered that Soap, of all people, might hunger for immortality. 'Pardon? You'd rather be a werewolf than a vampire?'

Soap's eyes, in the flickering light of the boiler, were almost hungry-looking. 'I don't want to suck blood, although I'd take the rank that came with either and be grateful. But werewolves have fewer restrictions; even a sootie can make claviger. Plus, I like the idea of a pack, don't you?'

'Sort of like collecting a bunch of grown-up hairy sooties?' guessed Sophronia, feeling somehow hurt the more she considered it. *How could I not know this about Soap? My Soap? Stupid not to realise he wants more out of life than shoving coal in boilers all day long.* He had seemed eager for her reading lessons, but she'd suspected it was an excuse to spend more time with her. Now she thought there might be more to it: social climbing. Soap had his own plans, which he hadn't confided and which – worse – didn't include her.

Soap smiled at his fellow sooties rushing around. 'These old cusses, my pack?' Many of the sooties regarded Soap as a kind of unofficial mayor of the boiler room. There were firemen and greasers, adults ranked far above them, but if one wanted to mobilise the sooties, even the head of engineering knew it was best to get Soap to do it.

He nodded thoughtfully. 'Yeah, I suppose they are. Don't you like the idea of a pack, miss? You kinda got yourself one, what with all your projects.'

'Projects' was what Soap called Sophronia's various female friends.

Sophronia tried to be fair and consider life from Soap's perspective. It was jolly hard to imagine, since he was a different class, colour *and* sex. Still, if he hadn't any opportunities to further himself, and if that was what he wanted? Not to mention the chance of immortality?

'So that's why you've learned everything you can about werewolves?'

'Indeed. Miss Maccon's been bonny good with that.' Soap and Sidheag preferred to pretend he didn't know she had a title, made everyone more relaxed. Sidheag enjoyed being lowly Miss Maccon when she smeared around with the sooties.

Sophronia felt almost compelled to change the subject, but the more she thought about her dear Soap pursuing something so dangerous, the more the ache of worry in her stomach expanded. She tried to stay calm. 'But, Soap, indenture as a claviger? You're little better than a warden against moonmadness. You serve the pack's whims with no guarantee that they'll let you try for metamorphosis. It could take *years*.'

'At least there's a chance of clean, honest work in the

interim. Better than being a sootie, and better than being food, like a drone.' He sounded serious about the scheme.

Sophronia's stomach ache expanded into fear, clogging up her throat and thickening her voice. 'You do know how rare survival is and how dangerous?' She barked the words, her panic blossoming into anger. Statistics weren't published, but everyone was aware that few could withstand metamorphosis. It was a huge risk!

Soap's gentle tone did not rise to match her stridency. 'I know the odds.'

'And you'll wager your whole life on them? That's idiotic!' She switched tactics, forcing her voice to mellow. 'If, by some puny chance, you did survive a bite, then there's military service. Even werewolves die in the front lines.'

'And others come back war heroes and are granted a holding. Can you imagine, I'd be landed gentry?'

'You could be decades in some foreign land!'

'It's a chance to travel.'

'That's a stupid reason to risk werewolf!' *I wouldn't see you. You'd be gone. You'd leave me behind.*

Soap was clearly startled, perhaps even hurt by her rage. His posture altered, tense in the arms and shoulders.

Sophronia pressed her eyes with her hand and sensed Soap calm in response to her worried gesture. His slight slouch returned. She couldn't say that she would miss him, because she was afraid it might work and hold him back. And if this really was his dream? It would be as bad for her to hold him with empty promises as it would be for him to do this for the wrong reason.

She took a deep breath. 'I'm sorry, Soap, it's only that I worry.'

Soap softened and put his hand close to hers where it rested on the coal pile – almost touching. 'I know, miss, but it's my choice in the end. And it's not like I'd have a long, healthy life as a sootie.'

'No good options. That's what I'm afraid of.' *When did Soap get so stubborn?* Sophronia was amazed to find she was shivering.

Soap dared to move his hand and cover her shaking one. Sophronia found the hard calluses on his palm oddly comforting. They sat in silence for a moment, listening to the clangs and rattles of the boilers. Sophronia calmed, becoming quietly angry at herself for getting so emotional over a friend. A good friend, but only a friend. She extracted her hand from his, gently but firmly.

Finally Soap said, 'I may know where Miss Maccon is.'

Sophronia brightened, more at the switch in topics than the information. 'Oh, good. Where?'

'I think she and Captain Niall have gone to London.'

'Goodness, why?' Now her excitement was over the information itself.

'Because the captain is a strong werewolf loner. If Lord Maccon's got control problems, Miss Maccon is the type to use Niall as a solution. She'll do whatever she can to hold that pack of hers together.'

'Why London?'

'Rumour is, that's where Lord Maccon was last headed.'

'A Scottish werewolf in London? That will make the local

packs mad.' Sophronia shuddered. She'd seen Lord Vulkasin, Alpha of the Woolsey pack, only once, and he'd terrified her. If Lord Maccon was anything like that, London might not survive their meeting.

Soap said, 'That's why the dewan works for the queen. Keeps the peace between Alphas.'

'But for Sidheag to leave with no word to us? No word to the teachers?'

Soap shrugged. 'Bet she'll try to send word, soon as she can. I'd keep an eye fixed.'

'On the other hand, could be she doesn't trust someone here at school. In which case, she might try to reach me at home at that dratted ball of my brother's.' Sophronia stood, brushing down her trousers. 'It's getting late, I should go to bed.'

Soap followed the movement of her hands; her legs were plainly visible without formal skirts and petticoats.

Sophronia stopped, self-conscious.

Soap looked away, muttered something to himself. Then abruptly he said, 'You'll be dancing with that Felix nobbin, won't you? At this fool ball of your family's?'

'I will.' Sophronia, surprised by the question, temporarily forgot her policy of evading all things romantic around Soap.

'He's a snoot-airing toff.'

'He is.' Sophronia was at a loss to do anything but agree with Soap. She'd never seen him in such a tetchy mood, and they'd already argued once this evening. She didn't want to push her luck.

'Dad's a Pickleman, you recall that?'

'It's part of the attraction, I suppose.'

Soap glared at her. 'Never thought you would be one to steam in for naughty boys, miss.'

Sophronia stiffened, annoyed that Soap was pursuing this subject so doggedly. 'There's a certain level of appeal.'

'Oh, yeah, what's that?'

'Soap, I can't have this discussion with you!'

'Oh ho, why not? I wager you talk with the young miss projects about it.'

'They're girls!'

'And I'm not.'

'I certainly hope not, or you've been acting a better hoax than Vieve ever pulled.'

Soap moved in close, quick as a supernatural; perhaps he was halfway to werewolf already. He certainly looked fiercer than she'd ever thought possible. 'Happy to prove it by tossing that Felix blighter out of the hatch anytime.'

Sophronia couldn't help but giggle at the image – poor Felix would be so surprised, clutching his top hat and floating through the air. 'Oh, Soap, you are droll.'

Soap blinked and slid back into familiar friend territory. 'Well, then, miss, you tell that to the other sooties? Lately they been taking me seriously.'

'That's 'cause you been all over moody,' barked one sootie, moving past them at a trot.

'Goodness, Soap, imagine taking *you* seriously!'

'Yes, imagine that?' said Soap, all smiles, but Sophronia detected an edge of bitterness.

Sophronia made good her escape, unsettled by the whole conversation. Sidheag going to London. Soap becoming a claviger and then a werewolf! She wanted her old silly boyish Soap back. The one who didn't care for the state of the world. The one who made no plans to be immortal, who took no grave risks. The one whose eyes merely twinkled with mischief and nothing else. She wanted things as they were. *And I thought it would be such fun to grow up. I can't tell Dimity about it, either.* Dimity wouldn't understand. Dimity would tell her to stop visiting engineering. But as much as Sophronia was unsettled by the new Soap, she felt a sharp pain at the very idea of not seeing him at all. *Oh, bother,* thought Sophronia, *why is he trying to ruin everything?*

Next morning they told Lady Linette that Sidheag had disappeared. They said they thought she'd simply gone off to mope somewhere alone with her thoughts and her disturbing letter.

'You didn't see her leave the ship?'

They all shook their heads.

Dimity twirled a lock of golden-brown hair.

Agatha looked at her feet.

'You're quite certain? She wasn't with anyone? This could be important.'

'Perhaps if we knew something of that letter?' replied Sophronia, knowing it wouldn't work, but drawing a kind of battle line in the intelligencer sand.

'Indeed. Perhaps. But I'm afraid I don't know myself.'

Sophronia narrowed her eyes. Lady Linette's cornflower-blue ones were impassive. They both inclined their heads in acknowledgment. *At least we both know where we stand*, thought Sophronia.

'Very well, ladies, off with you. Breakfast won't wait.'

For a fortnight they learned nothing more. There was no mail delivered. With Captain Niall gone, there was no one capable of running to Swiffle-on-Exe for the pickup. They didn't go ground-side, either. Professor Lefoux took over their bladed fan lessons. They had never before realised how integral a land-bound werewolf was to their collective mental stability. Floating in the grey drizzle – the general aspect of Dartmoor in January – with nary a peep from the rest of the world gave them all a malaise of the emotional humours. Even Dimity, who might have held to her bubbly nature with a birthday and a ball in her immediate future, remained troubled by Sidheag's absence and stayed quiet.

Sophronia did not visit engineering. She was uncomfortable with moody Soap. Perhaps they both needed some distance. She wasn't sure if she was punishing him for the gripes and hungry looks, or scared that she might unwittingly apply some of her seduction lessons to him. And the last thing she wanted to do was encourage her friend in a hopeless cause. His intent to turn werewolf felt near to a betrayal.

Dimity noted Sophronia's lack of evening jaunts, as her repository of filched sweets grew ever larger with no clandestine distribution. Dimity felt it her ladylike duty to dispense tea-cake charity unto boiler room unfortunates. 'Had a falling-out with your sootie beau, have you?'

'No,' said Sophronia shortly. 'Just overly busy.'

'Busy with what?'

'Mastering the fan – I think I want it to be my trademark weapon. All great intelligencers have a trademark weapon.'

'And you're choosing the fan because it's both sensible and cooling?' suggested Dimity.

Agatha, who was spending time in their room as her own was lonely, perked up. 'I prefer the garotte myself.'

The others looked at her, startled. Aside from the theatre, and sleeping, Agatha rarely expressed an interest in anything. Let alone something espionage-related.

'You do?' Dimity encouraged.

Agatha nodded. 'You can wear it as jewellery, it hides away easily and it's a nice clean death.'

'I hate to say it, but I'm with Preshea on dealing down, poison's best.' Dimity was firm on the matter.

'No blood?' suggested Sophronia.

'Exactly!' Dimity twirled the bangles about her wrist and sighed. 'Enough of this morbid talk.'

Agatha was looking at her small weekly planner. 'Shouldn't we be heading into Swiffle soon? Without Captain Niall to give you two a ride, the school will have to meet your transport itself.'

The two girls looked at each other. 'Oh, dear me yes. Depending on where exactly we are right now, it could take weeks. I hope Lady Linette hasn't forgot about the fact that we are due at a masquerade in a few days.'

Sophronia agreed, 'We'd best make sure.'

They shouldn't have underestimated their teacher. Lady

Linette was, after all, a mistress of information. It was her business to keep track of details.

During breakfast, which, since Mademoiselle Geraldine's kept town hours, fell at around noon, the girls heard the unmistakable repetitive thudding of the school's propeller cranking rhythmically below them. This could only mean one thing: the airship had a focused direction in mind. They were no longer gliding idly about the moor.

Dimity and Sophronia exchanged excited glances. Mademoiselle Geraldine's floating finishing school was heading into town.

STEALTH MOUSTACHES AND STEALTHIER FLYWAYMEN

The school arrived at Swiffle-on-Exe late the following evening. It floated in over the River Exe itself, to take on water for the massive boilers in engineering. Then it took up its customary position, moored outside town, the mismatched turrets of Bunson and Lacroix's Boys' Polytechnic in view down a goat path.

Sophronia and Dimity were to depart early the next morning. They were excused from their last lesson of the night with Professor Braithwope, the idea being that they should get to bed before midnight. They tried to explain this to the vampire, who regarded them with a sobering eye, almost like his old self. The effect was lost, however, by the fact that he had taken it into his addle-brained head to shave off his moustache.

Professor Braithwope's moustache, which he must have had as a mortal before he was metamorphosed into a vampire, was a tiny caterpillar-like object that perched upon his upper lip with an air of great uncertainty, like an amateur diver. This seemed to trouble the professor of late, for he would sporadically attempt to rid himself of the fuzzy protuberance. Since he was immortal, this did not work, for the moment the razor was put away his moustache grew back to its exact former state.

Sometimes, like tonight, he'd only managed to shave halfway before getting distracted, so the moustache looked as if it had lost its purchase at last and slid dangerously to the side and was trying, before their very eyes, to claw its way back up. It was hypnotic and difficult not to stare because the facial hair grew as quickly as a vampire's wounds might heal.

'Young ladies, why are you leaving my class so soon, whot? I believe we have not yet even started. Wait a moment there! Don't I know you? Yes, I think I do, I believe you are dancers to perform this evening. Or, wait . . . '

Sophronia and Dimity curtsied apologetically.

'Sorry, sir,' said Sophronia, 'we're excused. There's this masquerade, you see?'

Dimity added, 'Her brother is engaged, very exciting. We have to catch transport tomorrow and we need our beauty rest.'

'Well, that is no lie,' said Preshea from her seat near the back of the room.

The vampire lost interest halfway through their explanation. 'Oh, yes, well, if you insist. Don't forget your sausage, whot.' His moustache had almost resumed full bushiness.

'Of course not, sir,' replied Sophronia with a perfectly straight face.

'I believe they are bringing Viscount Mersey, does he count as a sausage?' Preshea was inclined to be fresh.

Professor Braithwope turned on her. 'Bratwurst or banger?' he snapped.

'Banger, most assuredly,' replied Preshea.

The vampire thus distracted, Sophronia and Dimity made their escape, trying not to giggle.

They had already packed, terrified that they would forget something. And once in their room, they were far too excited to sleep, particularly not earlier than usual.

So instead they lay in their nightgowns talking.

'Are you pleased Lord Mersey will be there?'

Sophronia sighed. 'I suppose so.'

'He is very handsome. And very rich. And very titled.' Dimity's tone gave nothing away.

'Yes, but you're the one who really wants to marry those things, not me.'

'Then what *do* you want from a beau?'

Sophronia considered this question. It had been troubling her of late. Felix was good looking, but he rather knew that too much. And he was nicely mysterious. But as a Pickleman he would interfere with her espionage operations, and that really couldn't be countenanced in a beau. *Perhaps I can train him out of it?*

Before she could answer Dimity, a timid knock sounded at the door to the parlour. The two looked at each other. They were the only ones not in class; whoever was there must know this.

Sophronia climbed out of bed and pulled on a robe. She was less self-conscious about these things than Dimity. After her foray into dressing like a dandy, she'd given over most scruples concerning public appearances in impolite clothing. After all, her nightgown nicely covered her climbing outfit, even if it was intended for the bedchamber.

'Oh, Sophronia,' said Dimity, 'they can wait while you dress.'

Since dressing, at the best of times, took a quarter of an hour, this was probably not wise. That knock had definitely sounded clandestine; besides, appearing at the door in said nightgown might unsettle the visitor, thus giving her an initial conversational advantage.

So Sophronia disregarded Dimity and padded through the parlour to open the hall door. A tall, shrouded figure pushed in past her without ceremony.

'What?'

'Shut the door, quickly now!'

Sophronia did so, and the individual pushed back the shroud to reveal . . .

'Soap!' He'd never visited before. It was terribly dangerous for a sootie to be up top. If he was caught he'd be summarily dismissed without references. Not to mention the fact that Sophronia and Dimity would be ruined.

'What ho, miss? Guessed I'd catch you before you left.'

Sophronia wasn't sure how she felt about this. She had, after all, been avoiding him.

'Sophronia, who is it?' peeped Dimity from the safe confines of their darkened sleeping chamber.

Sophronia went over and stuck her head in. 'No one all that important; give me a few minutes, please?'

Dimity's white face peeked out from under the covers, which she'd pulled up to her chin in case someone untoward tried to see her. 'Must you receive callers in such a state of disrepair?'

'I'll be quick.'

'Who is it, then?' Dimity pressed.

'Just a friend.' Sophronia wanted to avoid explaining Soap to Dimity. Dimity was bound to come over with a surfeit of disapproval.

Dimity sighed, but there was no way she was leaving her bed to meet an unknown entity.

Sophronia shut the door, took a deep breath to steady her nerves and turned to face the sootie.

Soap was standing awkwardly in the middle of the parlour, the cowl pushed down to drape about his shoulders. It was made of ripped fabric sacking.

'Do sit down?' said Sophronia politely, with an elegant gesture designed to disarm the intruder with politeness, as Lady Linette had once instructed.

'I won't, miss, thank you kindly. I'll only smudge up all your pretty little seatlings.'

Sophronia stayed where she was for a moment, on the far side of the room. Then decided she would risk proximity for greater privacy in speech, in case Dimity was listening at keyholes. So she went over and sat, looking up at him expectantly. 'Well?'

'I scared you off, miss, didn't I? This last time. Should've known I was too blunt. Even you've got some finer feelings.'

Sophronia's pride was stung. 'You most certainly did not

scare me! And I've plenty of finer feelings, thank you very much. I was ashamed of my behaviour, shouldn't have yelled.'

Soap grinned, wide and cheerful. 'I'm glad you did. Shows you care.'

'Of course I do!'

'So you're avoiding me because you came over all lily-livered, afraid I'll chuck a little affection your way?'

Sophronia glared at him. 'I'm not frightened of you, Soap. I simply don't think of you that way, and I don't want to.'

'I know.' The tall boy managed to look both hurt and shamefaced. 'It's just, miss, that I wish ... I ...'

He stammered, unsure for once, and Sophronia took it as an opportunity to leap hastily in. 'And I wish you would please stop showing me so much affection.' If he said anything more, *she'd* have to say more, and then she was sure to lose his friendship for ever. So she hurriedly switched the subject. 'What are you doing outside of engineering?'

'Couldn't let you go ground-side smouldering like to choke with disapproval.'

'I am not smouldering!' she said, looking as if smoke might start to come out of her ears, as it did Bumbersnoot's when he was excited.

Soap smiled, but it was not his usual broad grin. 'No, I can see that. You're catching a train in the wee hours?'

'No, Mumsy is sending the cart. An undignified way to travel, but it'll get us there. And Roger is an old chum.'

Soap's eyes narrowed slightly. 'Well, I'll be off, then. Don't go dancing more than three with that Felix blighter.'

Sophronia sniffed. 'I'm not a complete idiot, to be trapped

so easily. Nor, for that matter, is he. It's most annoying of you to order me to do something I'm going to do anyway. Now it'll look like I'm obeying you!'

Soap shifted the cowl back over his head and let himself out. 'Wasn't an order, miss, only a request.'

'You could have fooled me!'

'Now I've gone and offended you again.'

'You have. And things used to be so jolly between us.'

Soap looked down at her, his eyes bright sparkles from the depths of the sack. 'Even a crafty little thing like you can't change the inevitable.'

Sophronia's mouth firmed and she got a distinct glint of determination in her eye. It was an expression most had learned to be wary of. Not Soap, though. 'We'll see about that.'

Unexpectedly, Soap laughed. 'Only you, miss, would try to stop us all from growing up.' With that he skulked off down the hallway.

Sophronia was left thinking the whole encounter very odd.

She made her way back to bed, fortunately not having to explain anything to Dimity – her friend was fast asleep.

Sophronia's mother sent the pony cart with Roger and another stable hand to act as escort. It wasn't a stylish means of transport. Preshea would tease them mercilessly if she found out. However, Dimity and Sophronia were off school grounds before Preshea was even awake. Most everyone on board was dead to the world at six o'clock, at which entirely uncivilised hour Sophronia and Dimity caught the goods lift ground-side.

They clutched sandwich boxes and flasks of tea – necessary sustenance for the long journey ahead.

Bundled in oiled mackintoshes, with hatboxes and carpet bags full of ballgowns tucked under for protection, the two young ladies were the last to arrive.

Roger and compatriot sat on the front box. Both were shrouded head to toe against the bitter cold and ceaseless drizzle. Roger gave them a limp wave of greeting. He looked thoroughly miserable. He'd have driven half the night to collect them all so early. The other stable hand had his nose buried in a dirty handkerchief and didn't even look up.

Inside the cart, nearest the driver's box, sat Pillover, Dimity's younger brother and escort to the ball. It was embarrassing to bring one's brother for a dance partner, but it was the best she could do at short notice. Any finer feelings between her and Lord Dingleproops had been crushed under the weight of a Pickleman-driven misunderstanding. *All the better for it*, thought Sophronia, who didn't like Lord Dingleproops, and not solely because of his reluctant chin and Pickleman leanings.

She did, however, like Pillover. He was a morose sort, a general failure at most aspects of life, particularly – to his great trial – at being both evil and a genius. Pillover could invent things, and he wasn't stupid, he was simply too nice. This was a shortcoming he found depressing.

He grunted at them, having long since elected to treat Sophronia as he did his sister, with a lack of deference and mild splats of brotherly affection.

Sitting as far away from Pillover as possible was Felix Golborne, Viscount Mersey. There was no love lost between the two boys. Sophronia was under the impression that this was mainly because Pillover was younger, practically middle class, and not a member of the Pistons. Felix was the oldest son of a very prominent family, a full Piston in bad standing, and deliciously sinister. The Pistons were a club of sorts, members of which distinguished themselves via fancy waistcoats, black eyeliner and Pickleman politics. Although currently Lord Mersey looked more damp and disgruntled than anything else, the kohl about his eyes having run to form sad rivulets down his cheeks. His bronze-beribboned top hat was sagging. Sophronia could feel her cheeks flush. This transport was miles beneath his dignity, and to have him sit waiting in the rain . . . How would she ever live it down?

Piston or not, Viscount Mersey was still a gentleman. Noting their approach, he jumped down to assist them. His expensive black boots became all over splattered.

'Miss Temminnick, Miss Plumleigh-Teignmott, delightful to see you both. It has been too long.' He tipped his hat. The hat dripped on him.

Dimity blushed becomingly. Sophronia mastered her embarrassment enough to smile apologetically. 'Good morning, Lord Mersey, terrible weather, isn't it?'

'I'll say!' His voice had dropped since she'd last seen him, and he was taller by a good few inches. He didn't tower over her the way Soap did, but he was exactly the right height to dance well.

Lord Mersey assisted Dimity first.

'Good morning, Pustule,' she greeted her brother affectionately.

'Hoy up, Fatty?' was his gloomy response. Pillover was certain to be even more grumpish than usual. His customary occupation when travelling was to bury his nose in a book, but it was raining too much to read in the open cart.

'Agatha not with you?' he asked.

Dimity blinked at him. It was not like Pillover to distinguish between females, let alone ask after one.

'What? I like Agatha. She's no fuss and doesn't chirrup on. Unlike some people I know.' Pillover huffed.

'She's well. I'll tender your regards, shall I, brother dear?'

'No need to fuss.'

Dimity sat next to him, bumping his shoulder with hers. Then, showing some modicum of delicacy, she dropped the subject. They began to talk softly of family and friends. This was a stratagem on Dimity's part to allow Sophronia private time to reacquaint herself with Felix.

Roger slouched, watching the aristocrats settle into as much comfort as was afforded under the circumstances. Then, at Sophronia's nod, he clicked the pony into a brisk walk.

Sophronia, labouring under the guilt of such incommodious transport, opened the conversation consciously at a disadvantage. Lady Linette would have been shocked. 'I do beg your pardon, my lord, for this. Carts are challenging, even on the best sort of day. The family carriage, please understand, was required to ferry Ephraim's intended from the station. Mumsy does so wish to make a good impression.'

'Advantageous match, is it?' suggested Felix, the implication being it would take quite a bit to outrank him in worthiness of a carriage. Which was true.

'Indeed it is. Did I not write on it?'

'Little of the particulars. Never you mind, it's a novel experience, this trap thing. My father tells me that soon such transports will be entirely obsolete, and private steam locomotives the thing.'

'Oh, do you think that likely? They would have to lay tracks practically everywhere.'

'I think our reliance on mechanicals should organically lead to ever more mechanical transport outside the home, don't you?'

It was a little shocking that a duke's son should be versed in rural matters and goods transport. 'Yes, I suppose that would be efficient. It will be sad to see the countryside so scarred.'

'So said many townships when the railroads were constructed, and now look how far they have taken us. Wouldn't you rather we had the option, now, for example, of a fast closed conveyance to one's home?'

'Indeed I should.' Sophronia was disposed not to argue with the boy right off. She was more nervous than she ought to be, at this reacquaintance. She had forgot how blue Felix's eyes were. He also had this adorable lock of hair that seemed compelled, in the rain, to fall down over his forehead. Unfortunately, his conversational deviation did not bode well for their relationship, such as it was. When Felix and the boys had travelled with them into London almost a year ago, he had been almost obstreperously intimate with her. His flirting had been blunt to the point of rudeness, designed to unsettle. He had stated outright he intended to court her, even with all the obstacles of family, school affiliation and politics. This, on the other hand, was an overly proper conversation, as if they were surrounded by polite society, or being monitored by parents.

Perhaps I was right, he really isn't interested in me any more. Sophronia nibbled her lip in aggravation. She didn't realise that little gesture of nervousness did more to endear her to the young man than anything Lady Linette might teach.

'Your family seems most complicated, my dear Ria.'

Well, *that* was reassuring; he still utilised her pet name. At first she had hated his assumption of affection, but now, uncertain of his interest, she found it comforting. She shifted a little closer to him on the bench of the cart.

'There are an awful lot of us. Eight at last count,' she said.

'Goodness, your mother must be exhausted.'

'So she says, most of the time. Often claiming we will be the death of her. But she can hardly complain. She would keep going having children and most unwisely ended with twins. Silly of her. Should have stopped with me, it would have made a world of difference.'

Felix ruminated. 'But then, how much more of a bother, between six and eight?'

Sophronia nodded. 'I suspect that was Father's argument. He seems happiest under a pile of children. Pity, as he works so hard away from home most of the time.'

'He *works?*'

'Only for the government. He's home during the hunting season!' Ministry was the only allowable occupation for the gentry, and Sophronia wanted it quite clear that her father was a *gentleman*. Felix's family might be on the rolls and extremely toffee-nosed, but there had been Temminnicks in Wiltshire for as long as Felix's father, Duke Golborne, had held his seat, possibly longer. Sophronia's family did not rank Felix's, but they were just as old, thank you very much!

'So Ephraim is the eldest?' Felix continued, trying to get her family straight.

'He's the eldest boy, there's two sisters above him, Nigella and Octavia. Then another brother after him, that's Gresham. He's at Oxford making *something* of himself. Then comes the horrible Petunia, you'll meet her right off. She's still at home and bound to set her cap at you. Then there's me, I'm the final girl. And after me come the two repulsive younger brothers, Humphrey and Hudibras.'

Felix looked properly gobsmacked. 'Quite the mouthful.'

'You should hear what Father named the dogs. Frankly, he goes a little overboard.'

'Gracious me.'

Sophronia giggled. 'Ephraim would come home from Oxford on holiday, and Father used to yell for all of us by name, and both beagles, before he got round to Ephraim. I expect it'll be the same with me now that I've been away. Nigella's been married for simply ages and she's off the recitation completely. Sometimes I think Father doesn't remember she exists. She netted the rather well-regarded Dr Chillingsrymple, have you heard of him?'

Felix shook his head so Sophronia prattled on. 'Publishes papers on the probable medical effects of aetheric travel.'

Dimity and Pillover were arguing vociferously, as only siblings can, over something utterly inconsequential – like the nature of apple sauce. Roger was stolidly facing forward, the road having turned into a bit of river and requiring all his attention. Roger's companion occasionally glanced back at them, but it was with the attitude of one who checks on packages to ensure they are all still inside the transport. Once or twice, Sophronia suspected him of snorting, but it was impossible to see his face.

Sophronia knew she was talking overmuch, like a real schoolgirl rather than one who was trained to flirt and should know better. But Felix's constant banalities were making her increasingly nervous. Chattering was Dimity's trait, but Sophronia seemed to have picked up on it, at least with Felix. He didn't appear to mind, asking encouraging questions and learning all about her family. He must not have siblings of his own.

They continued on in the vein of polite conversation for almost an hour. Sophronia would never before have thought how unsettling it would be to find that this unsettling young man was no longer intentionally trying to unsettle her!

Then, changeable and sudden, Lord Mersey pushed his dripping hair out of his face and lowered his voice. 'How are you *really*, Ria? Your letters are so impersonal.'

Sophronia was relieved, honest interest at last! So relieved, in fact, she was a tad unguarded in her response. 'As are yours! I searched between the lines for some indication of significance, and yet there was nothing.'

'I'm no great letter writer. Besides which, you gave me no encouragement!' Felix's eyes flashed in indignation.

Sophronia bit her lip, both delighted and terrified that she still had his affection. 'We have not yet learned how to write letters with purpose.'

The boy calmed and his voice became a purr. 'Have you learned how to do other things with purpose?' Felix often reminded Sophronia of a cat, always stalking something, seeming bored with life, and then the pounce, a flash of claw and the thrill of a hunt.

Sophronia felt on safer ground now that he was flirting. 'Lady Linette has been teaching us seduction techniques.' She lowered her eyes and then looked off across the grey moor, presenting him with her profile, which was rather a nice one, or so Mademoiselle Geraldine told her.

That statement successfully shocked Felix. He swallowed a few times before saying, his voice almost as high as it had been a year ago, 'Really?'

'Oh, yes indeed. Would you like me to show you? I could use the practise on a real man.'

This time he actually squeaked. 'That might be nice.'

Sophronia demurred, still gazing over the non-existent view, then said, 'We are to start with longing looks.'

'Oh, are we?'

With which Sophronia turned towards him and raised her lashes. She stared into his eyes, trying to convey alluring desire. She thought of the time they had last danced together, how Felix's hand had felt at the small of her back, the sweetness of his breath on her neck. She allowed a small smile to play over her lips.

Felix seemed physically paralysed by her eyes. His own pale-blue ones lost focus. Sophronia noted the remaining kohl about the outside. Daring. One of his endearing foibles. Evil geniuses in training were encouraged to develop eccentricities.

Sophronia let her eyelashes flutter, not too much, only a little.

Felix's breath hitched.

Now, *that* was an interesting reaction.

Sophronia tilted back her head, showing neck. This was a gesture of innocence and vulnerability. It also let the rain trickle right down her décolletage and under her stays, but she mentally gritted her teeth against the discomfort, allowing none of it to show on her face.

Lady Linette would have been proud.

Felix Mersey was well and truly hooked. He leaned in towards her, shifting closer on the bench as though drawn by a magnet.

His voice was so low as to be almost a whisper. 'My goodness . . . Ria.'

And then he was bending down, looking as if he might actually kiss her – in the back of an open cart! With Dimity and Pillover right there! Not to mention the stable lads.

Frightened of her own power *and* of what might happen next, Sophronia broke the look. She lowered her lashes completely and pulled away, offering up her wrist in recompense.

He grabbed her fingers, perhaps too roughly, and pressed his lips into the palm of her hand, kissing up to the small bit of exposed flesh between glove and hurlie strap. Sophronia never went anywhere without her hurlie.

She let him continue to kiss her for a short while, fascinated. It seemed to be some means of coping with an excess of physically manifesting emotion. It was all quite wonderful.

The experiment was spoiled by a scuffle at the front.

Everyone's attention was drawn to where Roger's friend seemed to have almost fallen off the driver's box. He righted himself, and Sophronia wondered if the lads had been at the drink, or if he'd simply dozed off.

Before turning back to her escort, Sophronia exchanged a sharp look with Dimity.

Dimity's expression clearly said, *Do you need me to intervene?*

While Sophronia's response was, *Not just yet, thank you. I believe I have it in hand.*

Pillover's said nothing. Dimity took up scolding her brother for some supposed transgression to do with shoe habits. Pillover sneezed, unexcited.

Sophronia returned her attention to Felix, careful not to look into his eyes any longer than etiquette demanded.

The distraction had provided enough time for Felix to recover control.

'God's bones, Ria,' he hissed, unacceptable language in front of ladies. Dimity heard and gasped, but Sophronia let it slide on the grounds of extenuating circumstances.

Felix said, 'I should have known better than to allow you to practise those wicked lessons on me. You are a sorceress.'

Sophronia liked that description very much. 'Oh, good. It worked, then?'

He dropped her wrist and rubbed at his face. 'You shouldn't do that to a man, not after almost a year of separation and an hour and a half of impersonal conversation at close quarters.'

'I shouldn't? Why, was it terrible?'

'No, quite the opposite, too much good all at once. You must be careful with those green sparkles of yours. You know

Calypso's green eyes trapped Odysseus on her island for seven years? I could live in those eyes of yours.'

'I think we'd both find that rather uncomfortable.'

'Oh, you know what I mean. Let's talk about something else, shall we? How about telling me more of your lessons at that school of yours, outside of seduction class.'

When Sophronia smiled quite wickedly at that, Felix changed his mind. 'Maybe that is unsafe, too?'

'Why don't *you* tell *me* a little of life at Bunson's? How are the Pistons? How is your father?'

'Oh, now, my father is definitely not a safe topic.'

Sophronia edged in, testing the waters. 'Pickleman problems? They do seem overly demanding.'

Felix didn't take the bait. 'Aren't all worthy causes? You know he still grumbles about your tricks at the Westminster Hive.'

'Indeed? How on earth did you get his leave to come to my brother's engagement party?'

'Fortunately for me, he doesn't know your name, so he did not make the connection. He still thinks Lord Akeldama was involved.'

'And you didn't tell him the truth?' Hope sprang so hard in Sophronia's chest, she swore she tingled with it. *If he covered for me against the Picklemen, perhaps I can change his mind about them.*

'I claimed one of your other brothers was a friend from my early days at Eton. You know I was at Eton before Bunson's?'

Sophronia nodded.

'I suspected you probably had some brother who was about

the correct age. You seem to be lousy with brothers. We might have been at school at the same time.'

'You're right. Gresham would have been older than you, but you could have crossed paths.'

'Father won't look into it thoroughly. He's been distracted recently. He'd check the name Temminnick and not a whole lot else. Whatever your father does for the government, it obviously does not impede Pickleman policies. So I'm allowed to attend.'

Felix's father, Duke Golborne, was something terribly high up in the Picklemen as well as a peer. The Picklemen were, so far as Sophronia could tell, evil. Not that there was anything especially *wrong* with being evil. But this evil seemed particularly centred on monopolising political control and undermining everyone else's power but their own, and that Sophronia didn't like. She was finding, as she grew older, that she was rather fond of balance . . . in all things. 'Oh, indeed. And what has been *distracting* the duke of late?'

'Now, now, Ria, you think I don't remember that look of yours?'

'What look?'

'Not unlike a hound on a scent. A very pretty hound, of course.'

Sophronia sighed. 'I know, it's my worst giveaway. I'm mostly good at schooling my features for anger and love and suchlike emotions, but curiosity gets the better of me.'

Felix, clearly thinking of Sophronia and Sidheag's spectacular rescue infiltration of the Westminster Hive, added sarcastically, 'I should say that it does so in more ways than one.'

'Now, now, my lord, you know it's part of my charm.'

Felix looked as if he doubted it. 'You do wear breeches well.'

'They are comfortable and mobile. Why should you boys have all the fun?'

'Next thing you'll have me in stays.'

Sophronia was surprised to find she rather liked that idea. She thought Felix would look well in a corset, perhaps a black-and-blue one to match his eyes and hair. 'Would you like to try? You might fit one of Sidheag's.'

Felix actually blushed. 'Oh, now, I say!'

'It was only an offer.'

Their conversation remained a great deal livelier after that, ranging on topics of interest both evil-genius and finishing related. Sophronia even successfully teased him about Pickleman politics, and he looked as if he might have been second-guessing the Picklemen's interests. Or at least actually thinking about the implications. Eventually, they moved towards the front of the cart to include Dimity and even Pillover in their conversation. The boys managed to put any animosity aside for the duration of the trip. It helped that tea and sandwiches plus hard-boiled eggs and winter apples were consumed. It was hard to be antagonistic over the comfort of food on a rainy day.

MASQUERADING MECHANICALS

It was a pleasant trip, in the end, despite the weather and the conveyance. They arrived at Sophronia's family estate early that evening. It was too late for tea, although Frowbritcher, the mechanical butler, laid out a reserve for the weary travellers.

The engagement party was Mrs Temminnick's opportunity to exhibit her hostess technique. With eight children, thrift was a matter of course, but this was her *eldest son* and no expense was to be spared. There were floating lanterns ready to launch as soon as the sun set. There were freight carriers full of goods and errand boys on donkeys arriving at an alarming rate. Sophronia was relieved to see that there were no cheese pies. Mumsy had borrowed extra mechanical staff from the neighbours as well. Sophronia spotted six clangermaids and two buttlinger models of the latest design, certainly not belonging to her family. Frowbritcher, who ordinarily had the most regal of bearings, as it were, seemed shabby next to the shiny new technology. Extra tracks had been laid down in the public areas of the house, criss-crossing the sitting room and card parlour and bordering the ballroom in artful waving patterns.

After tea, the girls and boys separated to change for the main event. Pillover and Felix were bound to be quicker and so were instructed to attend the other gentlemen in the billiard room once their toilette was complete. The young ladies were put in with Sophronia's sisters, a milling, giggling throng of primping and gossip.

All attention instantly turned to Sophronia and Dimity, much to Petunia's annoyance. Petunia was Sophronia's nearest older sister and, in consequence, a trial.

'Oh, Sophronia, is it true?' asked one of Petunia's silly friends.

'Of course it's true, isn't it always,' replied Sophronia, depositing her shawl and sundry unnecessary luggage in a pile on a settee. Bumbersnoot, lost under the mounds, seemed content to stay quiet. Dimity put her assorted garments on top.

Petunia bustled over, clucking. 'What on earth has happened to your hair, sister?'

'I travelled all day in an open cart in the rain!' Sophronia snapped.

Petunia always treated Sophronia as if she were still ten. At Dimity's startled look, Sophronia realised she was usually better at holding her temper, and took a deep breath, reaching for her training. She would outclass her sister if it killed her.

Petunia continued to cluck and fuss. Soon a gaggle of girls joined her, attacking Sophronia's flattened locks with curlers and rags, pins and puffs, falls and flowers. Sophronia stood composed under their siege. Of course, she knew what they wanted of her, but she was not going to make it easy. She allowed them to guide her to a chair in front of a looking glass without offer of information.

Dimity, ignored, drifted to a corner and popped open her carpet bag to extract her costume. It was a modification of her favourite gold ballgown. She'd ordered a new evening bodice for it and added crystals about the neckline in a gear-like pattern. The shape of the skirt, paired with copious gold jewellery, including an ornate tiara, made her look like the queen of mechanicals. It was a lovely effect with her pale complexion and riotous curls – Dimity did not need the benefit of curling tongs. Having donned a smooth mechanical-like mask, she looked enchanting, entirely guileless and completely trustworthy. She had learned well how to manipulate with clothing. There was something so unthreatening about household mechanicals. Dimity had managed to trade on that fact and still look regal. Sophronia wished she could carry off such a costume.

Sophronia let her sister's friends fuss. Only she knew that her hair was destined to be scraped back into a severe bun. Best let them have their fun. Behind the group, on the settee, Bumbersnoot awakened. Their pile of garments was weaving erratically. Sophronia drew attention away from him by answering questions.

'Sophronia, what we want to know is, is it true that you've brought two eligible members of the peerage with you?' Petunia had no subtlety.

'Dear sister, that should entirely depend on what you mean by eligible.'

'Stop being coy, young lady.'

There was a vast difference between coy and evasive, and Sophronia dearly wanted to instruct but said instead, 'I have brought Viscount Mersey and Mr Plumleigh-Teignmott. So far as I know, neither is affianced. For Mr Plumleigh-Teignmott's part, you might ask his sister. Although he is still young. Even Lord Mersey has not gained his majority.'

The ladies sighed in disappointment.

Sophronia took that as an opportunity to extract herself from their clutches and rummage through her own carpet bag. She also reached under the mackintosh pile and pulled out Bumbersnoot the reticule.

'Be still, you,' she hissed at him.

'What is that hideous thing?' demanded Petunia.

'Oh, dear sister, don't you know? This is the very latest in animal-shaped reticules out of Italy. You don't mean to tell me you are *that* out of touch with the current modes? How sad for you to be trapped in the countryside.'

Petunia said, through her teeth, 'Of course I heard of the craze, but I should not think myself so lacking in individuality as to adopt an accessory simply because it is the latest thing in some backwater foreign country!'

'It is the latest thing in London as well, or didn't you know even that much?' Sophronia was going to run with it. Bumbersnoot, for his part, remained perfectly still, like a good little dog. Although she thought she saw a twinkle of mischief in his jet eyes. She put him carefully under the settee, and then draped a shawl over the edge, as if protecting him from the avarice in the eyes of those around her. It would give Bumbersnoot a chance to explore discreetly.

Sophronia would have wagered her best *robe à transformation* that Petunia wanted nothing so much at that moment as to go to finishing school herself.

The girls around her murmured in distress as Sophronia began to dress.

'You don't have to wear that, do you?' said one.

Sophronia had begged an old dress from Sister Mattie. It was black and severe and could be thought a mourning gown, it was so plain. Over the last few weeks she had tailored it into a narrow silhouette, most unfashionable.

'Sophronia, dear, it's so ugly!' remonstrated Petunia.

Sophronia pulled it on. She looked well in black, and as a young lady with no deaths in the family, she rarely had the opportunity to wear it. It went on easily. Sister Mattie did not employ a lady's maid, so all of her dresses fastened up the front. But what Sophronia, Dimity, Agatha and Sidheag had spent their free time doing to that dress was ingenious.

They had cut it in and down at the collar so that Sophronia wore it over a white blouse. Both were low enough, however, to show a goodly amount of cleavage. Sophronia had very nice cleavage and was under orders from Mademoiselle Geraldine to take advantage of it. *One never knows when one might need to hide or distract; décolletage is good for both.* Hers were nothing on Mademoiselle Geraldine's own considerable assets, but then, whose were? The bodice was tailored all the way to her waist, nipped in further with a wide, stiff leather belt. The effect was almost like a blacksmith's apron, giving Sophronia a utilitarian, masculine look. The white underskirt was full enough to disguise the fact that it was actually divided down the middle and could act as trousers if necessary. Over this was draped the skirt of the black gown, split up each side so it looked even more apron-like. To it they had sewn multiple pockets in shades of black and grey, in variable sizes, largest and lightest at the bottom, smallest and darkest near the waist, forming a pattern. In those pockets Sophronia had stashed useful objects. Not that she expected trouble, but she had the pockets so she might as well use them.

'Sophronia, what *are* you meant to be?' Petunia was disgusted.

Sophronia pulled out her mask; it was an asymmetrical slash of black lace, like a large smudge. 'I'm a sootie, of course.'

The young ladies all gasped. Imagine going to a masquerade as something lower class! There was some muttering about the fact that at least Sophronia wouldn't be competing for masculine attention.

'Well,' sniffed Petunia, 'I suppose we should be glad you didn't actually don masculine attire.'

Sophronia blinked at her. *Yes, yes you should.* She said, 'Oh, dear, do you think this too plain?'

'Of course it's too plain!'

'I was thinking of your finer feelings, sister dear. I wouldn't want to distract the gentlemen. After all, I'm not officially out yet. You're on the market; you should have first crack.'

'Oh, well, that's very thoughtful, Sophronia.' Petunia fluffed the skirts of her shepherdess outfit, trying not to look pleased by the consideration.

Dimity grinned from behind her mechanical mask.

Sophronia winked at her.

They both knew the truth. The very plainness of Sophronia's dress would make it stand out in a sea of colour. Besides, Sophronia had the figure to carry it off. After a stint at Mademoiselle Geraldine's, she also had the bearing. Also, the simplicity would make others underestimate her, never a bad thing. Sophronia loved the gown for its practicality and for its nod to her friends belowdecks. Soap would have thought it a great joke. After all, it looked like a feminine version of the apron he wore to shovel coal.

The ball had started, but there was still an hour or more before they could safely go down without being thought desperate. Sophronia and Dimity made their way to the settee corner. Sophronia occupied herself checking the sharpness of her scissors and letter opener and wishing for a bladed fan while relaying softly some of her conversation with Felix in the cart.

Suddenly an excited twittering emanated from the door, opened by a very uncomfortable-looking Pillover. He cleared his throat.

Before he could say anything, Dimity pushed through the crowd to face him. 'Pill, you aren't supposed to *be* here. We're dressing!'

Pillover grumbled something unintelligible. Dimity nodded. She replied sharply and then shut the door in his face.

The hubbub died down and the young ladies returned to fixing masks and fussing with hair, now accompanied by discussion of Pillover's finer points. This startled Sophronia and Dimity – who would have thought he had any? Apparently his complexion was considered lovely, and he was a nice height for dancing, and the sullen glumness came off as deliciously mysterious.

'Don't you want to cuddle and console him? Poor darling, he looks so unhappy,' said one, pulling on long white gloves.

'I wager he's had his heart broken,' suggested another. She wore the costume of a Greek goddess – swathes of white silk draped over a turquoise ballgown and large crinoline. She was one of many who had opted for the classics. 'I should love to be the one to repair his tortured soul.'

Dimity made her way back to Sophronia, not bothering to advocate for or against her sibling. Pillover would suffer the slings and arrows of willing young ladies without her help. 'Pillover needs to talk. Alone. He's been trying to all along, apparently, but Felix has always been there. I told him to wait in the gazebo. I knew he'd remember it from before.'

The gazebo had been the location of all the fuss with the prototype and Monique the first time Dimity and Pillover had attended a party at the Temminnicks'. It burned down as a result, but Sophronia's mother had had it rebuilt bigger and better. Sophronia had used the reconstruction to hide her stolen air dinghy. The small aircraft seemed a part of the roof structure, hidden in plain sight like a basket figurehead on top.

Sophronia looked around at the excited young ladies. 'We'll never escape unseen. Too many people at too close quarters.'

Dimity nodded. 'I think he mainly needs to talk to you. I'll create a distraction. If the message was meant for both of us, he'd have told me himself while you were flirting with Felix. It'll be easier for you to get around with all the borrowed mechanicals. In that outfit you might be taken as staff, so long as you avoid family.'

Sophronia reached below the settee, grabbed Bumbersnoot and shoved him under the throw rug in one corner of the room with an encouraging 'Go ahead.'

Bumbersnoot began to explore, a moving lump under the carpet.

'There's your distraction. You can keep him safe?'

Dimity smiled. 'In this crowd? Of course. Most of them will faint, and the others are silly.'

It was a fair assessment. 'Yet you still want to be one of them?'

'It's not the deceit I object to, Sophronia dear, it's the danger.'

With which Dimity made her way to the settee. For a short moment she stared fixedly at the rug where the Bumbersnoot lump moved. Then she threw her head back and shrieked at the top of her lungs. 'Rat! Eeeeeek!' With which she hopped up on to the settee, upending the mound of discarded clothing on to the floor and on top of poor Bumbersnoot once more. 'Eeek! There it goes, get it! Eeeeeee!'

Without even seeing the alleged rat themselves, the girls in that corner of the room all fainted. Those near to a couch or chair got up on top of it, screaming themselves. This proved challenging on the cushier furniture and with longer skirts. One or two fell over; a few pushed others off in order to gain the high ground. This caused more shrieks. Still others cried out in sympathy, for the sake of exacerbating the hysteria. The chaos was instant and intense. With all attention on Dimity,

Sophronia slid out into the hallway, closing the door behind her.

After a year and a half of ghosting about a finishing school for intelligencers, a place riddled with tracks and malevolent mechanicals of all kinds, she found her own house easy by comparison. Most of the human staff were already downstairs attending to early guests and dressed gentlemen. A few mechanicals trundled along, under orders, none of them equipped with proximity alarms or remotely interested in Sophronia. She belonged here; why should it matter that she was out and about?

Her parents and sundry older siblings were already at the ball. Petunia was upstairs screaming at Bumbersnoot, so there was only the twins to worry about. They must be off causing mischief for her mother, as Sophronia made it through the house and out into the garden without attracting attention. Or perhaps she had learned more than she thought at Mademoiselle Geraldine's.

'I have a message from Lady Kingair,' said Pillover, without the courtesy of a greeting. He was slouching on a rail of the gazebo, plucking dolefully at a camellia bush.

Sophronia respected brevity. 'I was hoping someone might.'

'I'm the best and most trustworthy option of a bad lot, I suppose.'

Sophronia held out her hand.

Pillover shook his head. 'Naw, it came via Vieve, verbal only. Too dangerous to keep written, scamp said.'

Sophronia flipped up her hand, looking about to make absolutely certain they were enjoying complete privacy. A few stable hands walked towards the front of the house from the barn. Carriages were beginning to arrive. They were out of earshot. Above them the basket of Sophronia's misappropriated air dinghy nested comfortably. Someone could hide in there, she supposed. Quickly she pulled out her letter opener and jabbed through the wicker of the gondola. No one screamed and there was no blood, although Pillover watched her do this with mild disgust.

Sophronia jumped back down and nodded at him to continue. She stashed her letter opener.

Pillover said, 'Sidheag says her werewolves are in trouble. The Kingair pack has been disgraced.' Pillover looked as if he had swallowed something unpleasant. 'They were caught planning to murder Queen Victoria. Lord Maccon has abandoned them and is contemplating challenging Lord Woolsey to take over the pack near London.'

'Oh, my goodness!' said Sophronia. 'Treason?'

'Attempted treason.'

'*And* Alpha abandonment.' Sophronia could understand the Laird of Kingair's anger, but it put everyone at risk. A werewolf pack without an Alpha could be very dangerous. Quickly, she calculated the next full moon. Right around the corner; without an Alpha, the pack's madness could be particularly brutal. 'I hope the claviers are ready.'

Pillover continued, 'Sidheag has gone to London to intercept Lord Maccon, try to turn him back to his duty. He's needed to keep the Kingair pack in order, especially now. Seems his Beta planned it all and Lord Maccon killed him before heading south.'

Kingair had no Alpha *and* no Beta? Sophronia paled. She'd never heard of such a thing in the whole history of openly accepted supernaturals. *Who is controlling the pack? They could run mad.* Every one of those werewolves was an uncle to Sidheag; this would account for her upset. Her one and only family was fractured beyond all possible repair. This was the werewolf version of those unspeakable divorces so popular on the Continent! 'Poor Sidheag! What are we to do?'

Pillover shrugged, sublimely unconcerned. Or perhaps he always expected bad news and thus was never surprised by it. 'I'm only the messenger.'

Further discussion was stopped by a whip crack of a cry. 'Ho there, young man!'

Pillover jumped away from Sophronia, barking his elbow on the gazebo railing. 'Ouch!'

Sophronia turned to face the house. 'Mumsy!'

'Sophronia Angelina Temminnick, what are you doing alone in the garden with a *boy*!'

'Um,' said Sophronia.

Pillover rubbed his elbow.

Mrs Temminnick turned her wrath on the unfortunate young man. 'Mr Plumleigh-Teignmott, this is too bad! I am shocked, shocked, I say. After we welcomed you into our home last winter! I trust you will make an honest woman of my daughter?'

'Mother! Pillover is *only* fourteen!'

'Oh ho, *Pillover*, is it? What have they been teaching you at finishing school? To meet a young man in the gardens, alone and unchaperoned ...'

'Really, Mother! He is a veritable hobbledehoy. Don't be silly.'

'Oh, thank you for that,' muttered Pillover, utterly dejected. Which fortunately made him seem less threatening.

Sophronia said smoothly, 'My school has trained me to recognise when a young man offers no risk. He is my dearest friend's younger brother. I asked him to see me around the garden. I was feeling most unwell after that cart ride, and the rain has abated somewhat.'

'Don't you dare talk back, young lady!' Mrs Temminnick looked at Pillover with new eyes. He did seem as if he could barely muster enough energy to hold his own head up, let alone menace her daughter. It obviously took great effort for him to speak to, let alone kiss, a lady. There was clearly no threat to her daughter's reputation, aside from the fact that they had been caught alone together. Mrs Temminnick checked to see if anyone else had noticed. No one had. Still, the value of having her youngest daughter trussed up at only sixteen?

Sophronia perfectly followed her mother's thought process. 'Mumsy, the ball is to start soon; everyone must be looking for you. If you leave quickly, Pill and I will return separately, with no one the wiser.'

Mrs Temminnick wasn't going to let them get away that easily. 'I will be looking into the Plumleigh-Teignmott family. If Mr Temminnick thinks them suitable, we will arrange the match. I know what is happening here, daughter, even if you are both too young. I demand an *understanding*. Do you understand, Mr Plumleigh-Teignmott?'

Pillover shrugged, which was his response to everything.

Sophronia blinked. 'If you insist.' There was no point in arguing further at the moment.

Shortly thereafter, Sophronia slid back into the dressing room full of primping ladies. No one had noticed her absence.

'Well?' hissed Dimity. 'How'd it go?'

'You were right, Sidheag had a message for me. Although I don't know what I'm supposed to do with the information.' She quickly relayed the bulk of Pillover's communications.

Dimity was suitably appalled. 'Treason *and* murder? Lord Maccon's abandonment is totally understandable, of course. To conspire against the queen is to conspire against the Alpha.'

Sophronia nodded. It was the stitching that kept the fabric of an integrated society together. Supernatural leaders, in their way, were Queen Victoria's strong arm. To betray her was to betray them. Sidheag was the one who'd taught them that very fact. 'Anything else, dare I ask?'

'Yes, unfortunately, I seem to have got myself secretly engaged to your brother.'

Dimity raised her eyebrows. 'Oh, dear. Although I should like to have you for a sister-in-law, of course.'

Sophronia glared at her.

'Well, yes, Pillover is *perfectly* ghastly. But does that really matter? He'd make an amenable husband. You could do whatever you liked, take any patron you wanted. Secretly run the empire as Her Majesty's Mistress Intelligencer and he'd never notice. So long as you kept him well-supplied with bacon and books.'

Sophronia smiled. 'I suppose we could play with it for a while. But I will have to find a nice way to jilt him, eventually.'

Dimity sighed and twirled her mask. 'Of course you will. But it will be fun to torture Pillover in the interim.'

Sophronia's smile turned into a grin. 'Not to mention Felix Mersey.'

Dimity's eyes sparkled. 'My, yes!'

So it was that Sophronia attended her brother's engagement masquerade secretly engaged herself. Mrs Temminnick insisted Pillover be Sophronia's escort and take the first dance. A very surprised Lord Mersey was forced to lead in Dimity. Thus paired, they undertook the opening quadrille with great discomfort on the part of everyone, except perhaps Sophronia, who was starting to view it all as a joke. She flirted shamelessly with Pillover, who told her to stop it in tones of such abject misery she almost pitied him.

The ball was certainly up to snuff. Sophronia felt proudly that it was good enough to impress even a man of Felix's standing. Preshea would have found flaws, but it was a vast improvement on last year's ball. The masquerade dresses were divine. The masks were varied, and Ephraim looked ridiculously happy dancing with his fluff of a bride-to-be. She was a pretty, jolly sort. It was impossible to determine her costume, with so many layers of white and pink. Sophronia settled on cupcake.

She recognised most everyone in attendance, even with masks. After all, the society afforded by the local gentry was not varied. There were a few unknown young ladies, friends of the bride, and a gaggle of older folk of a similar jolly roundness that suggested familial relations. Behind them stood a tall young man who held himself beautifully, if a little stiffly, wearing a full mask of black velvet and a wig of a style popular some hundred years ago among the French nobility. His costume matched the wig, complete with velvet coat and satin breeches of dark silver, and waistcoat and gloves of blood red. He reminded Sophronia of her vampire friend, Lord Akeldama. Had the vampire sent her a message via drone? The young man did seem intent on watching her movements. This when there were a number of young ladies without partners who might benefit from his attentions.

In and around the glittering throng, the extra mechanical staff trundled, bearing trays of enticing nibbles. The mechanicals were also dressed for the occasion. These were not the faceless utilitarian creatures of Mademoiselle Geraldine's, but proper household issue, with shiny – if impassive – metal faces. They blended nicely with all the masks. Dimity could be seen posing with one or another as they passed, for her costume was much admired. The mechanicals all wore small black evening cravats or crisp white aprons. Their protocols were simple and they moved smoothly from crowd to dumbwaiter and back, engaged in a dance of their own.

Felix demanded an explanation the moment they began to waltz. He was dressed as a particularly handsome jester, his mask so small as to be a mere nod to the theme. Sophronia contemplated playing coquette but decided that would be cruel. Felix seemed genuinely enamoured, and she didn't want to hurt him. So she explained that Pillover had needed to deliver a message from a friend and that they had been caught in the garden together.

Felix found the whole thing amusing. 'Would you like to walk out into the gardens with me, Ria, my heart? I could arrange to get us caught.'

Sophronia twinkled up at him. Her heart fluttered at the idea of a night-time stroll with such a handsome boy. *I could practise some other bits of seduction class.* 'Oh, now, my dear lord, I think that might be jumping from toast fork into fire. You are far more dangerous a proposition for me, and far more desirable a prospect to my mother. I should think you would wish to be more discreet.'

'For you, my Ria, I would sacrifice my reputation.'

'Now, now, Lord Mersey, you are perfectly aware that you would be sacrificing *mine*.'

He whirled her into an elaborate twist. He danced divinely, his frame always a little too intimate but not enough to shock the chaperones. The hand at her back was warm and supportive; the one clutching hers to lead was direct and assertive. He looked into her eyes in a melting manner, but only long enough to let her know he was interested and not so long as to lose track of the others around them. He could have been a dance instructor had he not been born the son of a duke.

A duke who would see all vampires and werewolves dead. Sophronia tore herself away from his blue eyes to find she was the object of envious glances from nearly every young lady there.

'Felix, my dear, do me a favour after this dance?'

'Anything for you,' he said, rather unguardedly. Then quickly, 'You aren't going to leave me to finish the set alone, are you?' There was real fear in his voice; twice Sophronia had abandoned him in the middle of a dance.

'Not tonight, I hope. No one I know has been kidnapped, and the prototype is beyond my control.'

Felix tilted his head. 'Indeed it is, as it should be. It was the Picklemen's by right. Ours by right. Not something for you to worry that pretty head about.'

Sophronia wanted to argue that point, but mid-waltz was not the time; besides, she liked it when Felix underestimated her. More room to manoeuvre. 'Mmmm. No, I was going to ask ... My sister Petunia is there, the one dressed as the fluffy shepherdess? Dance with her next, would you? Otherwise she'll never forgive me.'

Felix looked over, winced a tiny bit, then said gallantly, 'Of course. It would be my pleasure.'

'Oh, thank you.' Sophronia nearly slipped up and applied another longing glance at that juncture, she was so grateful.

Felix noticed and leaned in. 'Careful, my sweet, we are in a public place. All eyes are upon us. And you are affianced to another.'

That made her smile again.

The dance was nearly finished when the tall, stiff young man dressed as a vintage dandy appeared at Felix's elbow.

'If I may?' he said, insinuating himself between them like oil into a mechanical and dexterously depriving Felix of Sophronia.

Sophronia had never been removed from a dance partner before, although she had been trained for it. Felix certainly had never had anyone dare to cut in on him! At a loss, he bowed out politely. He was angry, though. There was a good chance that he, like Sophronia, was thinking of Lord

Akeldama when he saw this man's costume. And Felix did not like vampires.

The dandy guided her, clumsily it must be admitted, through the final refrain of the waltz. He relaxed noticeably at the end and whisked her to the punch bowl, taking proprietary control of her dance card so that she could not find her next partner. As it happened, she had no partner. She was, after all, not out, and could really only dance with her escort or her brothers.

Sophronia glared at him, waiting for some kind of sign.

'You're awfully friendly with that young man,' said a horribly familiar voice from behind the velvet mask.

'Soap!' hissed Sophronia, backing them both away from the punch and into a corner behind a potted plant. 'What on earth are you doing here?'

'Swilling punch with the aristocracy. Keeping an eye on you.'

'I can take care of myself!'

'Not from what I hear. Rumour around the floor is that you got yourself engaged!'

'Oh ho, trust you to be in on the gossip.'

'The ladies like me, what can I say? What do you have to say for yourself?' He was glaring at Felix, who held court across the crowded ballroom and raised his glass at them in a challenging, cocky way.

Soap inclined his head.

Sophronia could almost feel the sharpness of Felix's glare.

Sophronia was convinced these two shouldn't encounter each other when Soap was pretending to be a gentleman. Duelling might result.

'Silly Soap, it's not to Felix. Mumsy has decided to engage me to Pillover.'

'What?' That took the coal out of Soap's boiler.

'Misunderstanding.'

'I should hope so. He's a child.'

'Sadly, he doesn't look like it any more.'

Soap stopped staring angrily at Felix and turned to follow Pillover's slouched form as he led an excited lady through a reel in a competent – if desultory – manner. The young woman clearly thought he was *the* most wonderful thing.

'Oh, dear,' said Soap.

'Who knew Pillover would turn into a lady-killer?'

'Who *indeed*?' Soap could do a fair imitation of an upper-crust accent when he put his mind to it.

If Sophronia hadn't been so annoyed with him for putting himself in danger, she might have said something complimentary on this subject. 'I think it's the general air of bleakness and dyspepsia; women want to save him and administer good cheer.'

'Poor old Pillover.'

As if knowing he was the object of their discussion, Pillover spotted them lurking behind the palm and, with an air of desperation, began to bend his set in their direction. Felix extracted himself from a flock of eager young ladies and desperate mamas and circled in on their location as well.

Sophronia panicked. 'Soap, you have to get out of here! You haven't been invited. What if someone finds out who you are? I'm sure there's a law against it. You could be cashiered or whatever it is they do upon encountering unsanctioned mixing of the classes.'

'I thought my accent was rather good!'

'Soap, and I don't mean to be rude, but you do *know* you are of African descent, don't you? What if your mask slips?'

Soap shrugged. 'I like your costume, miss. You look a treat, almost like you was one of us down below.'

'You're impossible! Why, I . . . Wait a moment. You were Roger's friend, on the box! How did I not know it was you?'

'I bundled completely up and I slouched so you wouldn't recognise my posture. And I stayed quiet so you wouldn't know my voice.'

'How did you persuade Roger to go along?'

Soap grinned. 'You think I don't have just as many tricks as you, for all your education?'

That was fair; he had taught Sophronia a whole mess of dirty fighting techniques.

'Who are you? You upstart poodle faker!' demanded Felix, interposing himself between Soap and Sophronia in an over-bearing white knight way.

Sophronia was instantly annoyed. Felix should know she was perfectly capable of dealing with things!

'That is none of your concern,' replied Soap, sounding even more the toff, his speech patterns influenced by Felix's accent.

'Oh, now, if you are focusing in on *my* lady here, I should *make* it my concern.'

'Ho there!' said Sophronia, in a low hiss, attempting to get both young men to lower their voices and not cause a scene. 'I'm no one's lady, thank you kindly. Despite what my mother thinks.'

The boys ignored her, squaring off rather like two hounds after the same smelly old carcass.

'Oh, really,' said Sophronia, annoyed at being ignored. 'I'm not really important in this situation, am I? You two simply wish to bicker.'

This was probably unfair to Felix, who didn't recognise Soap. *Where did Soap get such an outlandish outfit?* Felix would consider a sootie so far beneath him as to be unworthy as a rival, if he knew.

Soap, on the other hand, had taken an active dislike to the young viscount the moment Felix entered Sophronia's life.

Things might have got quite out of hand, except that Pillover pulled up, panting. 'Oh, Sophronia, thank goodness. Save me? Please? All those young girls, in pastels, talking about the weather. I shall go and jump off a bridge, I swear I shall. Do you have bridges in Wiltshire? They chatter, they chatter worse than Dimity ever did. Oh, the chattering! The chattering, it haunts me.'

That broke the tension.

Felix looked at Pillover as if he were some yappy dog.

Soap chuckled.

'Well,' said Pillover truculently, 'if we're secretly engaged, she's obliged to save me.'

Sophronia did not want to leave Soap and Felix together. 'Oh, Pill, I really would like to help, but we seem to be in the middle of some kind of whose-top-hat-is-the-biggest contest.'

Pillover looked between the two young men in question. 'Well, I don't know who you are, sir,' he addressed Soap, 'although I respect the courage of a man who wears satin breeches *that* tight, but in the end you'll have to cede to Lord Mersey. He's too much of a peer, you understand? And a bit of a prick as well.'

'Pillover!' gasped Sophronia.

'Well, he is. Girls never see it, but it's true. All I'm saying is, he's going to win no matter what you do, stranger. So you might as well give up.'

Felix looked as if he had been given some kind of caped weasel – part gift, part insult, part utter confusion. 'Thank you, I think.'

Pillover glared at him. 'Pistons! Trouble, the lot of you. Now that's settled, you'll save me, Sophronia?'

'Pill, I don't think you've solved the problem.'

'People tell me that all the time.' He turned about. 'Oh, belter, here they come!' A gaggle of pastel puffs mixed with wings and very pretty flowered masks headed purposefully in his direction. Though, to be fair, they might have also been after Lord Mersey.

Sophronia followed Pillover's gaze, only to have her attention caught by a hubbub at the door to the ballroom. Within a very brief space of time, it escalated into a loudly voiced argument of the type that ought never be conducted in public, not even between tradesmen. It had everyone's attention. Even Felix and Soap left off their animosity to focus on the astounding breach in social etiquette.

Frowbritcher and a human footman were barring the door against some highly excitable interlopers.

'How thrilling, I do believe someone is trying to infiltrate our party,' Sophronia said. 'I had no idea an invitation was so desirable. Mumsy will be pleased. We have *arrived* in society at last.' She realised that might sound like bragging. 'Or there is nothing on at the theatre this evening.'

Then she caught sight of one intruder. The lady wore no mask and displayed no extravagance of fancy dress. She wasn't trying to attend the ball; she was trying to get inside for some other reason. She turned to face the crowd.

'Good gracious me, Lady Kingair!' said Felix.

'Sidheag!' said Sophronia at the same time.

Standing to either side of Sidheag, visible only when the ebb of the throng allowed for it, were two huge wolves. One of them had a top hat tied to his head. The other was bigger and shaggier. And hatless.

'Captain Niall?' squeaked Sophronia.

'And a strange werewolf,' added Soap.

Felix looked alarmed. 'Werewolves? Unknown, *uninvited* werewolves? Here? How revolting.'

'You do know the by-invitation-only thing is just vampires, don't you?' said Pillover, under his breath.

Sophronia wasn't certain if her mother would take the presence of an underdressed Scottish aristocrat and two beast-form werewolves as an honour or a horror. So she stepped forward. She had better make certain it was thought an honour or they'd all be in trouble. 'If you'll pardon me, gentlemen, I believe I have a situation to rectify.'

None of them objected.

Helpful Barnaclegeese

S ophronia pushed her way through the crowd. Her mother was at the top of the stairs, agitating like a malfunctioning mechanical. Her father seemed to be already at the cards. Sophronia was glad to note his absence. One less parent to bamboozle.

'Who are you and why have you brought those *animals* to my party?' Mrs Temminnick demanded. She must be near hysterics, for she knew better than to address a werewolf with anything but the strictest courtesy. Poor Mumsy did not like chaos, which made it all the odder that she had eight children.

Sophronia stepped up. 'Mumsy, I believe I may be of assistance.'

'Sophronia, this wouldn't be your fault, would it? Did you invite these ... these ... hirsute interlopers? Is that academy a complete failure? I thought you were doing so well.'

'Now, Mumsy, I brought the son of a duke to Ephraim's party, didn't I?'

'That *is* something.'

'Well, this is Lady Kingair, daughter of an earl, a very important person indeed.' Technically it was slightly more complicated than that, but daughter of an earl was good enough for Mumsy.

Mrs Temminnick looked at Sidheag doubtfully. Not for the first time, Sophronia wished her dear friend *sometimes* dressed the part of a peer. Today Lady Kingair was wearing a gown so drab that even a governess wouldn't have bothered.

'But, but, dear, that dress is tweed ... Oh, has she come costumed as a parlourmaid?' Mrs Temminnick was disposed to be optimistic on behalf of an earl's daughter.

'Now, Mumsy' – Sophronia was quick on the flip – 'don't you see? It's a symbolic allegory of the famous myth of Romulus and Remus. Since a werewolf is almost never female, Lady Kingair has dressed as a nanny to foil the wolf shape and properly represent the she-wolf who fed the great hero-founders of Rome.'

Mrs Temminnick balked.

Sophronia looked at her, eyes wide. 'Oh, dear, isn't it obvious? I thought it was obvious. I'm sure Sidheag did, too. Didn't you, dear?'

Sidheag balked almost as much as Sophronia's mother.

'Goodness, well, at least they are giving you *some* kind of education at that finishing school.' Mrs Temminnick liked that she hadn't understood a word her daughter had said.

'I could say it in Latin, if that would help?'

'No, dear, no, not Latin as well as tweed. Not in one night.'

'Oh, Sophronia!' Sidheag did not want to play along. Fortunately, she also seemed incapable of cogent speech. Solid, unflappable Sidheag was so relieved to see Sophronia, it seemed she might cry. Or cast herself into Sophronia's arms. Impossible options in public, the both of them.

Sophronia had thought Sidheag would be recovered by now, yet she seemed to have got worse.

Since she was unable to console her friend with intimacy, Sophronia's training kicked in. 'Mumsy, Lady Kingair appears to have misplaced her mask on the journey. Was it terribly distressing, Sidheag dear? Why don't I take her to the family parlour for a restorative cup of tea? I might be able to settle matters, find another mask. This would get us all away from the ball. Ephraim would like that.'

Brought back to the purpose of the masquerade, Mrs Temminnick could think of no better solution.

Dimity appeared at Sidheag's elbow.

No one mentioned the werewolves, although Sophronia and Dimity both nodded at them. Politeness deemed they only be acknowledged, not addressed directly. When in wolf shape, they couldn't exactly engage in polite conversation. It was thought best not to remind them of this fact by attempting an introduction.

Mrs Temminnick threw her hands up to heaven. 'Fine, fine, but the young gentlemen *all* stay here dancing!'

'Of course, Mumsy. They can make up the numbers.' Sophronia sent a silent prayer to Pillover to keep Soap and Felix from murdering each other.

'This way, Sidheag dear.' Sophronia grabbed her friend's hand. It was icy cold. Sidheag must have ridden through the rain for hours. Sophronia guided Sidheag hurriedly away from the ball.

Captain Niall and his unknown companion followed. It was a mark of how little, if ever, Mrs Temminnick fraternised with werewolves that she had decided to categorise both as friendly dogs, rather than naked men. Otherwise, she would never have permitted them to accompany her daughter.

The family parlour was a cosy enclave of puffy furniture and unbreakable objects much used by the Temminnick children over the years. They settled Sidheag on the couch nearest the fire. Dimity sat next to her, patting her on the arm, trilling consoling banalities.

Sophronia sent one of the clangermaids off to retrieve tea. She then suggested to Captain Niall and the strange werewolf that they find some of Gresham's old clothing in the nursery and requested they go change shape there. She worried about the second werewolf, who was a good deal larger than the captain. It meant he would be a good deal larger as a man as well, and Gresham was not particularly large.

With werewolves gone and fire stoked, Sidheag stopped shaking. The tea, once it arrived, had its customary effect – engendering comfort and loosening the tongue. *That's tea for you*, thought Sophronia, *the great social lubricant*. Soon they had the whole story out of her. No wonder tea was considered a vital weapon of espionage.

'I begged Gramps to go home.' Sidheag's Scottish accent was thick in her distress, or perhaps from arguing copiously with her great-great-great-grandfather recently.

Dimity hadn't the strength in the face of such distress, so Sophronia said what they all knew had to be true.

'It's treason, Sid. You know he can't. They betrayed him as well as the queen.'

'But the pack should stay whole. He killed ... he did what had to be done, let that be an end to it. Why can't he forgive the others?' Sidheag adored her pack; she only wanted it to stay together.

'You know he won't,' said Sophronia softly.

Frustrated out of her sadness, Sidheag snarled, 'Of course I bloody know it! Worse now, he can't. He did as he said he would! He up and challenged for the Woolsey pack and won. He's garnered himself a new family! A replacement pack.'

Sophronia's mind whirled. 'Lord Vulkasin is dead?'

Sidheag nodded, her anger abated and the tears returned.

Sophronia was strangely relieved. She'd only seen the were-wolf Alpha of the Woolsey pack a few times, and had never been introduced, but he seemed cruel and unhinged. Knowing the world was without him was oddly cheering. But it didn't solve Sidheag's problem.

'And now he's lost to me. I had to choose.'

Sophronia's eyes widened as she grasped Sidheag's meaning. 'Are you saying you had to choose between the Kingair pack and your grandfather?'

Dimity's face was white with distress. 'Whyever would you have to do that?'

Sophronia felt faintly ill. Poor Sidheag.

'I canna maintain a relationship with both – Gramps killed his Beta. Killed him! Yet the pack betrayed Gramps. I just ...'

Sidheag paused, struggling to explain why she was rejecting the only father she had ever known. 'It's up to me to fix it, don't you see?' Normally so taciturn, she became loquacious in her despair. 'No matter what they tried to do, I love them. Someone has to look after them. Hold them together.'

'Oh, dear Sidheag.' Dimity fairly crumpled in sympathy.

Bumbersnoot, having been set on the floor by Sophronia, bumped up against Sidheag's ankle, his tail tick-tocking slowly.

'So if it's not Lord Maccon with you, who is the other werewolf?' Sophronia asked.

'Don't you recognise him?' Sidheag seemed to think his identity obvious.

'No. All the werewolves I've ever seen were in human form, except for Captain Niall.'

Sidheag looked enquiringly at Dimity, who also shook her head.

'That's the dewan.'

'The dewan!' Sophronia and Dimity said it together, shocked. Only the werewolf in charge of *all* other werewolves. Only the queen's *personal* adviser. Only the werewolf representative on the Shadow Council. Only the man who saw to werewolf assignments in the army itself!

If Mumsy knew who she just called an animal she'd be mortified.

The door opened and in came Captain Niall, decidedly too tall for Gresham's clothes. The trousers were short as a cocklehunter's and the shirt was basically cuff-less. Still, the important parts were covered. The captain, who was a bit of a fancy lad, for a werewolf, was uncomfortable in his shrunken get-up, but presentable enough to be among humans. He came to crouch next to Sidheag, his handsome face deeply concerned, his trousers straining alarmingly. He put his back to the fire and placed a hand on the arm of the couch near Sidheag's repulsive tweed skirts. His fingers twitched slightly, as if he would like to stroke her hand in sympathy. Sidheag, for her part, leaned into his presence, taking reassurance there. Neither had the courage to actually touch.

They exchanged a single brief yet deep look of … *sympathy? Something more?*

Sophronia couldn't pinpoint what, but something significant had occurred between them on their recent journey. A connection had shifted, as if they saw each other as equals now.

Then Captain Niall said, as there was no point in hiding the fact that both werewolves had overheard the conversation, 'If I may present the gentleman in question?'

Sidheag said, airily, 'Oh, of course, no secrets here.'

'There are always secrets,' corrected Sophronia softly.

The dewan entered the Temminnicks' shabby family parlour. *Oh, how chagrined Mumsy will be.* Then again, perhaps not. As silly as Captain Niall's appearance was, the dewan looked sillier.

He was a large man who had been metamorphosed somewhat late in life. He had dark hair tinged with grey, and a wide face with deep-set eyes. His mouth was a little too full, reminding Sophronia of Felix. He had a cleft in his chin, and his moustache and mutton chops were quite bushy. For a werewolf who was at least a hundred years old, the facial hair was stylishly modern. Unfortunately, Gresham's clothing was stretched to indecency. It was doing little to disguise the necessary, and looked as if it might stop doing that at any moment. All the protruding parts, of which there were a great deal, were covered in such a quantity of hair as to make the young ladies present wonder if the dewan was not partly wolf *all* the time.

Sidheag did not show the leader of all English werewolves any deference. She didn't even bother to stand, merely saying, 'Lord Slaughter, may I present my dearest friends, Miss Temminnick and Miss Plumleigh-Teignmott?'

The dewan, with great dignity for a man so experimentally dressed, answered with, 'Young ladies, how do you do?'

Dimity and Sophronia curtsied, careful not to show any neck, as custom demanded. 'My lord,' they said in unison.

Sidheag said, lip curled, not looking at the great man, 'He says there is nothing even he can do to change this outcome and I must stay out of it.'

The dewan sighed the sigh of an older gentleman dealing with a hysterical young girl. 'Lord Maccon has made his bed and must lie in it. That bed is Woolsey. Frankly, with Vulkasin the way he was, it is not so terrible an outcome. Politically, Lord Maccon will be good to have closer to town. I'll give him plenty to do, keep him out of trouble.'

Sidheag wailed, 'But he has left Scotland for ever! I must be allowed to attend my pack!'

'Admirable sentiments, as I have said before, young lady. But they aren't your pack, you are not a werewolf, and this is not your concern. Allow Captain Niall and me to manage Kingair, and me to deal with their punishment for attempted treason. Exile, I think, for a decade or two. Now that we have delivered you back to the safe bosom of your friends, we must be on our way. Captain, shall we?'

Captain Niall stood, unhappy, and cleared his throat. He said to the assembled young ladies, 'I do not blame Lord Maccon for his choices. For an Alpha werewolf to be betrayed by his Beta – there is no worse pain. It cuts through the heart and mind, but also what is left of the soul. It tears at the bonds of pack, the instinct that holds us as one unshakable group. Lord Maccon could never unify Kingair again after this, nor would he want to. But he is still strong enough to hold a pack. Woolsey will do well for him. Please, take care of your friend, and keep this in mind? Try to get her to understand?'

Sidheag looked betrayed and unreasonably angered by his statement. She jumped to her feet, hands fisted at her sides. 'I dinna give two tail shakes about Gramps! He has abandoned the others. What are they to do? What are *we* to do? How will my pack survive without an Alpha? Who will look after my uncles? Who will plead for a lesser punishment?'

Captain Niall shook his head sadly. 'Please, give us time, Lady Kingair. This is not your concern.'

Sidheag said, softly, looking to Sophronia for understanding, 'I asked Gramps to bite me.'

Sophronia gasped.

Dimity let out a squeak of alarm.

Bumbersnoot trundled in a shocked circle, as if he actually understood what was happening.

'Oh, Sidheag. You didn't.' Sophronia tried to be gentle. Sidheag was suffering so much, but such a request was plain *idiotic*.

Sidheag growled, sounding rather werewolf-like. 'He refused that, too! Too young, he said. Last of the Maccon line, he said. Not ready, he said.'

'Female!' cried Dimity in frustration.

Sidheag shook her head as if tossing aside the very fact of how unbelievably risky such a request was. Maybe one in a thousand men survived the bite and managed metamorphosis into a supernatural. And for women ... well, Sophronia knew of only three female werewolves in all history.

Sidheag looked to Captain Niall. 'So, what *are* we going to do?'

The werewolf said, not unkindly, '*We* are going to do nothing. You three are going to return to school, like good girls. I've written a note explaining Lady Kingair's extended absence.'

The dewan had grown increasingly impatient. 'Niall, we really do not have the time to humour children further, not even Lady Kingair. As it is, we will lose a night's travel tomorrow. It's full moon, after all. We shouldn't have come here. We should have tried for Kingair before the moon.'

'We'd never have made it,' said the captain. Then, like a good loner, he acquiesced meekly to the dewan's insistence, saying politely to the ladies, 'I will take my leave of you now. Best wishes for safe travels back.'

Sidheag looked for a long moment at the werewolf captain. It was almost one of those longing looks Lady Linette made them practise. Only this one, Sophronia thought, had a modicum of sincerity to it that she herself had yet to master. She felt guilty watching Sidheag expose her emotions in such a way – intrusive.

So Sophronia turned to make her farewell to the dewan. 'You will not stay to meet my mother? She'll be sorry to have missed you, as Lord Slaughter, of course. I do not believe my parents play in the same political arena as the dewan.'

He looked at her, concentrated on her as a person for the first time, and not an inconvenient schoolgirl. 'And you will not tell them of your lessons at finishing school? Or of this conversation?'

'Absolutely not.'

The great man nodded. 'Lady Linette does good work.'

Dimity said nervously, 'It was kind of you to escort Sidheag here.'

'I should not have done so but for Captain Niall's insistence. And he is necessary. Speaking of which, Captain? Now, please.' It was not a request.

With the barest of courtesy, the two werewolves strode from the room.

When Sophronia and Dimity turned back, Sidheag was trying to pull herself together, eyes glassy.

'I can't believe you rode through the night from London on wolf-back!' said Sophronia, gently applying admiration.

'I can't believe you requested the bite,' said Dimity, more accusatory.

'I can't believe my own gramps turned me down,' huffed Sidheag, a little colour returning to her cheeks.

'Thank goodness for small mercies,' said Sophronia.

'You called, Ria, my love?' said Lord Mersey, letting himself into the room.

'Oh, *mercies*, Lord Mersey. Yes, I see. Ha ha,' Sophronia was quick to respond.

'Don't call her that,' said Soap, still entirely masked, following the other young man inside.

'I tried to stop them, but goodness, it's nice to get away from all those ruffles,' said Pillover, trailing in last of all. He bent to pat Bumbersnoot, who clattered in greeting.

Sophronia said, 'This is wonderful.' She walked to the door, stuck her head out, and said, 'Would any other eligible young men like to join our party? I don't know, to attract *more* of my mother's unwanted attention?'

Dimity said, on a slight smile, although still tending to Sidheag's finer feelings, 'Be sensible, Sophronia, we don't *know* any other eligible young men.'

The boys must have missed the two werewolves, for they made no mention of having seen the dewan. Lord Mersey, at least, would have recognised him and made some derogatory remark.

Pillover and Soap settled easily into the group. Pillover being Dimity's brother, and Soap Sophronia's friend, they assumed levels of intimacy that would have given Mrs Temminnick hysterics. For one thing, they sat far too close to the young ladies.

Felix stayed to the outside, held back by society's protocols. He pretended keen interest in Bumbersnoot.

'What's the dilemma, ladies?' he asked, perceptive enough.

This was too much of a crisis to stand on social airs. 'Come sit, Felix,' Sophronia said, intentionally dropping his title. 'This is an emergency, no time for folderol. Soap, take off that ridiculous mask.'

Felix started when Soap removed the mask. 'You! The chimney sweep.'

Soap swept him a seated bow. 'The same.'

Felix spluttered.

Sophronia interrupted before things could get out of hand. 'Both of you, behave. Now, Sidheag, what do you need from us? More tea?'

Dimity began pouring for everyone. When it became clear the pot was likely to run dry, she went to the door, corralled a clangermaid, revived the pot, and returned, having wedged the door shut with an armchair as added precaution.

'We have about a quarter of an hour before Mumsy realises the boys are missing,' said Sophronia, consulting a pocket watch.

Felix was glaring at Soap. Now that he knew who Soap really was, Felix was upset at being challenged during a dance by a sootie.

Soap was focused on Sidheag. He considered her a friend – they had sparred on occasion. He liked her masculine ways and acerbic attitude. He respected her as a decent gambler. No icing on Miss Maccon, he was prone to saying. 'Miss Maccon, I've never seen you upset afore. What's happened?'

Pillover sat cross-legged on the floor, Bumbersnoot in his lap, attitude mostly sympathetic. Although he did seem morosely pleased to be in the company of someone as unhappy as he.

Dimity relayed Sidheag's tale of woe, avoiding mention of the dewan. It was intelligencer instinct that caused her to withhold that bit of information, but Sophronia agreed with her decision. Felix didn't need to know everything; his father was a Pickleman, after all. The Picklemen were probably elated by the werewolf crisis.

During the telling, Lord Mersey, unaccustomed to all attention being on someone other than him, came timidly over and drew up a small hassock to sit on, joining the circle by the fire. He wisely held his tongue, but Sophronia could practically read his mind: *Who cares what happens to a pack of werewolves? Good riddance to bad rubbish.* But he knew himself to be in the minority. He was also, Sophronia hoped, a genuinely decent enough person to sympathise with Sidheag over the loss of a loved one – whether or not he approved of that loved one's condition. Maybe seeing her distress would make him think that not all supernaturals were bad. Then again, Kingair had just tried to kill the queen. What a pickle this was.

Sophronia wasn't sure what to think. She wished, inexplicably, that she could get Lord Akeldama's perspective. Vampires and werewolves were mainly uninterested in one another's private affairs, except where they crossed into alliance with the Queen of England. They were protective of their unusual acceptance in British Government and guarded it jealously as the only supernaturals in the known world with legal status. Which explained the dewan's involvement. He had to fix this. The stability of the nation depended on it. *There you go*, thought Sophronia, *perhaps I don't need to talk to Lord Akeldama to understand after all.*

They sat drinking tea and suggesting possible plans of action, consoling Sidheag with words and imagined deeds.

Sidheag remained mainly monosyllabic but after her third cup took a deep, shaky breath. 'Thank you all for being so kind. But I know what I have to do. It's only ... Sophronia, I'll need your help.'

'Of course.' Sophronia looked up, eager to be of assistance. She hated the feeling of helplessness her friend's misery engendered.

'I have to go home to Kingair. Now. Right away.' Sidheag's expression pleaded with her not to argue.

Sophronia nodded. Her mind was already on it.

'You want to follow Captain Niall?' Dimity had seen that intimate look exchanged between their tall, angular friend and the handsome werewolf.

'My pack needs me. Kingair needs me.'

The train is probably fastest, Sophronia was thinking. 'You can help them?' was what she said. *The right train and we might even beat them there, as the werewolves have to lock down tomorrow night.* She did some quick calculations in her head.

'I am the Lady of Kingair, after all. There is power in the title.' Sidheag sounded confident.

'What good could you possibly do?' Felix asked. The others would have simply supported Sidheag, however illogical or emotional her choice. She was their friend and they would do what was needed.

Sidheag spoke, peer to peer. 'You don't understand. Pack is more than a group; it is a container. Like a jug of water that can hold a great deal if it is intact. Without an Alpha, the jug fractures and the water drains away.'

'You think *you* can patch the leak?' Felix's lip curled slightly in genuine disbelief.

Sidheag snorted. 'Bad analogy. But, yes, in a way I do. I think I am more than a little Alpha by nature. My uncles, they trust me.'

'To become a kind of Alpha yourself? Or help one of your uncles take the position?' Sophronia was confused as to what Sidheag thought she could do.

'Either, both, I don't know, something. Just offering emotional support I'm sure would help.'

Sophronia thought this was foolhardy. But she had no better plan. She didn't know werewolf dynamics well enough to predict their reaction to Sidheag's interloping. But if this was what would make Sidheag feel better, to commit a mad dash across England to Scotland, then Sophronia would arrange a mad dash or die trying.

Sophronia had made her decision before she'd even finished that thought. 'We'll need to get to a train station. Mumsy will have all the horses tied down, but I have an idea that I think will work.'

Sidheag looked relieved. She herself was a decent leader, but under current conditions she trusted Sophronia to get the details sorted. 'Good, I like trains.'

Sophronia continued to scheme. 'I think it'd work best if we went as young men, fewer questions.'

'*We?*'

'I'm coming with you, of course.'

Dimity said, instantly, 'Then I'm coming, too!'

Felix Mersey added, 'I as well. Sounds like a lark. Besides, can't have you ladies running around the countryside without some kind of supervision. Especially not if werewolves are involved.'

'If he's going, I'm going.' Soap's tone of voice brooked no argument.

Sophronia did weight sums in her head.

Everyone else turned to look at Pillover, the only one still silent.

'No, thank you,' said Pillover primly. 'I loathe adventures. I'm sure Bumbersnoot will join you, though.'

Bumbersnoot blew smoke out his ears in agreement.

Sophronia said, 'That's good, because I don't think it can take six.'

'You don't think *what* can take six?' Sidheag seemed to be perking up now that the others had agreed so readily to her need to head north.

'The air dinghy, of course.'

Dimity knew exactly what Sophronia was talking about. 'The one we stole and stashed? It still works?'

'Don't see why not. Mumsy hasn't lit her floating lanterns yet; we could steal the helium meant for those.'

She was interrupted by a rattling at the door.

'Sophronia! Let me in this instant,' said an autocratic female voice.

'Oh, dear,' said Sophronia. There was nowhere for the boys to hide; they were about to get in serious trouble.

The knob rattled again. Then the door crashed open with a splintering sound, overturning the chair Dimity had wedged against.

In strode Mrs Barnaclegoose.

*

Mrs Barnaclegoose was a dear friend of Mrs Temminnick's. A country lady much feared by gentlemen of all ages because she was decided in her ways, firm in her opinions and interested in impressing both upon everyone around her. She was an inveterate gossip who favoured stylish gowns designed with far less substantial figures in mind. Tonight's ensemble was a blue-and-white-check dress with a wide collar from which dangled an impressive quantity of fringe. The fringe shook much in the way a finger of reprimand might.

Everyone was terrified by the intrusion. Mrs Barnaclegoose had an aura of imminent discipline. She was the type of female who would report to Sophronia's mother on the situation in the family parlour in such vibrant terms as to make it seem a veritable orgy.

'Oh, there you are,' she said calmly to Sophronia, completely ignoring the others.

'Good evening, Mrs Barnaclegoose. I did not see you arrive at the ball, or I would have tendered my regards immediately.'

'Very prettily said, dear. As you can tell, I'm not dressed for a masquerade. I hadn't intended to come. I'm only here to deliver something. Oh, there's the nice little doggie! Good evening, Bumbersnoot, how do you do?'

Bumbersnoot submitted good-naturedly to having his leather ears scratched. Mrs Barnaclegoose loomed over him, breasts heaving, stays creaking alarmingly.

'Such a good little man,' said Mrs Barnaclegoose to Bumbersnoot. She straightened and handed Sophronia a long, thin package. 'Just this once, mind you. A similar request from anyone of less standing and I should have considered it an insult. Imagine asking *me* to deliver a gift as if I were a messenger boy.'

She turned to leave the room, trailing a strong scent of lavender in her wake. At the door she paused to say, 'Now, dear, you will be careful with that one? He's too old for his own good.'

It must be from Lord Akeldama. Sophronia seized the opportunity. 'You would recommend against his offer of patronage?'

'Gone as far as that, has it?'

'Not formally. I'm still in school, after all, but I think he might ask.'

Mrs Barnaclegoose hinted darkly, 'I expect other contenders.'

'Oh?' Sophronia looked at her hard. Mrs Barnaclegoose had guided her into espionage. And despite her once having covered Mrs Barnaclegoose with trifle, Sophronia liked her. 'Would you care to elaborate?'

Mrs Barnaclegoose glanced about at the assembled party as if only just noticing them all. 'Interesting collection, Miss Temminnick. Is that Golborne's get? I was engaged to him once, you know? Before we found out about his political leanings. The duke, I mean, not the get. Now, dears, I'd scatter if I were you. Mrs Temminnick is soon to send one of her other spawn to check up on Lady Kingair's condition, and they aren't as' – she paused, knowingly – 'discreet as I.'

Sophronia could imagine the delight in Petunia's eyes. 'Thank you very much, Mrs Barnaclegoose.' She curtsied deeply.

Mrs Barnaclegoose left, closing the door behind her.

The room erupted into confused questions. Dimity's higher tones resolved into the only one Sophronia felt like addressing.

'Who was she?'

'Oh, Mrs Barnaclegoose? She's the one who recruited me.'

'I forgot you were a covert. I never would have guessed *that* woman a product of Mademoiselle Geraldine's.'

'I believe that's the idea,' said Sidheag, sounding almost like her old self.

'Who is her patron, do you think?' Dimity seemed particularly curious; perhaps she saw Mrs Barnaclegoose as a model for her own future lifestyle.

Sophronia answered because she wanted Felix to know she had options. She wanted Felix to know *he* had options. 'Queen Victoria, I suspect. She acted as if this delivery was a favour to a friend, and the same when she recruited me to the school. I've never asked her outright, but I think her patron must be someone very important. The queen matches her personality.

'Speaking of which, I find it's generally best to follow her advice. Ladies, we should go down directly. Gentlemen, in about fifteen minutes Lady Kingair will have a fainting fit that will result in our needing to retire from the ball early.' Sidheag nodded her willingness to participate. 'Dimity, are you ready with the assist?'

'Of course.'

Sophronia looked to Soap. 'If the gentlemen would meet us in the gazebo in a quarter of an hour? Pillover will show you where. Soap, can I trust you to requisition sufficient supplies from the kitchen?'

Soap nodded.

'Lord Mersey, you're on clothing. The nursery is four doors down on the left. There are masses of Gresham's old things stashed there. Mumsy is keeping them for when the twins are big enough. Bring enough for all of us, lots of sizes and such. I trust you have a good eye for the figures of ladies?'

Felix's kohl-rimmed eyes were mellow behind the slim jester mask. 'I've seen you in trousers before, both of you. Although not Miss Dimity, of course.'

Dimity blushed. 'Must I?'

Sophronia said firmly, 'I think it best. Then we're only a bunch of lads – ladding it about. Young ladies on the loose get noticed.'

Dimity winced in anticipated humiliation.

Sophronia gave her team a quick look-over. They all seemed prepared for action. Sidheag had bucked up, less worried about life now that Sophronia had a scheme in play. Pillover looked like Pillover, the weight of the world oppressing him. Nothing to be done about that. She worried about Soap. Would he be sacked for being away from engineering for so long? Would he refrain from popping Felix in the snoot?

Sophronia reached down and scooped up her mechanimal. She fed Bumbersnoot the gift from Lord Akeldama. It was almost too long to fit into Bumbersnoot's storage compartment, but he managed it. She marched from the room, clutching Bumbersnoot under one arm. Dimity and Sidheag trailed after.

They re-entered the ballroom.

Just in time, as it turned out. The grandfather clock in the hallway behind them was striking midnight. Speeches were soon to commence, then more nibbles, then more dancing. Ephraim was leading his cupcake lady up to the dais in front of the quartet, for some concentrated adoration and praise. The mechanicals circled in a pattern, herding people to stand on the dance floor, passing out glasses of bubbly. Sophronia, Sidheag and Dimity hustled to the front, in prominent position to be seen by Sophronia's mother and cause a maximum amount of distraction with sudden illnesses. They each took a glass of champagne, knowing that flying crystal and spilled drinks could be almost as bad as the faint itself.

The clock finished its final gong. The musicians stopped playing and everyone stilled, turning expectantly to face the dais crowded with proud parents and the happy couple.

All was in readiness.

Sophronia prepared to give Sidheag the signal.

Then every mechanical in the house went completely and utterly unhinged.

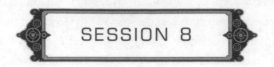

A CRISIS OF OPERATIC PROPORTIONS

There was no other way to put it – they went bonkers. One moment, mechanicals were passing out the champagne. The next, they were engaged in a high-speed romp along their tracks. Those that had the bearings to do so twirled in place. Those that were less dexterous twirled only their heads, like owls. It was a synchronised ballet of sophisticated engineering. A feast of mad pirouetting, as much as conical metal contraptions attached to tracks could be said to pirouette. Such a ramp-up in action, so different from their ordinary sedate trundling, caused internal engines to crank. The lower part of the ballroom became steamy. Sophronia closed her mouth on a hysterical giggle. No one had any feet. The masqueraders looked to be bobbing gently in a white sea.

The mechanicals stopped as suddenly as they had started, going perfectly still as if hit by a blast from Vieve's obstructor. Everyone relaxed, thinking it some strange glitch, now ended.

But before the guests could completely recover, the mechanicals began to sing, all together, in perfect unison. Sophronia hadn't even known one could instil such complex group protocols into mechanicals.

The mechanicals sang as loudly as their voice boxes allowed. The tune was startlingly patriotic. Although, afterwards, no one would claim that 'Rule, Britannia!' sung in such high, tinny tones was particularly stirring. The fancy new models, on loan, threw themselves into their dramatic roles. Even Frowbritcher, at the top of the stairs, the most sophisticated mechanical in the Temminnick household, was participating. Such nonsense ought, by rights, to be far beneath his dignity!

Bumbersnoot, dangling from his lacy cord over Sophronia's shoulder, looked as if he'd like to join. But he had no voice box and no track. So he beat out time to the tune with his tail, slapping the side of Sophronia's hip rhythmically. The mechanicals sang the full length of the song, drawing out the chorus at the end on a long 'slaves!' Longer than any human could hold the note.

Then they stopped.

Instead of going back about their duties, they stayed stopped. All their little steam engines cycled down, as if they were dying in their tracks. Silence descended. Only the tick-tock of Bumbersnoot's tail continued. He seemed the only one immune to a massive turn-off.

There was a moment's stunned silence, and then pandemonium reigned. Only this time, it was humans. No one there had ever seen anything like it. Mrs Temminnick's amazing hostess abilities were praised by all. Imagine the exorbitant expense in mechanics' commissions alone! But Mrs Temminnick was no Sophronia; she could not hide her surprise and claim credit where none was due. Thus the shock and awe, initially translated into delight, quickly changed to fear that such a spectacle was *uncontrolled*.

This, soon, was the least of their problems, as it became patently clear that every mechanical in the house was dead without possibility of revival.

There was no one to serve the food. No one to respond to the bell rope. No one to open the doors. No one to clip the wicks and replace the candles. No one to turn down the gas. No one to carry the wood and lay the fires against night-time chill. Worst of all, there was no one to refill the champagne glasses. The party was ruined. The evening was considered a loss. The whole week was looking pretty bad. How on earth would they function? What were they to do? No one could imagine life without servants. Of course, there were a few human staff; everyone kept *some*. But they were intended for complicated tasks. It was beneath one's human staff to do the work of a mechanical, not to mention the fact that there was simply too much of that work!

The gentry at the ball spiralled into panic. What if it was not just the Temminnicks' mechanicals malfunctioning? What if their own servants were broken? Who would make the tea in the morning? Several of the ladies began to have hysterics. Even a few gentlemen succumbed to overwrought nerves.

Sophronia, Dimity and Sidheag participated briefly in the confusion. After all, they also had never seen anything like it.

But it only took them a moment to realise they should take advantage of the situation. Such a crisis as this, mass mechanical revolt of an incomprehensibly passive variety, would occupy the adults long enough for them to make good their escape.

Thus, without any fainting necessary, they left the ball and made for the gazebo.

The boys were already there. Soap had found a number of large wicker picnic baskets and stuffed them with food filched from the kitchen. Felix provided a pillow sack containing a collection of menswear. Pillover was standing off to the side with these items, watching as the other two attempted to extract the air dinghy from its intimate relationship with the gazebo.

While Dimity went to point out how it had been incorporated, Sophronia dashed off with Sidheag to find Roger. He might know where Mumsy was keeping the helium.

Roger proved amenable to repurposing the transportation nodules, so long as Sophronia took the blame. He hooked up a donkey to the helium cart so quickly, it was almost as if he had been expecting never to use it for the party display.

Sophronia gave him a sardonic look.

'This much helium, miss, for a lantern show? Bloody great waste.'

'My thoughts exactly, Roger.'

They returned with donkey and helium just as the air dinghy basket tumbled off the roof of the gazebo with a crash. Fortunately, it survived intact. Felix and Soap righted it and jumped inside to throw out the four balloons. While they wrestled the sail and mast up the middle, the girls and Roger unrolled the balloons and began to fill them with helium. There was no way to rush this part, although Sophronia kept glancing back to the house, where the shifting lights were her only clue that all was still chaos in the ballroom.

None too soon, the four balloons were filled. They tugged up the basket so that it rose sedately into the air, shedding decorative bits of gazebo in its wake. Felix and Soap managed to raise the centre sail. It was a pity they disliked each other so intensely, for it was clear that they made an efficient team. Sophronia appreciated efficiency.

Dimity and Sidheag climbed inside, awkward in long skirts and with no ladder. Sophronia swung Bumbersnoot over. Pillover passed up the hampers. Roger tossed in the sack of clothes.

'Everyone good to go?' Sophronia asked, wondering what they were forgetting.

Four faces peeked over the edge, nodding. Soap and Felix extended their arms down while Dimity and Sidheag went to the other side of the gondola against the lean.

The balloons caught a breeze and they bobbed up a bit.

Sophronia held up her hands to be lifted inside.

'What in heaven's name is going on *here*?' came Petunia's shocked voice. She appeared as if by magic around the side of Mumsy's rhododendrons.

'Cut us free, Pillover!' yelled Sophronia, dangling off the side. Felix had both his hands wrapped around one of her wrists and Soap the other.

'Sophronia Angelina Temminnick, what on *earth* are you doing to the gazebo now?'

Pillover unlashed the air dinghy from where it had been tied to the gazebo columns.

It lifted sedately upward.

'Wait,' cried Petunia, 'come back here this instant! You can't just drift off with a duke's son. That's not sporting!'

Felix and Soap hauled Sophronia into the gondola. She blessed the split skirt of her costume; it allowed her to leg over and land on her feet inside. She turned to look back at her sister.

'Sorry, Petunia, but this is an emergency. I'm only borrowing him for a bit.'

Petunia stood, head tilted back, watching them float away. Pillover slouched over to stand next to her. They were outside earshot, so Sophronia had no idea what he said, but to everyone's surprise, Petunia seemed mollified. She took his arm, and he led her with great dignity back towards the house.

'He's coming out well, for a pustule,' said Dimity, with evident pride.

'He may have found his calling at last,' said Sophronia. 'Hoodwinking my sisters. That's no mean feat. We have brothers, too; we're usually immune to their charms.'

Dimity chuckled. 'Imagine Pill, with charms! What a hoot.'

Sidheag said, in all seriousness, 'He should be at Mademoiselle Geraldine's, he'd make a great intelligencer. No one should ever believe it of him.' She turned to face inside and assess how they were handling the air dinghy.

Soap was concentrating on manning the sail, as if he actually knew what he was about.

'Do you know what you are doing, Soap?' Sophronia asked.

'Not really, miss, but someone's got to.'

'So, which way is north?' asked Sidheag.

Sophronia leaned over the side of the basket, squinting into the night, looking for the lights of Wootton Bassett. The basket tilted and Dimity hurried to counterbalance.

Sophronia pointed. 'That way, more east than north for now. Everyone look out for a big clock face. That'll be the nearest railway station.'

With no propeller, they had to drift up and down, searching for a breeze headed in the correct direction. Finally, they hooked into one that carried them along at a sedate pace. This was not exactly a high-speed, high-risk endeavour. Fortunately for them, Pillover seemed to have adequately distracted Petunia, and the mechanical malfunction seemed to have adequately distracted everyone else. Sophronia kept looking back, but no carriage or horseman came galloping after them.

Dimity gave a little cry. 'There it is!'

Indeed, there it was – a small clock tower, peeking up above the other buildings of the town. Soap grabbed at the tiller and the air dinghy obligingly slid to one side. Thus they approached the station silently, a small bobbing craft within the damp night.

While Soap and Felix bickered mildly over how best to steer, Sidheag turned to Sophronia. 'We can catch a train north there?'

Sophronia hated to disappoint. 'Wootton Bassett's not very big and, as a general rule, people are going through it to somewhere else. Not many trains stop, and when they do it's either east to London or Oxford, or west to Bristol.'

'Well, I certainly don't want to go back to London.'

'Nor do you want to go to Bristol. Who would?' said Dimity, a decidedly snobbish tone to her voice.

'We need one heading to Oxford?' suggested Sidheag.

Sophronia nodded. 'From there we can switch to a north-bound line. I'm worried there won't be one until morning, but it's worth a try. Wootton rarely gets night-time passenger trains.'

The other two knew what that meant. If a passenger could get somewhere quickly, and with all the modern conveniences of first class, there was no need for overnight service. Vampires couldn't leave their territory, and werewolves could move faster on four paws than a train on rails.

Nevertheless, Sophronia had hopes. 'There *are* sometimes freight trains puffing through at night – out of the ports. We might be able to jump one of those, although freight will be going to London. We'd have to scramble to hop a passenger halfway to get to Oxford.'

Sidheag looked doubtful. A freight train wouldn't stop at Wootton Bassett unless they flagged it down. 'Do you have a plan?'

'Of course,' said Sophronia, but then added in confusion, 'except it doesn't look like I need it. See there?'

They were coming in over the station, and lo and behold, there was a train, sitting patiently, as if waiting for them.

'My, that one is a peculiar-looking beast,' Sophronia said, tilting her head in confusion.

'Looks pretty enough to me,' responded Sidheag, who clearly had great, if blind, affection for the railway.

Sophronia summoned Felix. 'Lord Mersey, stop bothering Soap and come and look at this.'

'I'm not bothering anyone!' Felix left off trying to fly the airship and came to stand next to Sophronia at the side of the basket. Dimity and Sidheag stayed to the opposite side. It was a dance they'd been conducting since they floated off, in order to properly weight the four balloons.

'Have you ever seen a train like that before?' Sophronia assumed that Felix was well travelled.

The young lord shook his head, equally mystified. 'Goodness, no. It looks as if someone crammed a first-class passenger train and a freight train together. Most abnormal.'

Sophronia tilted her head. 'That's exactly what I thought.'

'What's going on?' demanded Dimity.

'It looks like someone took four carriages from a passenger train and then added two from a freight in between them.'

'Could it be a circus or some other kind of acting troupe?' suggested Dimity.

Felix said, 'I think it's more likely a special delivery – military, perhaps. With the freight carriages in the middle like that? It's as if the passengers are needed to protect them.' He craned his head over the edge and to one side, as if trying to see the side of the train.

'Careful,' said Sophronia.

'Aww, Ria, you care.'

'Don't be silly. I prefer not to clean up the mess if you fall out.'

'I'd miss you, too, my lovely.'

'Would you stop leaning!' Sophronia actually was worried. Felix wasn't trained to fall overboard the way she was.

'Looks like there is writing on the side of one of the freight cars. Can't read it, though. Might be a hint.' He finally pulled himself to safety.

'Well,' said Sophronia philosophically, 'since it looks to be headed in the correct direction, shall we try for it?'

'Why not?' said Sidheag.

They floated on with greater purpose, if no greater speed.

Unfortunately, the little breeze they were riding wasn't fast enough. The engine of the train puffed to life, without the customary toot of warning. This peculiar beastie was apparently interested in being stealthy. Or as stealthy as possible, for a train.

'We aren't going to make it in time.' Sidheag looked resigned, but no closer to tears than normal. That was a relief. She seemed to be getting her gumption back.

Felix rounded on Soap. 'Can't you make her go faster?'

Soap did not dignify this with a reply. Air dinghies were designed for secrecy, not speed.

Sophronia took out her hurlie and lashed one of the air dinghy mooring ropes behind the grapple.

Dimity followed this action with wide, troubled eyes. 'I do not think what you are about to do is a very good idea.'

Sophronia looked at Felix and Sidheag. 'Can you rig something up with one of the other mooring ropes?'

Felix looked doubtful but went poking about the gondola for something sharp and curved.

Dimity produced an umbrella, but it was not strong enough.

'What we need is an anchor,' said Sophronia.

They closed in on the train; it was now spitting distance away.

It steamed up and began to leave the station with a quiet chug-chug.

Sophronia took aim and shot her grappling hook.

Felix leaned over the side and took a swing with an improvised lasso. He missed whatever protrusion he was aiming for.

Sidheag tutted at him and took the lasso away to give it a try. Being a gentleman, he let her, although he was clearly not pleased with ceding a sporting endeavour to a female. Sidheag, however, managed to loop the lasso over a finial-looking thing on the last passenger carriage on her first try.

Sophronia's hurlie scraped along the top of the same passenger carriage and then hooked into the front top lip of the last coach. Now they had purchase on two points of the same carriage.

The train picked up speed out of the station and both ropes jerked. Sophronia, for added security, unstrapped her hurlie and fastened it to the railing of the gondola. She trusted Vieve to have built the hurlie to hold her weight, not necessarily to haul an air dinghy full of people.

The air dinghy leaned dangerously as it was suddenly being dragged along by a moving train. Luckily, the locomotive wasn't moving fast. Nevertheless, an airship had not yet been built to be dragged along by something big on the ground.

'Soap,' yelled Sophronia into the wind, 'we need to take her down, land her on top of the train.'

'Oh, miss, that's not your best idea.'

'We can do it.'

'You, my dear, are overly optimistic!' said Felix, agreeing with Soap for once.

The gondola leaned all the way to one side. Dimity shrieked and almost tumbled over the edge. Sidheag grabbed on to her and the railing at the same time. Soap braced himself against the tiller, and then realised there was no point – the sail was now useless.

The train slowed. The air dinghy partly righted itself.

Soap pulled in the sail.

Sophronia said, 'Everyone take a corner of the basket and let out the helium, slowly now, not too fast.'

'Oh god oh god oh god,' murmured Dimity, who up until that moment Sophronia would never have categorised as particularly religious. 'This is bad.'

Sidheag agreed. 'Cut us loose, Sophronia, you're hurting the poor train. There'll be another one along soon.'

But Sophronia *knew* they could do it. Plus, she was wildly curious about that strange-looking train. 'Brace for it, and hold tight!'

Sidheag took one corner, Dimity another, Felix the third, Sophronia the fourth, with Soap holding the centre and manning the controls.

Each of the four balloons had various dangling cords, but one cord in particular, lined with small red flags, was connected to the helium release flap at the base.

Sophronia nodded and they all tugged on their red flags at once.

The air dinghy jolted and sank like a stone.

'Whoa, stop, too much!' yelled Soap.

The train below them picked up speed and the gondola tilted in response.

Only Soap managed to hang on, possibly because he was the strongest among them. Everyone else cried and fell. Sidheag landed with her feet near Dimity's head. Sophronia landed on Felix. The picnic hampers landed one on Sidheag's foot and the other on Soap. Soap caught it by the handle and lashed it down to the base of the tiller with a few quick loops of spare rope. Sidheag grunted in pain but seemed no more than bruised.

'Well, Ria, this is nice,' said Felix.

Sophronia was plastered against him. She struggled to roll away. He put one skinny arm about her, keeping her close.

It was a bit too good a feeling. Sophronia had a brief hysterical thought that perhaps Felix was like figgy pudding. Rich and delicious but best sampled in moderation. A seasonal treat. He smelled amazing.

Sophronia righted herself and shrugged Felix off. 'Ready, everyone, let's try again. Little more gradual this time.'

Soap was tall enough to lean over and pull down on one release cord and then another. Sophronia rolled to one side and Dimity to the other, pulling on those flags. The basket sank some more. Felix and Sidheag began to ratchet in the mooring ropes. No easy task against the pull of the train, but they did their best.

It was working. By careful degrees they sank down, taking care to go towards the train before sinking further; otherwise they might be dragged directly behind and fall to the tracks.

The mooring ropes had winches attached to the top. Sidheag and Felix strained against the levers.

Then, with a clunk, the gondola landed on the top of the rear passenger carriage. The basket was still on its side, which made for an awkward crash. The last of the helium escaped the balloons, and the balloons collapsed half on top of the train, half on to the basket and everyone's heads. Quickly as they could, the five stowaways untangled themselves and climbed out. Sophronia knew they had made too much of a racket on the roof, but no one seemed interested in checking the source.

Everyone was bruised and shaken, but otherwise unharmed. Dimity was white-faced but still functioning. After all, there had been no blood. Sidheag was looking, if anything, buoyed by the experience. Soap was stoic and calm. Felix was grinning.

'Jolly good,' he said, sounding a bit too much like a toff out on the town.

Sophronia gave him a quelling look and tried not to think about being pressed against him.

After a brief discussion, they decided to leave the air dinghy where it was. Its usefulness was weighed as superior to the fact that its discovery would alert others to their presence.

'Here's hoping we don't go through any tunnels' was Sophronia's opinion.

They extracted their supplies. Mercifully, the picnic hampers had stayed latched during the landing, although Sophronia couldn't vouch for the condition of the contents. The hard-boiled eggs had probably coddled in shock. They had to collect the clothing, scattered about, and stuff it back into the sack.

Sophronia's heart was in her mouth. 'Oh, no, where's Bumbersnoot?'

She began frantically rustling through the collapsed balloons, her world in crisis. Had he fallen out? Was he lying damaged and alone in the middle of the moor?

Soap produced him from within the second picnic basket. 'Stashed him there for safety when we first took to the skies.'

Sophronia clutched her mechanimal gratefully. 'Oh, thank goodness!' She resisted a near-overwhelming urge to embrace Soap.

Bumbersnoot wagged his tail at her and tooted a bit of smoke out of his ears in excitement.

The train rattled along at a snail's pace, for which Sophronia was grateful. They lashed down the gondola and rolled up the balloons as much as they could. Then they cautiously made their way to the side and peered over the edge. Like most first-class carriages, this one had three doors along its side for boarding at a station, one to each separate compartment. There was no ladder or way to climb down, and simply a footboard at the coach door.

Soap, who'd only ever seen a train from above, was intrigued. 'It's like they stuck three horse coaches together.'

Sophronia smiled at him. 'I believe that was the basis of the design, yes.'

'We'll have to all share one coach, then, won't we, miss?'

'I know, terribly uncouth, girls and boys travelling together without a chaperone.' Sophronia gently mocked his prudishness, especially since they'd recently been tumbling all over one another in a balloon.

'I suppose we need to be able to communicate,' relented Soap, who nevertheless looked wistfully down at the footboard of the middle door, as if he actually wanted to be separated from the girls and alone with Felix for the rest of the evening.

Felix, who by rights ought to have been more gallant than Soap about everyone's sensibilities, only gave the sootie a scornful look.

Sophronia selected the very last of the three doors.

She looped Bumbersnoot's reticule strap over her neck and went first, without discussion. Carefully, holding fast to the roof railings, she eased over the edge and lowered herself down. She was tall enough so that when her arms were fully extended, she only had a short drop. It was tricky, as the footboard wasn't very wide. She wobbled dangerously on the landing and nearly tumbled off the train entirely. Sidheag and Soap, who were tall, would have an easier time of it, but she'd have to watch Felix and Dimity carefully. She peeked in the small window of the coach door. Inside, it was dark and apparently vacant. She motioned for the others to wait while she fished her picks out of a pocket and jimmied the lock. The tumblers went over without protest. She scooted along the footboard, out of the way, and the door opened easily.

It was eerie inside. Moonlight filtered in from the windows opposite the door, slanting across the two facing blue velvet benches and dust motes in the air. The compartment was definitely empty, and she would lay good money on the other two being vacant as well. This entire first-class carriage seemed deserted. The coach held no luggage and no evidence that occupation was ever intended. It was odd, like a ghost train.

Sophronia, thinking of her exhausted friends, made a quick decision. It was unlikely anyone else could climb down as they had, so they should be safe until they reached a station. Climbing back to the roof and down to the next-over footboard seemed like an excess of precautions when this coach was safe and empty, and she was exhausted. She put Bumbersnoot down on the floor to snuffle about in the dark. If he came across anything unusual, he'd swallow it either to burn in his boiler or to be kept in storage. Which reminded her of the present delivered by Mrs Barnaclegoose. There came a clattering behind her, and she forgot once more.

Soap swung down and in. With the door open, the narrowness of the footboard was not such a challenge. One could simply dismount by falling forward into the coach. Which was what he did.

'Ah, good, you managed it,' greeted Sophronia.

Soap gave her a dour look.

'I know, stuck with all us girls, must be tragic for you.'

The others began leaning over from the roof and passing or throwing down the supplies, with Sidheag and Dimity, trained in stealth, trying their best to keep Felix muffled. There could, of course, be occupants in the other carriages, but they were either heavy sleepers or the sound of the train covered any noises made by the five new passengers in first class. Six if you counted Bumbersnoot.

They crammed inside the coach. As Soap had feared, it was a mite intimate for society standards. Sophronia closed and bolted the door, drawing the curtains over both it and the windows opposite in just such a way that she could peek out of a corner if needed. From the outside the drapes would appear messy enough to have unintentionally rattled loose, to the untrained eye.

The five sat down and looked at one another in profound relief. The three girls took the forward-facing bench. The two boys sat opposite. This seating arrangement ensured a respectable distance between them, one that even Mrs Temminnick might approve. First-class coaches were *luxurious*. Although, after falling on top of one another in an air dinghy recently, such concerns seemed silly. And Soap still looked uncomfortable with the arrangement.

Save Sidheag, they were all still wearing masquerade outfits, without masks, hair sticking up or fallen loose.

'We must look a treat,' said Dimity into the exhausted silence.

Sophronia shook herself. 'You're right, we should change. Best if we look more like stowaways, in case we do get caught.'

The boys rose and made as if to leave the coach.

Sophronia had no idea where they intended to go, perhaps outside to balance on the footboard or climb back on to the roof? She shook her head. 'We should stick together. We'll have to trust you two to turn around and not look.'

Dimity went white as a sheet, more terrified by this than the hair-raising ride they had recently endured. 'Must we? If anyone finds out, our reputations will be in absolute tatters, so . . .'

'We must ensure no one finds out,' said Sidheag, already unbuttoning her hideous tweed dress.

Then Soap, still facing them, went red as a beet at Sidheag's action and hastily turned to face the back of his seat, eyes screwed tightly shut.

Felix, after one startled glance, did the same. He did not look quite so embarrassed.

Sidheag continued with her changing while Sophronia upended the bag of clothes. She rummaged through for something that looked to fit her friend, realising that they'd have to cannibalise the train curtain cords for belts. Dimity helped Sidheag remove her corset, tight-lipped with disapproval. Sophronia envied her the fact that she didn't have to wrap. Sidheag donned a shirt, vest and trousers. Her boots were already so practical as to be almost masculine. Once out of her dress, she looked very like a boy, lanky with mannish features. Were it not for her long hair, she could pass without further mussing.

'We could cut it,' said Sophronia, who already had out her sewing shears to strip a petticoat for chest wraps.

She would never have thought Sidheag vain, but the girl looked genuinely perturbed at the suggestion.

'It's her best feature,' protested Dimity.

Sidheag said, very quietly, 'Captain Niall prefers long hair.'

'Oh, does he indeed?' said Sophronia, struggling to keep a straight face. 'We'll leave it, then.'

Dimity whispered, 'How did you find that out?'

Without answering, Sidheag plaited and wound her hair up tight to her head. She pulled a cap on over it and transformed, suddenly, into a rather good-looking young man. She then helped unbutton Dimity's beautiful gold gown. Sophronia stuffed it unceremoniously into the sack, which made Dimity look as if she might start crying. She refused to remove her stays, and chose some of the baggiest of the clothing so that she looked like a strangely top-heavy vagabond. Even in plaits, Dimity's hair was quite poufy and held her cap out about her head. In the end, she resembled nothing more than a walking, talking mushroom. With her round, feminine face, one really had to squint to see her as male.

After brief discussion, they added a smudge of moustache to her upper lip with a bit of coal from Bumbersnoot's stores. It wasn't much help.

Sophronia stripped self-consciously, including her stays, before pulling on a shirt and jodhpurs. She had a passing good figure, but fortunately it wasn't overly generous. She put her masquerade apron back on, instead of a waistcoat. Over that she added a tweed hunting jacket. It made her look like a butcher's boy with a pocket obsession, but she liked how useful the apron was and wasn't going to let it go.

'You can turn back around.'

The boys did so. Felix snickered at Dimity's appearance, but Soap was still so embarrassed he kept looking anywhere but at them.

'What's he up to?' Felix asked, pointing to where Bumbersnoot, near the door, made a funny little circle of discomfort.

'Oh, dear,' said Dimity. 'Look away, do.'

Felix did not, as there was nowhere else safe to look, watching with interest as Bumbersnoot squatted and ejected, out his back side, the gift Mrs Barnaclegoose had passed along. It was a most undignified and anatomically accurate expulsion mechanism.

'Oh, yes,' said Sophronia, reaching for it.

A bladed fan! Far nicer than the ones they had practised with, this one was steel, with filigree handle elements, making it lighter and more delicate looking. It had a leather sheath that was beautifully embossed, looking almost like a piece of mysteriously large and elaborate jewellery as it hung from a little strap with a tassel.

'That's a pretty thing,' said Felix. 'Gift from an admirer?'

Sophronia wasn't going to give him any quarter. 'I have a certain connection in London,' she said. Letting him think in terms of suitor rather than prospective patron.

Felix's face went slightly sour. He clearly didn't like the idea of a London rival, a man already finished with his education, based in town, with funds to spare.

Sophronia had no idea how Lord Akeldama knew she wanted one. Nor how he knew Mrs Barnaclegoose could get it to her. The dandy vampire had more than a few tricks to go along with all those fancies. However, she was rather in love, she hated to admit. With the fan, of course, not Lord Akeldama. She tested the edge, finding it beautifully sharp, and then carefully fastened the guard and put the bladed fan away in one of her larger pockets.

'What kind of connection?' pried Felix.

'A sharp one,' answered Sophronia coyly.

'Come with me to London, Ria. I'll buy you such pretty things.'

Soap jumped in, gruff and annoyed. 'Miss Temminnick doesn't want your kind of patronage, Pickleman's get.'

'Did I say anything about patronage?'

Sophronia sighed. 'Hush up and change, please, both of you.'

Then it was the young ladies' turn to look away while the boys stripped. Sophronia peeked – of course she peeked! – and she wouldn't have been surprised if the other two did as well. Sidheag, raised by werewolves, had seen men bare before, but these were *boys* their own age – how could she resist? Besides, Sidheag wasn't shy. Dimity rarely had the advantage, or disadvantage, but she was terribly curious about the opposite sex. Soap, Sophronia noted, had layered on more muscle than she'd expected. Felix seemed slight, white and lean next to the sootie. Sophronia was ashamed of herself, but that didn't stop her from taking a great number of mental notes. She'd been well trained in how to do so. It would be a while before she and Dimity could discuss the matter, and she wanted as much detail as possible for the purposes of compared opinions.

All too soon, Soap's dandy and Felix's jester costumes were added to the sack. The first-class coach now looked, by all accounts, to be occupied by a gang of scruffy lads bent on postal fraud or meat pie heists.

It had been a long night and everyone was glassy eyed – particularly Sidheag, who'd undertaken an entire wolf-ride from London before their balloon excursion. They agreed to take watches. Sophronia, still excited by the hunt and accustomed to prowling about late, chose first watch. She added, quite firmly, that she would take it with Soap, to forestall any bickering. Dimity stretched out on one bench and Sidheag on the other, with Felix gallantly taking the floor in the middle, using the bag of costumes as a pillow. Bumbersnoot curled up comfortably at his feet. A fact for which the young man was no doubt grateful, as the mechanimal was an excellent foot warmer.

Soon regular breathing and soft snoring meshed with the clatter of the train.

Soap stood near the door, peeking out into the night. Sophronia, after an awkward silence, edged past Felix to look out of the opposite window and see if she could guess the distance to Oxford junction. There was no clear sign of anything. Clouds had moved in, obscuring the nearly full moon. There was nothing of significance visible but damp black.

Sophronia returned to the door, standing on the other side from Soap, uncomfortable because he was uncomfortable. She examined his face, but it was closed off. Even if he wanted to talk, he didn't want to do so here, with the possibility of three sleepers shamming and listening in. Sophronia wasn't certain, but she thought he looked more sad than upset, and that confused her.

Casualties on all sides, she thought. *I get Sidheag sorted and now Soap's gone sentimental on me.*

She tilted her head at him and tried a small smile.

His mouth twisted. He blinked slowly, looked away and then glanced back at her.

Sophronia tried another smile.

He puffed out a short sigh, loss and resignation rolled up into it. Then he seemed to give himself a mental shake and smiled back. It was almost his old grin – only without the twinkle.

Then it was Sophronia's turn to feel lost and forlorn. Soap

had withdrawn from her, and it was her fault. *Was I too tough when I yelled at him about turning claviger? It's only that I'm worried. He should know me well enough for that. Did something happen on the journey just now? Is he still overly embarrassed about us changing? Is it Felix?* Sophronia knew, at that thought, that she would lose Soap to the clavigers, if he was given half a chance. If not, he'd see her through finishing, because he was loyal, and then take off in pursuit of a pack. She wouldn't put it past him to go for Kingair. If they managed to get Sidheag ensconced, it'd help to have Lady Kingair vouch for him.

Sophronia couldn't have explained, if asked, how she knew Soap's intentions so clearly. But she did. She also couldn't have explained why it hurt so much. But it did.

They stood watch in a silence so awkward it burned the backs of Sophronia's eyes.

TRANSMITTER ON A TRAIN

Sophronia woke Dimity with the firm shoulder grab of silence. It was a technique they'd applied before they even knew it was trained into intelligencers.

Dimity awoke quietly, automatically reaching beneath her nonexistent pillow for a weapon. It was an instinct ill-suited to Dimity, like watching a duck eat custard. But sometimes Dimity was surprisingly stealthy. She would have to unlearn a great many things, if she actually ended up as a real lady.

'Your watch, my dear,' Sophronia whispered. 'The sun is almost up.'

Dimity knuckled her eyes; only four hours' sleep, but she was willing to do her duty – true friendship, that.

Soap, still at the door, stretched languidly, looking exhausted.

Sophronia went to wake Sidheag.

'Let her sleep,' said Felix's voice from the floor. 'I'll take it. She needs the rest.'

'Very gentlemanly of you, Lord Mersey,' approved Dimity, offering him a hand up.

Felix looked at her aghast. As if he would accept aid from a lady! He wasn't in that sorry a state, although Sophronia was sure it had been an uncomfortable night on the floor. The kohl was smudged about his eyes and his hair was sweetly rumpled. Sophronia found it most disturbing – it made him look less aloof and more approachable.

Sophronia said, 'If you're sure. You know you actually have to *keep watch*? Do they teach you useful things like that at Bunson's?'

Felix gave her a dirty look. 'I suspect Miss Plumleigh-Teignmott can demonstrate the particulars.'

'I intend to climb up top to watch the sun rise, check on the air dinghy, and get the lay of the land.'

Soap paused at that, before folding himself reluctantly to the floor. Sophronia had expected him to insist on accompanying her.

But it was Felix who said, 'Is that wise?'

Sophronia answered, 'The wise would never have left the ball in the first place. I'll be quick, and I want to retrieve my hurlie, my wrist feels bare without it.'

Felix looked to Soap for support. 'You aren't going to stop her?'

Soap said, 'Kind of you to think I could, little lordling.'

Felix glared.

Soap leaned back against the sack of costumes, head under

the window, eyes heavy lidded, watching the door. He pointed at Bumbersnoot, who had moved to sit expectantly under a bench in one corner. 'Can't be too important or she'd take him with her.'

Sophronia felt a glow of pride. Soap understood her! And he trusted her. Why couldn't Felix be more like that?

Felix, strangely, took that to heart and raised no more objections.

So with Dimity and Felix posted by the door, Sophronia creaked it open and, hugging the side of the train, inched her way out on to the footboard.

It was wet and nasty, and had she not had practise on the damp exterior of Mademoiselle Geraldine's she certainly would have lost purchase.

Sophronia felt exposed and vulnerable. She jumped, trying to catch the top railing. She wished fervently for her hurlie as she missed and slid on the landing. She tried again, putting her will and strength into it, and managed to catch the railing and hoist herself up on to the roof. Strangely, she felt less exposed up high. As she had learned during her climbing adventures about the school, people rarely looked up.

The sun rose and the clouds lifted a little. She could see, far ahead on the horizon, the tall tower of a junction box. This train, unless she was mistaken, was not expected, and no one would be manning that switch. They'd have to stop, check it and change it over to the desired direction. She was about to witness their hosts. Would they look back at the train and see the balloon?

Sophronia crawled along the top of the carriage to the air dinghy, which was still safely strapped down. She considered knocking it off, and then decided it would make too loud a crash in the morning quiet. So she merely detached her hurlie and strapped it back in its customary place on her wrist.

She should have returned to the others at that point, but this was her first opportunity to explore without having to worry about their safety. She was dying of curiosity. What was the valuable freight in those middle cars?

She walked to the front of their carriage, jumped the coupler and climbed across the roof of the next carriage. She moved softly and slowly, so her footsteps could not be heard by any possible passengers. She sensed that this carriage was as empty as theirs, but she didn't *know* that. In front of her was the first freight carriage. From the air she'd thought it looked like a cattle cart, but up close it was a shock.

The top part of the freight carriage was, in fact, completely open to the sky. It seemed to be transporting a structure of some kind, a horse shed or similar, which boasted its own wooden roof. She suspected that there was an entrance from the front of the carriage, but in order to get there, she would have to climb across that roof, and she had no idea if it was secure or not. She risked it anyway.

Cautiously, she crawled about, examining the shed for clues. There were some funny-looking protrusions out of the roof. One of them like a big metal spittoon, another like the top part of a tuba. Eventually, she found a hatch. It was made so that something from the inside could telescope out. It didn't seem big enough to fit a person, but she could fit her head.

She cracked it, careful to shield the opening with her body, worried that even the dim light of early morning would creep in and alert those inside. She put an eye to the crack and waited patiently for her pupils to acclimatise to the gloom. The coach was empty. She flipped the hatch open completely and stuck her whole head inside. She was now bottoms up, like a duck, on top of a moving train. She wedged her shoulders to block out the light so her eyes could adjust and see as much of the interior as possible.

She stifled a gasp. There *was* someone inside! Fortunately, the gentleman in question was asleep – slumped sideways over the arm of a chair, mouth slightly open, snoring softly. He was a very handsome man, with long, wavy hair and an oval face. He was dressed well. Almost too well. It made Sophronia think of Lord Akeldama. She dragged her eyes away to examine the room.

The inside of that shed was awfully familiar.

Sophronia had seen something like it before, only smaller, on the roof of Bunson and Lacroix's Boys' Polytechnic during her debut at finishing school. Vieve called it a *communication machine*. Then it had looked like a deformed cross between a potting shed and a portmanteau. The appearance of the technology had not improved. The one at Bunson's was divided into two human-sized compartments, each filled to bursting with a peculiar assortment of tangled machinery. Sophronia would wager good money that those two were now represented, in larger form, by the two freight carriages. This one was filled with hundreds of tubes and dials. In front of the sleeping man was an upright glass box filled with black sand. Nothing was happening, but Sophronia knew the receiver of an aetherographic transmitter when she saw one. *An aetherographic transmitter on a train, oh dear.*

She wished fervently that Vieve were with them. Why had she brought a toff, a sootie, a lady and a werewolf's daughter, but not an inventor? Of course the inventor would be the one she needed. Sophronia tried to remember what Vieve had said about Bunson's aetherographic transmitter. She had been so excited about point-to-point messaging across long distances. One thing was certain, it wouldn't function while the train was moving. Vieve had insisted it needed silence to operate. For another, it needed aether to communicate from one transmitter to another. So that fairly explained why the freight carriages had no proper roofs. Was this some kind of communication train? However, they were hardly close to the aether now, so there must have been improvements to the prototype if that was the case. Vieve was now at Bunson's, with the original prototype, and Sophronia wouldn't put it past her to have worked on an upgrade herself. Was this train from Bunson's, then? That explained its presence at Wootton Bassett. Did that mean there were Picklemen on board?

Sophronia narrowed her eyes, straining to focus.

Is that . . . ? Oh, yes, of course it is. Why should I be surprised? Sitting in the cradle next to the receiver, all innocent and unassuming, was one of the crystalline valve prototypes that everyone was constantly fussing over. She supposed that transmitter technology had probably evolved to require the prototype at this point. Although it wasn't technically a *prototype* any more, but was now officially *in production*. The vampires had tried hard to stop that, but Picklemen had won the day. And now, there it was, in use, bright as may be.

Sophronia gave the interior one more cursory glance, then

withdrew her head, closing the hatch behind her. She lay back on the roof to think, eyes closed, enjoying the weak sun on her face.

Vieve used two crystalline valves to communicate commands from her hands to her sputter-skates. Perhaps the transmitter in the freight carriage is somehow steering the train in a like manner? Communicating with the engine? Why bother? And why put a man to sit watch over the receiver portion under those circumstances? It was very confusing.

Then a horrible thought occurred to her. *Felix! Does Felix know? Did he come along because Picklemen are involved? Did he know it would be their train in the station?* Sophronia quelled anger and a keen sense of betrayal at that idea. She tried to stay logical. She had no direct evidence as to who was in charge; no need to take it out on Felix, just because she didn't like his politics.

The train closed in on the junction box. Sophronia flattened herself to the roof and waited to see if a green-banded top hat came walking up. They stopped at the switch and the door to the engine popped open. A stocky driver with a gargantuan moustache swung himself down and lumbered over to fiddle with the switch. *No top hat. No green band.* Sophronia couldn't tell for certain, but she thought he was turning the direction towards London.

'No,' said a demanding female voice from the cab door. 'We aren't going back yet.'

The man looked up, unhappy with this order. 'But, miss, we've not much coal left, we need a restock.'

'Do it in Oxford,' commanded the unseen woman.

Sophronia frowned; she was certain she knew that voice.

'But why? This is a *London* train. Besides, other lines will be starting up soon. We can't risk it, not on a popular track, not during the day. We'll be seen, or worse, cause a collision. We'll certainly slow everyone else up if you keep us at this snail's pace.'

'That's enough,' barked the voice. 'Orders are orders. Oxford, my good man. The path is clear this morning, I checked the schedule.'

The man muttered to himself but muscled the switch back over with impressive ease. This was a great relief to Sophronia; they wanted to go towards Oxford, after all.

Still, *that voice*. She'd definitely heard it before. Unfortunately, the lady in the engine room did not get out.

Luckily for Sophronia, the driver didn't feel the need to look up. Both she and the air dinghy remained unnoticed. She wondered if those were the only other people on the train, the sleeping man with the transmitter, the driver, his stoker and the lady. Could such a thing be possible, all six carriages for four people and an aetherographic transmitter?

The driver safely inside the locomotive, the train started up again.

Sophronia retreated in relief to the relative security of their first-class coach.

Dimity and Felix were waiting for her, looking frightened and impatient.

Soap was still awake. He cracked an eyelid from his prone position the moment she entered. He evaluated her from head to toe and, apparently satisfied, went back to sleep.

'Where were you?' hissed Dimity. 'Really, Sophronia, sometimes you are quite impossible.' She sounded snooty in her relief. She sounded almost like . . .

Which was when Sophronia remembered who belonged to that voice. Pieces began to click into place.

'You've been gone an awful long time for watching a sunrise,' added Felix.

Sophronia said, 'Wake up, everyone, we need to talk. I worked out what the freight is, and who's carrying it. Now we simply need to know why.'

Soap sat up and shook Sidheag awake.

She blinked at them. 'What's going on?'

Sophronia wished they had tea. Tea would do them up a treat right now. However, without tea, it would have to be gossip.

'On the positive, we are definitely headed towards Oxford, Sidheag. Hopefully, there will be a northbound train we can hop there. Unfortunately, this train we're on is almost certainly a vampire concern. For some reason they've got themselves an aetherographic transmitter fitted with one of the new crystalline valves, and are relocating it.'

'Gracious me,' said Felix primly, 'how on earth did you learn all that?'

'I overheard a woman giving orders to the driver. I recognised her voice. She sounds a little older and more cultured, but I'm pretty confident it was Monique de Pelouse.'

Sidheag gasped.

'Oh, dear,' said Dimity.

Dimity didn't know the half of it. Sophronia cursed inside. Was Lord Akeldama in on it, too? Vampires could be very tricky.

However, her tone was prosaic. 'At least we are familiar with her methods.' She explained for Felix's benefit, 'You met her on that trip to London. Older girl who was forced to sit at our table. Now she's drone to Westminster Hive.'

Felix's lip curled. 'So sad.'

Sophronia, annoyed by Felix's bias, found herself unexpectedly defending Monique. 'It's a valid option in our field, if perhaps not considered the most honourable. Not everyone has the same choices you have, Lord Mersey.'

Sidheag said, gruffly, 'Unfortunately, she's also had all the same lessons we have. So she knows all our tricks, just as we know all hers.'

Sophronia said, 'Except that she doesn't know we're on board. Unfortunately, she also knows our faces. There's no disguising ourselves from Monique.'

'When we stop, will she come and check this coach, do you think?' wondered Dimity, glancing frantically around the interior. There was nowhere to hide.

'I don't know. I couldn't tell if there are any other drones on board. There's a man asleep with the transmitter. Good-looking enough to be a drone. Perhaps this mission is one of such secrecy they could only entrust it to the two.'

'Vampires always muck everything up,' grumbled Felix.

'You mean, just like the Picklemen do? Everyone has their own agenda, Lord Mersey. The key is to manipulate motivations without being sucked into them.' Sophronia looked hard at Felix, hoping he might take her words as a lesson, think about his own position for a change.

Unfortunately, he seemed mainly annoyed at her tone of voice.

'So much for our grand escape to Scotland,' said Sidheag, slumping on to a bench. The lack of sleep was catching up on her.

'Of course it's the vampires.' Felix didn't seem surprised enough by Sophronia's revelation. And she was pretty darn certain it wasn't simply his bigotry talking.

Sophronia gave him a hard stare. 'Felix, do you know something you're not telling us?'

The young lord shrugged. 'It's only that I thought I recognised the writing on the freight carriage as we approached, but I couldn't understand what it implied until now.'

'You didn't think that might be relevant?'

'Not until I knew there was a vampire drone on board.'

'That's not the point; the point is, you might have said something sooner if you had suspicions! What did it say?' Sophronia demanded. Blast his Pickleman secrecy. What had they landed themselves in?

Felix was sullen. 'Well, I couldn't *tell* at the time. I didn't see much of it. But now, I believe it was the brand of the East India Company.'

'Bloody Jack?' Dimity was intrigued. She had a fancy to someday visit exotic lands. Most girls wanted to tour Europe after their weddings. Dimity had plans to visit *places with more colour*. After she caught herself a sensible, tour-minded husband, of course.

'Indeed,' acknowledged Felix. 'My father has always suspected they had vampire ties.'

Sophronia nibbled her lip in consideration. 'Has the East India Company, by any chance, put in an order for crystalline valves recently?'

Felix sneered outright at that question. 'How should I know?'

'Your father is a Pickleman,' pointed out Sophronia mildly, again, trying to make him understand his own bias.

'He's also a peer of the realm, and would never deal in trade! That's Cultivator rank responsibility.'

'Picklemen have a ranking system?' This was news to Sophronia. She altered her attitude to one of enquiry rather than instruction.

Felix winced. 'I shouldn't have said that.' After which he clamped his mouth shut despite Sophronia's big, pleading eyes.

She inched closer and tilted her head, looking at him from under her eyelashes. *Perhaps if I'm winsome enough, he'll tell me more and realise how misguided the Picklemen are.*

Sidheag interrupted her tactics by asking, 'Would Picklemen sell valves to the East India Company?'

Felix nodded. 'Of course. We haven't any *proof* of vampire backing.'

Another slip-up, he said 'we'. Sophronia genuinely liked Lord Mersey. He was, frankly, adorable. But if Piston membership really was a means for recruiting Picklemen, she and Felix were ill-matched. Sophronia bit her lip, looking disappointed.

Felix tilted his head at her, enquiring, the corner of his mouth tilted up in a 'forgive me?' smile.

Why does he have to be so pretty? 'You know, Lord Mersey, so far as I can tell, supernatural creatures come some good and some bad. Just like everyone else.'

Felix bristled. 'And the fact that they hunt humans for food doesn't bother you at all?'

'On occasion. But I'm not one to judge anyone's character based on diet. I myself have an unacceptable love of mincemeat.'

Felix couldn't seem to help but smile at that. Sophronia could be awfully charming when she was self-effacing. 'And the fact that we are apparently stuck on a vampire train doesn't trouble you?'

'Of course, but we aren't supposed to be here. Anyone would be in their rights to get annoyed.'

'And the fact that the hive kidnapped Dimity?'

Dimity looked up, startled at being suddenly dragged into an argument. 'Oh, now, see here.'

'To counter a Pickleman monopoly. Frankly, it struck me as something the Picklemen themselves might do, were circumstances reversed.'

'This is ridiculous. No matter what I say, you will always give them the benefit of the doubt. Even now!' Felix was losing much of his simulated boredom under Sophronia's pointed remarks, but he didn't seem to be losing his opinions.

'Just as you will always see them as less than human and unworthy of trust, or even decency.'

'They are monsters,' hissed Lord Mersey through gritted teeth.

That raised Sidheag's hackles because of the implied slur on werewolves.

Fortunately, a voice interrupted them before it could descend into an all-out fight. 'Um, pardon me?'

'Soap?' Sophronia was grateful for the distraction.

'It's not that I don't find this conversation fascinating, miss. I most assuredly do. I never seen you tongue-lash a lordling afore.'

'Soap!'

'It's the clouds, they's lifting a bit, and up and ahead of us there's a ruddy airship.'

'What?'

'Midsized, kinda disreputable-looking.'

'Is it attacking?' asked Sidheag.

'No, I think *we* may be following them.'

'What?' Sophronia and the others rushed to the window and forced it open, craning their heads to look up.

Just as Soap said, there was a dirigible. It was a bit scruffy, like a fur muff left too long in the attic. If the train hadn't been on tracks, Sophronia would have agreed that they were following it. They chugged along in its wake until the tracks inevitably steered them one way and the dirigible drifted in another.

'That was odd.'

'Coincidence?' suggested Sidheag, not sounding confident.

'I don't believe in coincidences, not in our line of work,' replied Sophronia.

'Escort?' Dimity wondered.

'Could be that's the reason we have so few drones on board – they're all up there,' Sidheag said.

'In which case we're in trouble because they'll have spotted the air dinghy.' Sophronia looked hard at Felix. 'Did you recognise that ship?'

Felix shook his head. Sophronia wanted to trust him but wasn't sure she could any more.

After a pause, Dimity said, 'What have we landed ourselves in the middle of?'

Sidheag looked guilty. 'Sorry, everyone, you're all here because of me. If I didn't want to get home . . . '

Dimity said, 'Nonsense. Be fair to yourself, Sid, we all insisted on coming with you.'

The two boys nodded.

Dimity grinned and added, 'Besides, did you forget? It's *always* Sophronia's fault.'

Sophronia nodded. 'Too true.'

They made it safely into Oxford. Although the train paused several times, no one ever came to look into their coach, or noticed the air dinghy on top. With the others diligently on watch, Sophronia and Soap finally napped. Soap took the floor, scooting partly under the bench on which Sophronia slept.

'I'm used to it,' he said when the others protested.

Sophronia's hand fell over the bench side as she dozed. She woke to find it resting gently on the top of Soap's head. His cap had fallen off. His hair was short and rough to the touch. Like the autumn heath of the moor, warmed by the sun. She liked the texture, her fingers stroking it without meaning to. Quickly, guiltily, she stopped herself and looked around. Dimity was staring out of the window. Sidheag was stationed at the door. Only Felix had seen the caress.

Felix narrowed his eyes and looked away, clearly uncomfortable.

Guilt washed over Sophronia. She snapped back her hand as if burned and sat up.

In silence she began to lay out breakfast on the bench opposite. When she woke Soap, he had a small smile on his face.

They ate out of the picnic baskets. Soap had filched mainly meat pies, a smart decision as they were self-contained and nicely filling. There were jars of barley water to drink, the only thing he'd found quickly transportable. No one liked it – who did? – but it was better than nothing. The stores were generous but weren't going to sustain them for ever. When they arrived at Oxford station an hour or so later, it was with considerable relief.

Unfortunately, the station was crowded with morning business. The unexpected private train was shunted off to the last platform. As they pulled in, window still open, they heard a station call boarding for the Deft Twelve Star bound for Glasgow.

Sidheag nosed out of the door, excited, but they were too late. Four platforms over, the train in question pulled out before they could even come up with a plan to sneak off their own train. Sophronia grabbed her friend and yanked her inside just as Monique jumped down from the engineering cab.

Monique, as ever, was dressed to the height of current fashion, her carriage gown one of tiered lavender taffeta with black satin ribbon edging around the bottom of the wide, full bell. It was exactly suited to the climate and the conditions of winter travel. Her blonde hair was perfectly done and she looked beautiful. She must have had very little sleep herself. It didn't show, which Sophronia found highly annoying. Monique was probably accustomed to being up all night, living among vampires.

The handsome man from the aetherographic receiver joined her. He signalled at someone down at the end of the vacant platform, and a human porter pushed through the gate and hurried towards them. Money changed hands and the porter scurried off again.

'No mechanicals,' said Sophronia, squinting into the distant crowd in the station proper.

'There's track down for them,' responded Sidheag.

'Yes, but not a one is running.'

Felix nosed in. 'Pardon, ladies, if I might have a look?'

They allowed him space. He slid in next to Sophronia, warm and sweet smelling. *Figgy pudding,* she thought again.

'That is odd,' he corroborated, but offered no other explanation.

Minutes later the human porter returned, carrying two cups of tea and a copy of the *Oxford Whistler.* Monique and her companion, secure in their solitary state on the platform, made their way to a long bench under an overhang and sat with the paper and the tea. Their discussion seemed civilised, but despite Sophronia's ear trumpet and Dimity's lip-reading ability, they could not make out the topic.

Sophronia said, 'Soap, now that I think on it, does Monique know you by sight?'

Soap replied, 'Nope. Not one for fraternising with sooties, that snotty Miss Uppity.'

'Perhaps if you climbed out of the off side and nabbed one of those big brooms? If they don't have mechanicals working to clean, they'll be hurting for human staff.'

Soap followed her reasoning exactly. 'Platform sweeper? Good notion. I can brush on past them; with my skin and these duds, no one would know me from the scenery.'

He climbed out of the window on the far side of the coach, lowered himself down to the track, and dashed off.

Felix seemed troubled.

'What is it, Lord Mersey?' asked Dimity.

'I just realised how little I notice my household staff and the human servants all around me.'

Dimity grinned. 'Scary, isn't it?'

He nodded. 'Very. I think I shall impress upon Father the necessity of raising their wages.'

Sophronia tipped her head at him. 'You think loyalty can be bought?'

'Don't you?'

Sophronia thought about her friends; money had never yet been exchanged between them. It made her feel sorry for Felix.

'Sovereign, sovereigns or seduction,' said Sidheag calmly, before Sophronia could stop her.

Dimity nodded in agreement. 'It's our second lesson after the school motto: *Ut acerbus terminus.*'

Felix looked confused. 'What does it mean?'

'"To the bitter end,"' said Sophronia.

'Not that. I do speak Latin, thank you very much. I'm not a complete imbecile. I mean to ask, what does "sovereign, sovereigns or seduction" mean?'

'The three possible ways to turn a man to a cause,' explained Dimity.

'What cause?' Felix was unsettled. His eyes on Sophronia.

'I see Soap,' said Sophronia, wondering if Felix was afraid she could turn him away from a Pickleman future. *I'm trying,* she thought. *Is it working?* Self-consciously she shifted so the whole length of her side was pressed against him. His breath hitched in a most gratifying manner.

They watched as Soap appeared at the edge of the platform near the front of the train and jumped up. He'd found a big broom and pushed it about, his cap pulled down over his eyes, whistling softly, until he was right behind Monique's bench. He slowed and did a bit of extra sweeping.

'Don't do overmuch,' hissed Sophronia, her nose pressed to the glass in worry. 'Monique will notice. Move off now, move off!'

Monique, occupied with tea, argument and newspaper, nevertheless shifted and gave Soap a sharp look just as the tall, lanky sootie obeyed Sophronia's silent order and moved on down the platform.

Then the young gentleman looked up, noticed the sweeper, and yelled sharply.

Run! Sophronia suppressed the urge to scream out of the train.

Soap turned back and ambled towards Monique and her companion, dragging the broom casually behind him.

Everyone in the coach held their breath, even Felix, who didn't give two figs if Soap got caught. He was no doubt worried that Soap might give them away. Felix probably believed that sooties had no honour.

Instead of grabbing him, or yelling for the constable, or making any other threatening movement, the man signalled Soap forward.

Monique ignored Soap entirely.

The man asked Soap something, hands spread.

Soap shook his head.

The man got upset, throwing his paper down to the ground in annoyance.

Soap tipped his hat at them politely and returned to sweeping.

Monique and her associate abandoned their teacups on the bench and returned to the train.

'Drop!' hissed Sophronia.

Watching from the coach door window, they all ducked as Monique faced them for a moment. Had she seen the balloon basket on the roof?

Apparently not.

The stowaways popped back up in time to watch the man hand Monique into the cab before returning to the transmitter carriage.

They turned away in time to see Soap reach down and swig the leftover tea.

Felix and Dimity both made noises of disgust. Imagine drinking someone else's leavings? How humiliating!

Then Soap hurriedly swept the rest of the platform, before disappearing around the front of the train.

TRAIN-NAPPING

Sophronia trusted in Soap's abilities to get back on board, but she was impressed with his speed. He reappeared only a few minutes later, squirming through the window, looking chipper and pleased with himself. Also, he was bolstered by pilfered tea.

Sophronia couldn't help glancing at Felix. She knew that all he saw was a dark-skinned boy who drank someone else's leavings, like a beggar. She felt hot behind the ears. Why had Soap done such a thing in front of everyone?

She shook it off. She might have done it herself, if no one had been watching. She was *that* in need of tea.

'What did you hear?' she asked.

'They were arguing over the morning paper. She said something about the need for greater range. He said that range was never discussed. She said that didn't matter, that they would get blamed regardless and that she would make sure they knew he was at fault. Then he waved the paper and said he'd made it possible to get this far. Then she said it wasn't their choice to question orders and that they would have to keep trying. That was it.'

'What did he say to you, when you spoke directly?' asked Sophronia.

'That was the strangest part. He asked about the mechanicals in Oxford.'

'The mechanicals? Why, are they not working?'

'That's just it, he didn't explain.'

'So what did you say?'

'I asked if I looked like my family could afford mechanicals. He got hot under the collar and said he thought I might pay attention to the world around me and threw the paper on the ground. Then the driver signalled for them to get back aboard.'

Sophronia nibbled her lip in thought.

Soap looked disappointed, as if he wanted something more from her than just lip nibbles. Then again . . .

'I brought you a present.' With a flourish, Soap pulled the morning paper out of his shirt front. He must have lifted it while drinking the tea and stashed it when they ducked for cover.

Sophronia grinned. His drinking the abandoned beverage was entirely forgiven.

'Good on you!' said Sidheag, slapping Soap companionably on the back.

Both Felix and Dimity looked askance at such familiarity. Dimity was concerned with Sidheag's dignity, Felix with the dignity of the peerage. Lady Kingair should not go around touching sooties!

Sidheag was oblivious. 'What does it say?'

Soap handed the *Oxford Whistler* to Sophronia without answering.

Sophronia opened it eagerly, reading the headlines. There was an announcement of the wedding of Jemima Smackadee to Wilfred Corkin, some threatened occupation of the Danubian Principalities and concerns over staff repairs. It was frustrating; nothing seemed directly tied to the conversation Soap had overheard, nor the aetherographic transmitter on the train.

Dimity sat next to her on the bench, reading as well. Felix and Sidheag took the opposite side of the paper. Sophronia held it up so they could all read at once, scanning for relevant information. Soap, without having to be asked, took up a position at the door to keep watch. After lessons with Sophronia, he could read a little, but not well. He was only on the second-level primers.

The train lurched and began to pull out of the station.

Sophronia caught Sidheag's eye. If they didn't go northward, then they'd be headed to London. Sidheag would blame Sophronia for their not switching trains. Sophronia knew it and accepted responsibility. Sidheag ought to have been her priority. They should have got off along with Soap and left Monique and the vampires to their own devices. They could have pooled their resources to pay for a northbound ticket for Sidheag without them. But now?

Sophronia admitted to herself that perhaps she was following this new trail of intrigue because it might delay Sidheag's departure. The more she thought about it, the more she worried about her friend's choice. Should Sidheag really hole up with a pack of traitorous werewolves? Chugging across the countryside with an aetherographic transmitter might give Sidheag a chance to rethink her options. *Then again, if I were in Sidheag's shoes, I wouldn't want anyone to delay me or question my judgment.* Feeling guiltier, Sophronia went back to reading the paper.

Felix, sitting opposite her, leaned all the way forward to read the fine print. Did he need glasses? That was sweet. He reached out to straighten a corner of the paper, brushing her fingertips. She caught his eye around the side and he gave one of his little half smiles. She was trying to decide how to respond when his attention diverted back to reading and his face went ashen.

'What did you find, Lord Mersey?'

'It could be nothing. . . .' He flipped the paper and pointed out an announcement box. Sidheag came around the other side of Sophronia, and the three girls read the small section together.

'Well, ladies?' prodded Soap from the door.

Sophronia read out. '"The mechanical manufacturers Messrs Brine, Boottle and Phipps very much regret the minor malfunction of servant units experienced by the residents of northern Wiltshire last night. Housekeepers are advised that a return of the steam tax for the time period in question will appear during the next accounting cycle. Please accept our profound apologies for any inconvenience."'

'That's what they call a bunch of mechanicals singing "Rule, Britannia!" and then dying? A minor malfunction?' Dimity scoffed.

Sophronia said, 'I wonder if the breakdown has spread to Oxford and that's why none of the station ones were working. If it happened after last night's incident, this paper would already have been in production. We'll have to check the evening rags for another apology.'

'There's a proper article here.' Dimity pointed below the announcement.

Felix sat back on the bench, crossing his arms over his chest, face sinking into its customary expression of manufactured boredom.

Sophronia read the article out as well, for Soap's benefit. '"Members of the gentry and other key families in several towns in North Wiltshire experienced an unexpected performance at midnight."' She paraphrased, 'He describes exactly what we saw with the dancing, although he doesn't name the song. Apparently, everyone's staff did exactly the same. Certain older models, or those not recently upgraded, were immune. The manufacturer won't say for certain, but inside sources hint at sabotage.'

Sophronia passed the paper over to Dimity. 'Mumsy did say she'd recently had Frowbritcher serviced. I wonder if that service included extra unexpected protocols?'

She looked hard at Felix. He seemed upset – why? They had all seen the malfunction at the ball; he could hardly have hoped they would forget. The only new information was that the malfunctions had extended over a much larger area than only Sophronia's house. What did that matter? What else had they learned? The name of the manufacturing company. Perhaps that was what had shaken him.

Casually she said, 'Does anyone know anything about Messrs Brine, Boottle and Phipps?'

No one said a word.

Sophronia contemplated the initials *BBP*. Had she seen them somewhere before? At that moment, all forgot in the excitement of the morning's events, Bumbersnoot tooted smoke at her.

'Oh, dear me yes, poor Bumbersnoot, you haven't had any breakfast. Anyone have something he could burn? His boiler will die down soon otherwise.'

Soap produced a lump of coal. He seemed to like having them stashed about his person for Bumbersnoot.

Sophronia picked up her little mechanimal, petting him affectionately, even though she knew he couldn't feel it. While the others talked quietly about the implications of a wider-ranging malfunction, Sophronia fed Bumbersnoot coal. At the same time she surreptitiously checked the underside of one of his ears. There, branded into the leather, was a string of letters Sophronia had always thought some kind of illegible maker's mark. Now she suspected the letters were *BBP*. Bumbersnoot was a mechanimal that'd come to her by way of the flyway-men, but she was sure he'd originally been made by Picklemen. After all, they had been around when she'd first acquired Bumbersnoot. Picklemen, in her experience, were very fond of mechanimals. Considering Felix's reaction, she thought it pretty darn likely that the company of Messrs Brine, Boottle and Phipps was a Pickleman front. But what did that signify for the 'Rule, Britannia!' malfunction? Had the vampires triggered it to sabotage the company and discredit the product, sort of like a character assassination on an industrial scale? Sophronia thought that if so, the sabotage could have been carried out by this very train. It had, after all, been in a station close to her house, in North Wiltshire.

Was the aetherographic machine being used to transmit protocols to multiple mechanicals simultaneously, telling them to sing 'Rule, Britannia!'? Why would the vampires reveal their hand to the Picklemen like that? Character assassinations were supposed to be subtle. Vieve had specified that crystalline valves only worked point-to-point. By rights, that meant that for every mechanical commanded to sing, there would need to be one crystalline valve inside the mechanical and a sister valve to do the sending on board the train. She counted on her hand. For her brother's party alone, with twelve mechanicals, that meant twelve companion valves on the train. Yet she had seen only one in the freight car. Perhaps the other freight carriage was absolutely full of valves?

Sophronia's mind buzzed. She said, 'It's possible that the very train we are on is responsible for all this madness.'

Sidheag waved the paper about. 'Why do you think that?'

'It's too conveniently in the right place at the right time. Plus, vampires are open in their mistrust of mechanicals. I think the operatic performance may have been some kind of test.'

Dimity said, 'Would they be so bold as to run a test like that in front of everyone?'

'I wondered the same thing. Perhaps the test was a mistake?'

Soap said, 'Monique did say something about *range*. Perhaps the mistake was that it didn't take out more mechanicals? Or that it hit too many?'

They looked at each other in silence for a long moment.

'Is it possible that the vampires are trying to take control of all mechanicals, throughout England?' Sophronia wondered, looking at Felix.

Felix said, his voice soft, 'Of course it's possible. *Anything* is possible with vampires.'

Sophronia thought of her bladed fan, a gift from a vampire. Was Lord Akeldama trying to buy her cooperation? Though he was a rove, and unattached to a hive, he could be acting in the interests of all vampire-kind. 'There is another possibility. They could be trying to discredit mechanicals and through them the new crystalline valve technology. Remember, vampires missed out on the monopoly.'

Felix liked this guess. 'They get the politicians on their side.'

Dimity said, in a small voice, 'There are sides? Whose side are we on?'

'The werewolves,' said Sidheag instantly.

'Goodness, are they involved, too?' wondered Sophronia, trying to fit that into her various theories.

Sidheag considered. 'Vampires and werewolves aren't particularly friendly, but they will band together against an anti-supernatural enemy as needed.' This was said pointedly for Felix's benefit, but then she returned to Sophronia's question. 'However, in this case, I think, no. Werewolves are less likely to tinker in industrial politics than vampires. Plus, we've got our own dilemma right now, remember? What do wolves care for the politics of machines?'

Felix shot back with, 'Yet it's interesting that the vampires are making this power play right after one of the most powerful packs in Britain has been fractured beyond repair. Isn't it? Perhaps they want to take advantage of the dewan's distraction.'

'Are you implying that the vampires somehow caused it? I think that highly unlikely,' objected Sophronia.

'Lady Linette always says there are no coincidences, only opportunities,' said Dimity, trying to play the peacekeeper.

'If anyone is likely to take advantage of this kind of situation, it's the Picklemen,' said Sophronia.

'What does *that* mean?' demanded Felix, for some reason annoyed. 'Do you support vampires against Picklemen?'

Vexed by such a direct questioning of her loyalties, especially when she felt she had made her thoughts plain, Sophronia took the unprecedented step of stating her position outright. 'I support balancing out power. Perhaps you might want to think about the broader scope yourself.'

'Vampires have enough power already,' hissed Felix.

'Would you please try to be logical, without prejudice?' Sophronia couldn't help it; some of her frustration with Felix's myopic perspective leaked out. *Why isn't he trained like we are, to think about motives and manipulation? Why doesn't he understand that this damages my affection for him?*

Felix was having none of it, although he kept his voice low. 'As if you weren't prejudiced against Picklemen.'

If Sophronia had had a temper, it would have flared up at that accusation. As it was, she only gave Felix a pitying smile. 'They destroyed my mother's gazebo and tried to kill me with a huge mechanimal. Then again, the vampires kidnapped and nearly killed Dimity. For that matter, the werewolves just attempted treason. *Everyone* is bloody-handed. That's my point.'

'Sophronia, language!' barked Dimity.

'Whose side are we on, then?' reiterated Soap, mildly, looking strangely cheered by the dissent among his travelling companions. He watched Sophronia and Felix bickering with something bordering on delight.

Sophronia was wondering that herself. *Perhaps I'm better off making a patron of the queen like Mrs Barnaclegoose.* Then she remembered that she had to hold this whole impromptu expedition together, and that they were still hiding out in an enemy train. They all needed a patron right now. She drew herself up.

'We are on Sidheag's side,' she said firmly.

'Well, thank you very much, Sophronia,' said Sidheag. 'But I'd rather not take responsibility, if I don't have to.'

'Then we are on the side of curiosity and even-handedness. Once we know what's really going on, then we choose.'

'That's a very murky position,' objected Felix.

'So's the weather. But this is England, we must learn to live with uncertainty.'

Their train did not head to London, but trundled roughly northward on one of the lesser-used regional tracks, out of the way of faster engines. Sidheag occasionally looked longingly across the landscape, where black smoke indicated a faster locomotive, but she didn't say anything about it. At least they were moving in the general direction of Scotland, even if it was at a snail's pace. Occasionally they paused before starting up again, probably so that the transmitter could be used.

Around noon they stopped for twenty minutes at a station

so tiny there was no point in Sidheag's jumping down and taking a risk by waiting for another train. Any train that came through would be, if possible, slower than the one they were already on. The only interesting thing was the continued absence of station mechanicals. Had they broken down again, or were people now scared to use them?

'If this goes on for too long, at too many stations and wealthy households, there will be a public outcry,' said Dimity.

The group was getting a little lax about security. Someone still stood watch at the door, but it really seemed that no one else was on the train. When they paused, only Monique, the drone with the transmitter, or the driver was ever visible, although presumably there must be a stoker. No one was interested in checking the last carriage. Why was it even attached? To make the train look larger and more important?

Sophronia agreed with Dimity. 'Mumsy couldn't manage the household if Frowbritcher stopped functioning. She uses him for practically everything. That's why she's so diligent about maintenance. If he's still down today, the house will be in chaos.'

Sidheag said, 'Rather dependent, isn't that?'

Sophronia only shrugged.

'Doesn't Kingair keep mechanicals?' asked Dimity.

'No, we keep clavigers for the dirty jobs. The castle is far too old to lay tracks.'

Felix bristled at Sidheag's implications.

Sophronia suspected that Duke Golborne's residence, both in the country and in town, was littered with tracks. Felix seemed like the type to come from the sort of family that kept

188

a mechanical for every whim. *Perhaps his ideals are more entrenched than I thought. A true test of my persuasive abilities!*

Felix defended the status quo. 'People wouldn't need so many tracks if the supernatural politicians stopped restricting mechanical development. After all, mechanimals don't need tracks, but free rollers are illegal. It was the potentate that pushed that piece of legislation through.'

Sophronia frowned. 'Are you saying tracks are no longer necessary?'

'Might be implying it, but I'm not saying it.' Felix looked smug.

Sophronia thought of Bumbersnoot. He operated without tracks and was illegal. But he also wasn't very big and wasn't, by most standards, useful. Yet correlate track-free motion to the idea that mechanicals might be controlled by a distant third party via the crystalline valves? Sophronia felt very uncomfortable. She could almost see where the vampires were coming from.

Speculation died down after that and things got extremely dull. The day was grey and drizzly. The train moved slowly north. They played cards; Felix had some in an inside pocket. They bickered about inconsequential things. They were all getting a bit tetchy after being trapped in a coach for so long.

Around teatime Dimity threw down her cards petulantly. 'Sophronia, you never warned me adventuring would be so dull and tea-less.'

'No, but Lady Linette did. She said when one was stalking a mark that great patience was required.'

'I missed that bit.' Dimity leaned back. 'What I wouldn't

give for a nice pot of Assam with some of those little cream puffs with the sugar on top. This isn't the life for me. It really isn't.' She looked most unhappy. It lent her ridiculous get-up an air of self-sacrifice. She made for such an unconvincing boy.

Felix looked at Dimity, intrigued. 'I thought all of Mademoiselle Geraldine's girls wanted to be intelligencers.'

'Do all of Bunson's boys want to be evil geniuses, Lord Mersey?' Dimity responded, knowing with confidence that this was not the case. Her own brother objected to the principles of his school, and mooched through his studies in a very non-evil way.

'No, I suppose not. Then why bother?'

Dimity grimaced. 'You haven't met my mother.'

'No, I haven't had that pleasure.'

'I'd avoid it if I were you.'

'Duly noted.'

'Dimity means to get herself married to a nice safe country squire or tuppenny knight. Spend the season in London and the rest of the time out of all intrigue in the countryside. Although lately the countryside seems very excitable.'

'You mean, like a normal girl?' Felix looked not at all upset by this admission of limited ambition.

Dimity flushed and glared at Sophronia. 'You aren't supposed to tell *a boy* that!'

'As if he weren't well aware of the marriage market? If he isn't yet, he should be. Once he circulates in society, he's going to be prime nosh.'

'I don't know whether to take that as a compliment or not, Ria. You make me sound like a bun from the baker's.'

'And a very tasty hot cross bun, unless I'm very much mistaken. Full of currants,' said Sophronia, speaking for all the chaperones in Felix's social future.

Felix actually blushed.

Soap looked as if he might be moved to speak against such outright flirting. His face wore an expression of disapproval not unlike that of Professor Lefoux upon encountering something she deemed particularly frivolous.

Felix turned the conversation elegantly back to Dimity, saying gallantly, 'Don't you worry, Miss Plumleigh-Teignmott. I respect that choice. It seems eminently reasonable for a young lady of quality.' Was he purposefully testing Sophronia with that statement?

Sophronia couldn't say anything. If she objected to his support of the normal path, she would insult Dimity. If she condoned it, her own choices were in question. *Very nicely played.* She gave Felix a nod of credit.

Sidheag, however, took offence. After all, she was off to probable spinsterhood and a very abnormal life choice – nanny to a band of discredited werewolf soldiers. She would have argued with Felix, but Sophronia put a hand to her arm and shook her head. Sidheag jerked away and went to stare out of the window, annoyed now with both of them.

We are exhausted by each other's company. Lady Linette had warned that such things were apt to happen at house parties. The only ones who seemed to be weathering the confining quarters well were Soap and Bumbersnoot. Sophronia supposed Soap was accustomed to being confined to engineering. Plus, he was content to let Sophronia handle bickering aristocrats.

Bumbersnoot, on the other hand, was disposed to enjoy himself no matter what. A very doggy quality.

Sophronia wanted to ask Soap's advice. He was unofficial mayor of the sooties; how did he lead them without constant dissent? She thought back over the course of their friendship, only now realising how often he had given her counsel. Had this untenable romantic affection of his destroyed that as well? *What will I do without him? When he's gone off and turned claviger, I'll no longer have any balance.*

Soap saw her looking at him, her green eyes grave and pleading. He tilted his head at her in query. But there was no privacy to ask him anything. An uninformed decision had to be made. Fortunately, uninformed decisions were Sophronia's speciality.

Sophronia said, into the silence of discontent that permeated the coach, 'Are we agreed that there are few people on this train, possibly only Monique and three others?'

'Sophronia, what are you planning?' wondered Dimity, knowing that tone in her friend's voice.

'Soap, how different are steam engines in trains from steam engines in dirigibles?'

'Not a great deal. I believe the basics are pretty much the same, miss.'

'Sidheag, you did a bit of stoking when we were down with the sooties, yes?'

'Of course, you know me, I never mind getting my hands dirty.'

Speaking of dirty, Felix gave Sidheag a very dirty look at that statement. 'One simply can't trust the Scottish aristocracy,' he grumbled.

Sophronia nodded, decision made. 'Good. I think we should *steal this train.*'

Possibly as a result of being restless, possibly because they were accustomed to her outrageous ideas, there was no outcry at such a bold statement. Sophronia was a little disappointed.

Everyone looked mainly thoughtful.

'That sounds reasonable,' said Dimity. *Dimity, of all people!*

'We could get it going faster and straight towards home,' said Sidheag, brightening up substantially.

Even Soap, the voice of Sophronia's reason, looked excited, if slightly peevish. 'I've never driven a train before.'

Felix only blinked at them all in silent horrified wonder.

They pooled their resources.

Sophronia, with all her pockets, was the best equipped. Dimity and Sidheag both had red handkerchiefs, lemon-scented oils and sewing shears. Sophronia gave her shears to Felix and her letter opener to Soap, preferring to rely on her new bladed fan. There was some discussion over the use of the obstructor – was it better applied in the aetherographic chamber? Finally, they decided Sophronia should take it with her to the locomotive cab. In case they needed to stop the train in a hurry, it could, theoretically, seize up the engine. Although Sophronia had never used it on anything so large.

Soap said, while Sophronia checked the condition of her two gadgets and strapped one to each wrist, 'Funny, miss, how you've got the hurlie for the charge forward and the obstructor for the opposite, stopping an attack.'

Sophronia smiled at the symbolism. 'I guess I do, don't I?'

'Even-handed balance in this as in everything else?' suggested

Soap, mildly. Showing that he, at least, cared for her political beliefs.

Dimity shouldered Bumbersnoot in his lacy reticule disguise.

Only then did Felix throw his hands into the air. 'Are you all completely biscuit-minded? How will you steal a *train*? It's on tracks, you realise? And it's huge. It's not as if people won't be able to trace where you're going or see you coming.'

They hid it in plain sight, of course.

That was Sophronia's plan. They had thought the train might be transporting a circus when they first saw it, so they carried that idea forward.

Much to Dimity's distress, this involved ripping her gold masquerade gown into streamers. Sidheag and Felix hung these off the roof railings on the two passenger carriages. Soap, Sophronia and Dimity righted the air dinghy and draped the balloons to flutter off the back of the train. It did look rather like a carnival carrier.

'People won't question the presence of an odd-looking train if it contains entertainers,' insisted Sophronia.

Dimity grimaced, brushing off her hands and looking around. 'My poor dress.'

Finished with the streamers, Felix climbed over, looking harried. 'How will we get through stations, not to mention switches? You can't know how to work those. And what about, oh, I don't know, crashing into an oncoming locomotive!' His voice rose slightly in hysteria as he ranted. Sophronia was impressed; she hadn't thought he had it in him to get so upset. It was kind of adorable.

'They must have timetables in the engine room? Mustn't they?' said Sidheag. 'We'll stick to the regional tracks and avoid local passenger carriers. We'll be perfectly fine. After all, Monique is already doing it. What matter if we take over?'

It was always nice to have Sidheag on one's side. *Such a good egg.*

'And you think the vampires will let us simply trundle off with their aetherographic transmitter?' Felix scoffed.

Sophronia arranged the last collapsed balloon to her satisfaction. 'If this were a hive collective manoeuvre, they'd have more drones on board. I think this is Westminster's gambit. That's why so few passengers. The further we get from London, the less their influence.'

'This is obviously some shared delusion of ability. Unless' – Felix paused – 'you haven't been taught train stealing at Mademoiselle Geraldine's, have you?'

'Not as such,' admitted Sophronia, with a grin. She was enjoying Felix's discomfort. He so rarely got riled over anything, it was a pleasure to see his beautifully sullen face animated, even if that animation was frustration.

Felix ran his hands through his dark hair, sounding like a resigned maiden aunt. 'It'll all end in tears and coal dust, you see if it doesn't.'

'Well, since we've already started, might as well continue.' Sophronia led her little band over the top of the passenger carriage towards the aetherographic transmitter.

They stopped before the coupler.

'Sidheag, Soap and I will take the engine room. Felix and Dimity, you're on the drone in that transmitter.' She overrode

Felix's protests. 'Try not to kill him and try not to damage the machine. Both could be valuable. Your target is the crystalline valve. Get Bumbersnoot to eat it. Then if everything goes wrong, at least we have the one key piece of the puzzle, and evidence.'

'Has she always been this bossy?' Felix asked Dimity.

'Imagine being her best friend,' replied Dimity.

'Crikey.'

'Dimity, am I really? That's so sweet.' Sophronia was distracted from bossiness by affection. She thought of Dimity as *her* best friend, but they had never talked about it, and she'd no idea Dimity felt the same. After all, Dimity was more popular and gregarious, and had lots more friends than Sophronia. Possibly because she wasn't so bossy.

'Of course. Sorry, Sidheag,' Dimity answered with a grin.

Sidheag made a face. 'You two are attached at the hip, everyone knows that.'

To Felix, Sophronia said, 'I only get bossy when it's important. Speaking of which, you should let Dimity go first, she has more training. Besides, and I do apologise, Dimity, but the shock value alone of your outlandish appearance might give you the edge.'

Dimity's resigned expression, combined with the oddball clothing, gave her a marked resemblance to her brother in his younger, portlier days.

'Definitely bossy,' said Felix, resigned.

'Oh, hush up, you like it,' said Sophronia.

Felix grabbed her hand, and before she could protest, pressed a swift kiss to her arm above the hurlie. It was shockingly forward and very daring. Of course, Sophronia was delighted.

'I do,' he murmured against her skin, letting her go just before she would have felt it necessary to jerk away.

Soap hissed a little, like an offended cat.

Dimity clasped her hands together. 'Don't worry, Sophronia, I'll look after him for you.'

'Oh, I say,' huffed Felix, glaring doubtfully at Dimity.

So they left Felix crouched behind Dimity, ready to climb down and enter the freight carriage. They could only pray the drone had no gun. Sophronia hated to think her friends were going into danger on her orders. *The price of bossiness*, she thought.

But she had to trust in Dimity's abilities; it needed to be a coordinated attack. So she led the other two onward, over the two passenger coaches, hopefully empty, and then over the tender to the cab. The cab had open doorways on both sides. She crouched on the right and Soap on the left, ready to swing down and in. Sidheag held position on the roof behind them, to follow as soon as possible, whichever side seemed necessary.

Sophronia waved her arm back at Dimity.

Her friend signalled acknowledgment. Then Dimity and Felix disappeared from sight.

Sophronia looked over and was about to nod to Soap when he pointed up. Ahead and above them, through a break in the clouds, was that same dirigible. The one Soap had spotted before. No time to think about that. Sophronia spread her hands in mystification and then nodded at him, once.

They each crossed their own arms, grabbing on to the top

edge of the cab roof, then swinging out and twisting around feet first through the doorway to land inside the cab proper. Sophronia, trained in acrobatic execution, had had ample opportunity to practise as she climbed about the school. In trousers, it was easy as buttered crumpets. She had no idea why Soap knew the manoeuvre, but sooties were universally fit and Soap very athletic. He did get a bit tangled up in the doorframe, being taller than she, so his landing was one knee down.

A good thing, too, for Monique had taken a swing at him with a wicked-looking dagger. Her arm swooshed right over his head.

The driver with the huge moustache, who happened to be near Sophronia, was concentrating on the controls and only half noticed the intruders. It helped that the noise was deafening so close to the engine – the hiss of steam and roar from the firebox combined with clanging cables and pistons.

Monique hadn't noticed Sophronia yet. Her attention was on Soap.

Sophronia wasn't really a killer. She'd never particularly enjoyed the assassination part of her lessons, but she couldn't have the driver messing things up, either. So she simply tapped the man on the arm. 'Pardon me, sir?'

'Ho, there, lad, what are you doing . . . ?'

'I do apologise, but we require the use of your train.'

'You what?'

Sophronia grinned at him, very cheeky, in the meantime sliding around to his other side so he was near the open door and she was not.

He was very confused.

Meanwhile, behind them, Monique and Soap grappled, Monique hurling some very unladylike profanity at the sootie – what had she been learning among vampires? – and telling him he had no right, and to keep his dirty, nasty guttersnipe hands off her!

A small young man tended the stoker's box, the train's equivalent of a sootie. Hard to tell if he was a hireling or a minion, but he turned to face the fray, attracted by the noise. He seemed befuddled into inaction, but he *was* armed with a large shovel. No time to think on him further; Sophronia spun in against the driver, bumping him.

'What?'

'Oh, my god, what's that!' she screamed, pointing out of the open cab door. There was real fear in her face, as if she were seeing a poltergeist.

The driver turned to look.

Sophronia shoved him with all her might. It shouldn't have worked – she was too slight and he was too large – except that Sophronia nipped one foot out and behind his leg, tripping him up. The SOS manoeuvre – *startle, obstruct and shove* – was a classic tactic in which Captain Niall had trained them well.

Sophronia had never made it work before. When one was practising, one's opponent always knew the startle was coming. But the driver reacted perfectly, and as a result tumbled out of the train.

She stuck her head out after. He seemed to have fallen harmlessly to one side. The train was moving just quickly enough that even a fit human couldn't catch up.

She yelled up to Sidheag. 'Room for you now. Waiting for an invitation?'

Sidheag dropped down and swung in easily, no finesse but no wasted effort, either.

The girls turned to face the stoker.

He looked from one to the other.

Sophronia looked mean and scruffy and had just shoved his boss from a moving train.

Sidheag was awfully tall and imposing.

The stoker put down his shovel and put both his empty hands out in a pleading manner. 'They hired me, young masters. I'm only along for the pay and the ride.'

'Sidheag, if you would deal with this?' asked Sophronia.

Sidheag looked the young man up and down. 'Delighted.'

She said, in her most commanding Lady Kingair voice, 'You know, friend, I've always been terribly interested in the running of trains. If you wouldn't mind continuing to shovel? I'm sure we can match your pay. In the meantime, if you could please tell me everything you know about everything, that would be topping.' And, because Sidheag knew well how to recruit a willing participant, she added, 'Would you like a bit of kidney pie? We happen to have brought a few on board with us.'

Sophronia went to help Soap with Monique.

It was an awkward scrap of a fight. Soap was very conscious of his position in society, or lack thereof, and he was never one to strike a lady regardless of station. Therefore, he was trying to apprehend Monique without actually touching her anywhere indelicate or injuring her in any way. Monique was not correspondingly delicate. She had several more years of train-

200

ing than Sophronia and wasn't half bad, even if she had left Mademoiselle Geraldine's in disgrace. She was giving Soap a very challenging time of it, and she was armed.

Soap was mainly dodging out of her way and blocking her from doing anything drastic. She spat curses at him, lashing out with her knife. Soap hadn't drawn the letter opener to combat it.

Sophronia reached into her pocket and pulled out the bladed fan. Time to test its paces.

'Soap, if I may?'

Soap glanced over at her in relief. 'Oh, would you?'

'It would be my pleasure.'

Only then did Monique realise who had taken over her train. She saw right through Sophronia's boy's garb to the oval face and green eyes that had given her so much trouble at school. 'Of course, it would be you, wouldn't it? Always messing everything up, aren't you, Sophronia?'

'That's my sole purpose in life, Monique, to inconvenience you.'

The two girls circled each other warily. It was close quarters in the cab of a locomotive, particularly with three fellows. Sophronia was confident that Soap and Sidheag would, between them, get the train in hand. Out of the corner of her eye she saw Soap take the driver's station.

Monique nipped in and slashed. A real kitchen knife, too, no pretence at some more upstairs-friendly implement. Although it did have a nice ivory handle.

Sophronia whipped out her fan and shook off the leather guard.

'Had that lesson, have you?' sneered Monique.

Sophronia concentrated on the shift of Monique's shoulders under her travelling gown, hints as to where she might move to strike next.

'I never liked the fan. Too flashy,' said the blonde, nipping in again.

In Sophronia's experience, nothing was too flashy for Monique, so this must mean that Monique wasn't any good with the fan. Sophronia had been practising as much as she could since the first instance. This new one felt inexplicably natural in her hands.

She spun it in against Monique, a fancy wiggle and shift.

The girl's beautiful blue eyes widened in horror. She backed up a bit.

'Careful with that thing, Sophronia, you could hurt somebody!'

'I thought that was the idea,' replied Sophronia, twirling the fan expertly around her wrist in a blur.

'No, stupid, that's *my* task!'

Sophronia whipped the fan in, cutting away at Monique's sleeve and nearly chopping the blonde's hand off at the wrist where she held the knife.

Both girls gasped: Monique at the narrow escape, Sophronia at the very idea that she had almost cut off someone's hand. Shocking.

Odd, thought Sophronia, *that if Monique were a stranger, I'd have a much easier time hurting her. But because she's a person I know, even though I don't like her, I struggle to be ruthless. Do all intelligencers have similar scruples?*

They circled each other, a little more hesitant now.

I could really hurt her. I'm better than she is. It was a frightening kind of power. Sophronia would have thought to find it thrilling. After all, this was why they trained so hard. But it was merely scary.

Monique nipped in again, unguarded, aiming for Sophronia's chest – her knife sharp and focused. Sophronia might be a better fighter, but she wasn't as bloodthirsty.

Sophronia ducked out of the way and slashed at Monique's shoulder, cutting through the tightly stretched material there, above the older girl's corset, leaving a wide gash. Sophronia had thought Monique would now be accustomed to pain, offering up her neck to vampires on a regular basis. Perhaps vampire bites didn't hurt, because Monique dropped her blade and began to wail loudly.

Soap and Sidheag turned, surprised.

Sophronia kicked the knife off the train.

Sidheag gave Monique a dirty look and went back to chatting with the sootie. She was shovelling under his supervision while he consumed kidney pie with evident joy. Apparently, that was just the thing to alter loyalties. It probably helped that Sidheag was genuinely interested in locomotives. Strange, for until recently Sophronia would have said Sidheag cared for nothing but Scotland and werewolves, with the possible addition of small dogs and cigars. Not that she'd seen Sidheag with either; dogs and cigars were not encouraged at finishing school. But one could easily *imagine* Sidheag with dogs and cigars.

Sophronia returned her attention to the unpleasant Monique. She snapped her bladed fan closed in disgust. 'I had no idea you were so weak!' *I once thought this girl so very dangerous.*

Monique was petulant, clutching her shoulder. 'It stings something awful!'

Sophronia rolled her eyes. 'Well, there you go, stay away from bladed fans. Oh, for goodness' sake, shush! Here, let me bandage that up.'

She did so, Monique fussing the whole time.

'Toss her or keep her?' she asked Sidheag and Soap.

'Toss,' said Sidheag, without looking up from the boiler.

'I agree,' said the kidney-pie-filled stoker. 'That one is rotten to the core.'

'Keep,' said Soap. 'She might have vital information.'

'She's just like us, educated to resist.' Sidheag really did not like Monique.

'Still,' said Soap.

Sophronia was tempted to tip the annoying female off the train, but there was no knowing how useful she might be as a bargaining chip, if nothing else. She narrowed her eyes at Monique. 'Which would you prefer?'

Monique shrugged, but her eyes slid to the door.

That settled it; Monique was staying.

They'd had lessons from Lady Linette in how to escape bonds, so Sophronia tied Monique's hands above her head and then looped them up and over a protrusion on the outside of the doorway. Monique had to stand on tiptoe, occasionally swinging out of the door and back again in a most precarious manner. That would keep her distracted from slipping her restraints.

After that, it was a matter of ignoring the girl's whining and learning how to run a train.

Soap applied all his prowess as a sootie to monitoring gauges, throttle controls, and the brake lever. The stoker proved most helpful and most taken with Sidheag. Sophronia wondered if he saw through their disguises, or if he was merely the type of young man who preferred the company of other men. Whatever the case, he and Sidheag had formulated a relationship, even though nothing was left of the kidney pie. He was knowledgeable about trains in a way only a young man raised on the railways could be.

They chugged along happily, stoking the boiler up to a nice clipping speed, one that made Monique squirmy and discontented, swaying back and forth. Sophronia left her to dangle for a good hour, to contemplate her choices in life. They all ignored her pleas and attempts at bargaining.

Finally, they had to stop at a switch. Their young stoker friend explained the niceties of signalling. They waited politely at the switch for a local train to toot past them.

There was a moment of terror, wondering if the train would stop to find out who they were and why they were running on a normally vacant track. But the other train sped by, showing no interest whatsoever and no inclination to stop. It was mostly second class and clearly had its own problems to worry about.

If anyone saw Monique, a well-dressed woman of quality, dangling from the doorway, they apparently assumed everyone had difficulties in life and moved on.

Sophronia hopped out to handle the switch under the guidance of the stoker.

They were back on their way, hoping no other trains were due across that stretch of track. Had the vampires filed this journey with the appropriate offices? There was only one person to ask. Sophronia approached Monique as they clattered back up to speed.

'Oh, for goodness' sake, Sophronia, cut me down, do? My arms have come over all numb.'

'Riddle me this, Monique,' Sophronia responded. 'How dark are your masters keeping this journey? Did they file it with the controllers, or do we risk our lives on every new stretch of track?'

Monique would have shrugged if her shoulders hadn't already been up by her ears. 'That's why they have signals, isn't it?'

'That's a very lax attitude when hauling valuable equipment on an important covert mission.'

Monique looked away out of the window, past Soap and into the grey countryside. 'Little do you know.'

'So why don't you tell me? What are you really up to? Why are you intent on sabotaging mechanicals? Is it only to discredit the Picklemen, or is there something else going on? You realise society would crumble without mechanicals?'

'I wouldn't go *that* far. I've been living without their use for almost a year. I assure you, human staff are perfectly serviceable. Perhaps not quite so strong, but better able to follow complex instructions.'

They were getting off point. 'Why "Rule, Britannia!"?'

Monique looked genuinely confused. 'What *are* you on about?'

Monique had either got better at playing dumb or she didn't know that 'Rule, Britannia!' was the song malfunctioning mechanicals sang. It hadn't been named in the papers. Perhaps Monique was just executing commands without knowing the end result? But that idea didn't sit right; something was off here.

'How are you doing it with only one crystalline valve?' Sophronia persisted. 'I thought the technology meant you would need one for each mechanical.'

Monique looked confused again and shook her head. 'I assure you, Mr Smollet is perfectly capable of undertaking the necessary, with the system provided.'

Sophronia couldn't help feeling that they were talking at cross-purposes. If anything, Monique seemed as frustrated with Sophronia as Sophronia was with her. Monique would enjoy avoiding questions and being difficult, if she knew what Sophronia wanted. Clearly, she didn't.

Monique returned to griping. 'Really, Sophronia, I knew you were thick, but how can you be on *their* side? Don't you realise how dependent we have become on mechanicals? How lazy and slothful.'

'For certain, Monique. I can certainly see you washing your own laundry. Making your own tea. Dusting your own china.'

Monique almost growled. 'No, you idiot, not *that*! Who controls the mechanicals? Who controls the government? We have allowed them too much power. We have allowed them too much control.'

'Funny, there are many who say exactly that about vampires. It's all a matter of perspective.'

Monique actually squealed in annoyance. 'And you have the *wrong* perspective. Let me down, you idiot, you're going too fast. They are going to spot you.'

'Who is?'

Monique's gaze fixed on the side forward window near Soap. 'Too late,' she said. 'Too late.'

Sophronia, although she knew it could be a trick, turned to see what Monique was staring at.

Out of the clouds, a little to the front of them, floated that same dirigible. Now it was much closer. It was sinking down, and it was heading towards them.

'Outrun them,' advised Monique. 'Get away now, Sophronia. Shovel coal as if your life depends upon it, because your life just may.'

'Really, Monique, you can't frighten me. Who are they, anyway?'

'Flywaymen, of course. Who were you expecting, the British Navy? Get away *now*! They aren't going to take this lightly, and they are going to think it's coming from you, because I won't admit to anything.'

Sophronia only said, 'I think they'll see reason, if I explain myself properly.'

Monique let out a genuine bark of laughter. 'My dear, even you are not that persuasive. You do know what we have been doing, don't you?'

'Messing with mechanicals.'

Monique shook her head. 'Silly child.'

Sophronia turned away, suddenly worried. 'Soap, give her more power.'

Soap was already shaking his head. 'Another switch, we can't risk it. We're getting in closer to Birmingham and there's likely to be more trains sharing the tracks, even on rural lines.'

They had to stop at the signal.

The dirigible moved inexorably down towards them. It floated out of sight around the front of the locomotive, so that when they started back up again they had no idea exactly where it had gone.

Soap stuck his head out of the door to see, swinging wide so most of his body was arched out, holding on to the jamb with a free hand.

It had Sophronia's heart in her throat, but she knew better than to call him back or express concern. Soap would never question her abilities; it wasn't for her to question his. In this they understood each other completely.

'Nothing,' he said, returning to his station as driver.

Sophronia shoved Monique aside and did the same out of the other door, swinging out not quite so much.

Monique tried to shove Sophronia with her foot but was hampered by skirts.

Sophronia whacked her smartly with the backside of her closed fan in retribution.

The tracks began to curve enough for Sophronia to catch sight of . . .

'Soap, brakes!' she yelled. 'Those fools landed on the line!'

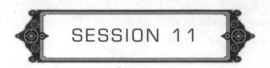

FELIX VERSUS THE FLYWAYMEN

S oap yanked on the brake lever. The locomotive
screamed in protest. Sidheag's eyes went wide in sympathy for the poor train. She and her little friend
stopped stoking and began scraping the coals out into
the grate in an effort to cool the boilers.

The engine stuck out so far in front of the cab that they had no
idea how much leeway they had before they crashed. They could
do nothing more than slow the train as soon as possible. Sophronia
was certain the wheels were sparking against the brakes.

The train squealed to a stop well before the dirigible. The
abruptness of the halt almost threw Sophronia out of the cab
door. She scrabbled for purchase and hoped Dimity and Felix
were adequately braced. She must rely on Dimity to act the
capable intelligencer, and Felix not to let his ego get in the
way of sensible precautions. She had no idea it would be so
challenging to depend on the abilities of others.

No time to check on her friends; the dirigible was settling with the clear intention of disgorging occupants.

'Soap, will you stay with Monique?' Sophronia took in the sootie from under lowered lashes.

Soap's expression said much that Sophronia couldn't interpret. Then he nodded and returned to checking gauges.

Sophronia faced Sidheag and jerked her head towards the door. The taller girl nodded and untied the apron she'd donned to help with the coal. 'It's all right, Dusty, you stay here. Mr Sophronia and I got this one for now.'

'If you say so.'

Sophronia appreciated Sidheag's continuation of their masculine personas. Monique had called her by name, but it was common among the gentry to refer to a man by his last name alone. Sidheag had turned it nicely in that direction.

'Ready, Sid?' Sophronia said, following the angle.

They swung out of the cab and crunched along the edge of the track towards the downed airship. It was fully inflated, only loosely lashed to the track, bobbing softly. It was big enough to boast a propeller, and proper ladders over the sides, unlike the air dinghy. Its gondola was more barge- than basket-like, a spacious transport indeed.

They heard a shout behind them.

Felix and Dimity were running to catch up. Dimity had Bumbersnoot slung over her shoulder. Lacy dog reticule combined with overly large clothing and corseted waist made her, if possible, even more incongruous.

Sophronia and Sidheag waited for them.

'Hello, lovely one,' said Felix to Sophronia, looking pleased with himself.

'Everything greased your end?' Sophronia asked, looking to Dimity.

'Topping, we dumped him out, shortly after you jettisoned the driver. Must be leagues away by now. Here, thought you might want this.' Dimity patted Bumbersnoot, grinning mischievously.

'Oh? Has he swallowed something interesting lately?'

'Only the vampires' crystalline valve frequensor.'

'Brilliant! You keep him for now? I'd rather stay unencumbered. Anything new to add to the puzzle of what the vampires are doing with that transmitter?'

Dimity nodded. 'Only thing we could get out of that drone before we chucked him was that they were only receiving information, not transmitting it. That valve was hooked into the sketcher component. The part on which letters appear. The drone was monitoring it and then making notes on a map.'

'You mean they weren't responsible for causing the mass mechanical malfunction?'

'It doesn't seem likely.'

Sophronia nodded, re-evaluating what was going on, her attention taken by the dirigible in front of them. Two men had climbed out and were striding aggressively towards them.

Flywaymen. Sophronia had met their type before. They were dressed like the highwaymen of olden days in baggy britches tucked into tall boots, with sashes about their waists. Sophronia thought the outfits a bit much, but she supposed if one was a criminal outside society one could afford to ignore all the rules of proper attire. They had handkerchiefs tied about their heads, instead of respectable hats, and cravats pinned with onion brooches. It was a hodgepodge of styles that Mademoiselle Geraldine had explained was 'only affected by the disenfranchised'. *Really*, thought Sophronia, *you'd think with a Pickleman alliance some style would rub off*. However, there was no way to know if these flywaymen were allies or not. There were many flywaymen and they didn't often work together. Besides, who was she to talk fashion? Sophronia pulled her tweed cap further down over her forehead, ensuring that her plaited hair was still tucked securely underneath.

Sophronia said to her friends, 'Ready, boys?'

Felix said, 'You sure you don't want me to talk?'

'Best not. Flywaymen have allied with Picklemen before. Your father could be involved. You could be involved.'

'Ria, you wound me!' He seemed genuinely upset. 'My father would never fraternise with the lower orders, not even for the good of the Empire!'

'And Picklemen do *everything* for the good of the Empire?'

'Of course.'

'It's just that they think that the Empire's good means every-thing under their direct control.'

Felix bristled. 'That's not fair!'

Sophronia realised she'd made an error. 'My dear Lord Mersey – Felix. It's not that I don't trust you. It's the Picklemen whose judgment is in question.'

Felix looked a bit mollified. She'd also trapped him neatly into thinking about his own instinctual alliance with the

Picklemen every time they were mentioned. She added a cautious 'You do realise that you still have the choice. Your father hasn't made it for you.'

He might have immediately reacted badly to that, accused her of trying to win him over, so she added quickly, 'That choice can always be to follow him. I know you are not the type to be told what to do by anyone.' She tried a little flattery. 'Far too strong in character. I simply wish to ensure you realise you are making a choice.' She tried a winsome little smile.

That seemed to help matters. Felix looked to be actually mulling over her words. *Am I getting through to him at last?* 'In that case, dear Ria, thank you for looking out for me. Such a supportive attitude.'

He leaned towards her and his tone, much softened, indicated that he now perceived her attempted influence as tantamount to wifely concern for his future. Perhaps she had taken it too far. He did have the prettiest eyes.

Sidheag interrupted what looked to become a lengthy flirtation. 'May I remind you that we have flywaymen to deal with?'

'I can handle a few flywaymen. I've done it before.' Sophronia spoke with more confidence than she felt. After all, the last time hadn't turned out at all well; Dimity had been shot.

They walked past the engine of the train.

Dimity referred to Monique in the doorway. 'Saw your nicely strung-up slab of bacon.'

'Don't insult bacon,' said Sidheag.

'I do my best work under stressful circumstances,' replied Sophronia.

The two flywaymen waved and hollered at them. 'What ho!'

The flywaymen approached with amicable expressions on their faces. And seemed quite delighted to find the train apparently under the command of a scrappy band of larrikin boys.

'Young squires, how do you do this fine afternoon?' enquired one, with forced jocularity. He was a squarish, stubby sort, wind-chafed, boasting a red nose in a round, pockmarked face.

The other, larger and angrier, had shaggy black hair and both hands shoved deep into his pockets, no doubt clutching some form of weaponry.

Sophronia was not one to abandon her lessons at a whim, so she played along by answering in kind. She forced her facial muscles and shoulders to relax. She splayed out her hands palms forward, tailoring her body movements to show openness and goodwill.

'Top of the day to you, my lords,' she said. 'May we be of some kind of assistance? You seem to have landed on our track.'

'Now, now, young squire, you know that there is Her Majesty's track,' said Stubby, still smiling.

'Indeed, indeed it is. How right you are, my lord. But, if at all possible, we should very much like to use it and are in a bit of a hurry.'

'Oh, are ye? And where are you off to in such a tearing rush with such an odd mix-up of a train? Are you not a little young for such heavy responsibility?'

Sidheag stepped forward, hackles up, less kind than Sophronia and in more of a hurry. They had played this hand before – the one pretending to be nice, the other . . . less nice.

'I am Lord Kingair and this train is under my commission.'

'Oh, is it indeed, lordly lad?' said Stubby, and then, with his smile made over nasty, he showed his intent in a manner most unwise. 'What if I were to say that we should like to borrow it for a while?'

'We should say,' answered Sophronia, placing a hand ostentatiously on Sidheag's arm as if to sooth Lord Kingair's ruffled aristocratic feathers, 'that you already had a perfectly serviceable dirigible. What would you want with our train?'

The flywaymen chuckled at this impertinence.

Stubby said, 'It's more what you want with us. Why have you been following us these three days?'

Now, that was interesting information. Was that what Monique had been doing? *Following* the airship by train? Why by train? Sophronia puzzled over the matter. *I suppose it's the only thing strong enough to haul two freights' worth of aetherographic machine. Which means they must have been using the machine to track the airship!* That was why the train kept pausing – they had to be still to use the valve. They must have known the ship would float over populated areas, or a train would be useless. But it would also explain why they wanted to stay secretive.

It took only a moment for Sophronia to realise all of this, and she weighed the merits of telling the flywaymen any of it. Best, she thought, to keep revelations about vampires as ammunition for when ammunition was necessary.

'I don't know what you are on about,' she said, smiling

broadly. 'We simply wanted a little play time, off Bunson's. A bit of a lark with a train. We found this one at Wootton Bassett and thought, why not? Lord Kingair here had a hankering to visit the relations, and Lord Mersey, Mr Dim and I thought we'd join him.'

Sophronia dropped each name and each nugget of information with purpose, paying close attention to the reactions of both flywaymen. The revelation that they were boys who had jumped a train on a lark appeared to engender relief. The fact that they were Bunson's boys struck a spark of recognition in Stubby. The name Kingair and the intent to head north meant nothing. If they knew about the fuss with the Kingair pack, they weren't connecting it to Sidheag. But it was the name Lord Mersey that really gave them pause.

Both flywaymen focused on Felix in a panic.

Obligingly, Felix stepped forward. He had gone back to his old looks and expression – a paragon of aristocratic boredom. His slightly full lips were too pouty. His blue eyes weighed the world and found it wanting. He slouched just enough not to mess with the cut of a fine Bond Street jacket – had he been wearing one – nothing more than the indolent son of a powerful man. Here was a boy accustomed to getting anything he wanted out of life. He thought he could have her just as easily, and she adored teasing him with the fact that he could not. In that moment, Sophronia again found him wildly attractive.

The flywaymen reacted to Felix's attitude. Even though they were criminals; even though they were little better than thieves of the sky; even though they were outside society – they could not deny hundreds of years of the British class system.

Sidheag was good at being autocratic. But her aura of command came out of an acerbic nature, from knowing that if upset she could eviscerate with her tongue. Felix, on the other hand, simply assumed superiority. One was compelled to obey him because of who he was, rather than what he might do.

It was wonderful to watch. Sophronia wondered if she could simulate such an aura of ennui and discontent or if it had to be trained from birth.

The two men trusted in Felix's stated identity.

'Lord Mersey,' said the leader, 'we know of your illustrious father, of course.'

So they are connected to the Picklemen!

Felix tilted his head. 'And you are tempted into contemplating ransom? You are thinking that here you have a train full of valuable cargo?'

The flywaymen looked more shocked than tempted.

Stubby said, 'I know the Duke of Golborne well enough to realise he would not respond well to such behaviour.'

Felix nodded crisply. 'Good, we understand each other.'

And Sophronia was beginning to understand their situation.

Felix did not mention that there was a fair chance these flywaymen were, untraceably of course, in his father's employ. If these flywaymen were up to something that would cause the vampires to track them, there was a good chance that something was a Pickleman plot. Sophronia's heart wrenched. He had to know this, yet he gave no hint, not even to her. Despite the fact that she had been expecting it, Sophronia felt a keen sense of betrayal.

Stubby whispered in his shaggy companion's ear.

Shaggy hurried back to the airship.

'Is that wise?' wondered Sophronia. 'You are now all alone with us.'

Stubby laughed. 'I am under the impression that you boys are not armed. Out for a lark, you said, didn't you? Childish prank, stealing a train.'

Sophronia cocked her head. 'Did we say unarmed?'

Dimity and Sidheag turned to look back at their train. The implication being that someone with a gun might be covering their backs.

The flywayman swallowed.

Sidheag added, 'More like *borrowing* a train.'

Felix said, 'You do *know* about Bunson's, don't you, Mr Flywayman?'

'Most assuredly, most assuredly. One or two of our number once trained there.'

Felix wrinkled his nose at the very idea. 'Hard times.'

Dimity and Bumbersnoot lurked to the back of their group. Dimity's was the shakiest disguise. Sophronia was beginning to regret having let her join them. Why hadn't she asked her to stay with Soap?

The flywayman was focused on Sophronia, Felix and Sidheag, who each commanded, in their own way, an aura of evil genius mastermind, junior level. Remarkable, thought Sophronia, how a girl intelligencer could so easily become a boy evil genius.

The other flywayman returned at a jog and the two conferred privately.

The angle was extreme, but Sophronia thought she could lip-read the second man saying something about Duke Golborne.

Stubby turned; his face was now closed and suspicious.

'It is not your style, we understand, Lord Mersey, to commandeer a train. And you still have not explained why you were intent on following us.'

'Pure coincidence,' said Sophronia. 'After all, there are only two directions to go on any given track.'

'Who are you to know anything of my style?' snapped Felix at the same time.

Oh, thought Sophronia, *he is so good at pompous.*

Shaggy spoke for the first time, his voice a low growl. 'We cannot allow our plans to be cocked up by a band of scruffy boys. No matter whose son they claim to be.'

The first man raised his hand for silence and said, 'Have you any proof, young squires, that you are who you say you are?'

Felix stiffened. 'I do not *need* proof. Show me any member of society and they will vouch for me. I am known well to anyone who is *anyone*! Besides, who are you to demand proof of *me*?'

Sophronia arched her eyebrows and watched him work. He might even be thought too good. It was so easy for him to be a toffee-nosed dunderhead. No wonder Soap didn't like him. She wasn't certain that she liked this part of him, either. However, it *was* working in their favour, so she allowed Felix to get more riled, prepared to rein him in only if he became careless with his information.

'You are but a schoolboy!' objected Shaggy, not so easily cowed by rank as Stubby.

'I do not need to be of age to have a presence in society!' Now Felix was genuinely annoyed.

Shaggy took offence at Felix's tone of superiority. He removed a deadly-looking little gun from a pocket and pointed it at him.

Sophronia felt it time to interject. 'Now, now, gentlemen, let's not be impetuous.'

That statement made Shaggy angrier. 'You've been stalking us. You got yourselves some pretty valuable equipment, and some pretty valuable young men, and you think, what . . . ? We just gonna let you boys continue trundling along on your lonesome?' This second flywayman was nastier than the first. Sophronia had thought Stubby the leader, but now she thought he was simply the speaker.

She appreciated Shaggy's directness, and, to a certain extent, his nastiness. She considered a judicious reply.

Felix, on the other hand, did not. 'That is *exactly* what I expect! You have no cause to interfere with our travels. Leave that to the authorities, if they can catch us.'

'I wonder what your father would say to that,' said Stubby.

'Father! Father! What do you know of my father?' Felix practically steamed, like an overwrought boiler.

'Lord Mersey,' said Sophronia, 'that is *enough*!'

Felix turned on her, red about the ears.

Sophronia gave him a little wink and a small smile, trying to lighten the mood with flirtation. It worked. Felix clearly remembered not only their need for caution, but also the fact that Sophronia and the others were ladies in disguise, and *he* must behave like a gentleman around them, whether these fly-waymen knew it or not.

His arms relaxed to his sides.

Shaggy came over all suspicious at this, perhaps because Felix, highest rank among them, had deferred to a winking Sophronia.

He said, 'Come to think on it, he doesn't look much like the duke. Do we trust his story? These boys could be with the hive.'

Stubby did not agree. 'In those get-ups? Never have I known a vampire drone to be anything less than perfectly turned out.' His gaze shifted over Dimity. 'That one is a positive *sight*.'

Felix bristled; now these criminals were insulting a lady friend.

'Who are you to judge?' he wanted to know.

'That's enough out of you, lordling,' replied the second fly-wayman, pointing his gun with even more surety at Felix.

Felix had clearly reached his limit. Short tempers, reflected Sophronia, were a severe liability in her line of work. The young lord jerked in Shaggy's direction. The flywayman was tenser than he seemed, for he shot Felix, right then and there.

The sound of the gun seemed particularly loud in the quiet countryside.

BUMBERSNOOT TO THE RESCUE

Time seemed to slow.

Birds in a nearby hedgerow took off in a small cloud.

Dimity screamed.

Sophronia leapt forward to Felix, her heart in her throat, absolutely terrified. 'Felix!'

He was rocking around on his back, clutching the side of his thigh, his pretty face screwed up in agony. It must be bad, for he was getting his clothes all over dusty from the track. They were borrowed duds, but Felix was generally respectful of all clothing.

Sophronia skidded in to kneel next to him. 'Where were you hit? Felix!'

The viscount took a short moment to look into her worried green eyes. His own blue ones were leaking tears of pain, even though he was patently trying to contain them. 'Curses, that burns! God, you're beautiful.'

Sophronia forgave him the bad language in fine company. This once. She also forgave him the compliment. It couldn't be too bad a wound if he was still able to flirt. Although the flywaymen were listening with interest and she was still dressed as a boy.

'Hush. Let me see,' she said.

Reluctantly, Felix took his hands away from his leg. 'Kiss it and make it better?' he pleaded, winsome as an injured child.

'Are you delirious? They're listening,' she hissed.

'Ria, my dove, I enjoy wearing kohl and favour well-tailored waistcoats. I already have somewhat of a *reputation*.'

Sophronia tsked and looked to his thigh.

Stubby said to his companion, 'Supposing that actually is the duke's eldest, do you think he knows his son is a prancer?'

Sophronia found the comment somewhat of a relief for her own part; at least her disguise held. Felix was remarkably untroubled by any questioning of his manhood.

She said, 'See what I mean?'

He whispered, teeth gritted under her gentle ministrations, 'All rumours will be put to rest once you agree to marry me.'

'Oh, of course,' replied Sophronia, 'because it always works out exactly like that. You're ridiculous. No wife ever cleared a man's character, not without a great deal of trouble on the lower decks. So to speak. I should know, we've studied somewhat on the subject.'

'Ouch, darling, must you be so rough?'

'Just stoppering up your silly mouth.'

'I know a better way.' He pursed his lips at her. He was still writing and crying, mind you. She was a little relieved – at least this meant he hadn't been in league with the flywaymen from the get-go.

Sophronia finished her examination of the wound, and in the absence of brandy extracted her vial of lemon tincture – it was alcohol based, after all – and poured it over the gash.

Felix shrieked. And then, panting, said, 'Thank you, fine physician. That makes it feel so much better, *and* all sweetly scented.'

'Stop your whingeing. It's not serious. It only grazed the surface skin, see there.' Sophronia pointed, face free of worry. Underneath, however, she was thinking that it was bleeding rather much. He wasn't going to be able to walk. She untucked her shirt and began tearing the hem for a bandage.

Behind her, Sophronia heard a faint sigh and a thud as Dimity collapsed in a faint. She must have caught sight of the blood. Wonderful.

Sidheag, bless her heart, held her position but had pulled out her sewing shears, which she now brandished in a threatening manner. It was odd for young Lord Kingair to be brandishing shears, but so much else was going on, and so much else was odd, this didn't seem to clue the flywaymen into anything in any substantial way.

Stubby did not seem to be inclined to charge.

Shaggy was actually looking guilty at having shot a peer in cold blood.

Then from behind the flywaymen came a shout of rage. Someone had been watching their confrontation from the airship, probably through a spyglass. Now that someone climbed out of the dirigible and trotted in their direction with the sedate upright steps of a hound on the scent.

This man was no flywayman but a gentleman. His suit was of impeccable heavyweight tweed, perfect for floating over the countryside on a damp afternoon. He had paired it with a daytime top hat banded in green, and carried a cane with a spiked wooden top and a silver-tipped bottom, a sundowner weapon designed for killing supernaturals.

It was the band that caught Sophronia's attention. She knew that the flywaymen occasionally allied with Picklemen; now she knew that *these* particular flywaymen were hosting a Pickleman of their very own.

The man approached at speed. He had silver hair and a very authoritative demeanour.

Sophronia knew him.

She finished tying up Felix's leg. 'My dear Felix' – she risked the intimacy of his given name as she whispered – 'please don't tell him too much. I fear this plot is bigger than any of us suppose, and our safety is in your hands. Do, please, be careful, for my sake?'

Then she calmly straightened to face the Duke of Golborne.

'What a surprise. Good afternoon, Your Grace.'

If Felix's father recognised Sophronia from their two previous encounters, he was very good at hiding it. Of course, the first time had been during a fight, at night, in a gazebo, and she had been wearing a ballgown. The second time she'd been dressed as a dandy drone at a carnival. This time, she looked like a scamp, with her cap pulled down and her body language that of a schoolboy, rather than a fop.

Besides which, the duke was understandably distracted by his son's being shot. Fathers were like that, even Pickleman fathers.

He strode forward and struck Shaggy hard across the face with his cane. Without waiting to see the flywayman's reaction, he bent over Felix. He did not kneel at his son's side. Dukes do not kneel on train tracks for *anyone*.

'Boy, are you alive?'

Felix blinked at him in genuine surprise. Perhaps it was true and he had never fully believed in the intimacy between his father's secret society and the criminal element. Here, however, the duke had come popping out of a flywayman craft. He was either their hostage or their accomplice. And he had not wanted his son to know, or he would have been the one to contact them.

Felix seemed startled enough to forget that he had been shot, or perhaps to think it slightly less important and put on a brave face.

'Father? What are you doing here?' he asked, tremulously.

'Oh, no, no. What are *you* doing *here*? You're supposed to be in school.'

'Technically,' answered Felix, 'I'm supposed to be at a ball. Remember, I wrote you of the invitation?'

'Ah, yes, some two-bit country gentry. Odd acquaintance to cultivate, but you thought the father's business interests valuable to the cause.'

Sophronia blinked, tempted to doubt all Felix's attentions. Had he been courting her all along because of something Papa was up to in civil service? Then she realised – hoped, really –

that Felix must have said this to get permission to attend the masquerade.

'Yes, but things change, as they do. It became necessary to borrow a train and head north.'

'Oh, it did, did it?' The duke did not look convinced. 'And you interfered with our business; why, exactly?'

'I didn't know, Father. We took this train off a handful of drones.'

Sophronia risked a small squeeze of warning in the guise of checking his bandages: *Please don't tell the duke too much!*

Felix ignored her and went on, 'And they happened to be at a station near the ball, and headed in the right direction. So we took their train and bumped them off.'

The duke nodded. 'And what happened at that ball?'

Felix frowned at this sudden change of topic. 'Well, the two-bit country gentleman, I don't think he'll be all that useful.'

'No, I mean to say, boy, did anything *unusual* occur?'

'You mean the mechanical failure in all the papers?'

'Ah, so you read about it. Did you see it in action?'

Felix came over suddenly quite still and suspicious. 'Father, what are you up to? What's going on? Did you . . . ? Was it . . . ?' He trailed off.

But Sophronia put *all* the pieces together at that moment. The Picklemen had chosen her brother's party on purpose because they knew Felix would be there. They knew he would give them a full report if asked. Perhaps they hadn't known how wide-reaching the effect would be, or that the papers would pick it up. Or perhaps they had run that test again in the Oxford area, to see what would happen. But Felix's father, these flywaymen, they were responsible for all of it. And the drones, Monique and the train, they had been tracking them: gathering data, staying out of the way. Sophronia and her band had come in and messed everything up.

The train hadn't fortuitously been at Wootton Bassett, and the mechanicals hadn't spontaneously chosen the Temminnicks for 'Rule, Britannia!'. As Lady Linette always said, there were no coincidences, certainly not with Picklemen, simply an endless stream of increased probability.

Because she wanted confirmation, and because she hoped Duke Golborne thought her one of Felix's Piston cronies and thus safe, Sophronia asked, 'You caused that entertaining malfunction, didn't you, my lord?'

The duke focused his attention on her. And because he, too, had training, he didn't give her the outright answer she wanted. He wasn't loose-lipped enough, or he didn't have that kind of hubris. 'Who are you? You're not one of my boy's usual associates. You do look awfully familiar, though.'

Sophronia said, 'I have that kind of face.'

The duke's eyes turned to Sidheag and the prostrate Dimity. Bumbersnoot had righted himself and was nosing her in the side in a worried manner. 'None of your usual companions, boy,' he said suspiciously. 'Are they even Pistons? You know I don't like you fraternising with the hoi polloi of the aristocracy.' He seemed genuinely angry about it; did he go so far as to control Felix's friendships? *How awful for Felix*, thought Sophronia, briefly distracted from concerns over her immediate welfare.

Stubby stepped in at this juncture. 'Sir, there is definitely something funny about those boys. Particularly that one.' He pointed at Dimity.

The duke glanced again at her fallen form. 'That one is the least of my concerns – he's got himself a mechanimal. He has all the *right* connections. No, it's these other two I don't know.'

Sidheag said, 'I'm Scottish,' as if that would explain everything.

The duke nodded, as if it did. 'Yes, well, we can't all be from the right side of the country. Would I know your family?'

Sidheag looked uncomfortable. The duke was probably aware of the Kingair scandal. She scrabbled for the right kind of family to call her own, but Scotland was a funny place, progressive as a rule, mostly not in favour of the conservative referendum. So she dodged the question. 'Probably not, Your Grace.'

That didn't mollify him, since he had practically demanded an introduction. He turned wrathful eyes on Sophronia. 'And you, little man?'

Sophronia said, 'I'm one of those two-bit country gentry, Your Grace.' She bowed. 'Mr Temminnick, at your service.'

At that precise moment, Monique decided to start screaming.

The duke looked at his son. 'And what *exactly* is that?'

'One of the vampire drones. We kept her for collateral,' explained Felix, happy for a change of subject.

'Is she always that noisy? Seems hardly worth the bother.'

Sophronia was growing uncomfortable with this encounter.

It was getting beyond her control. She wandered over, with the pretext of checking on Dimity. Dimity seemed perfectly fine, although deep in her faint.

Sophronia pulled out her smelling salts.

Dimity sneezed herself awake.

'What?' she sputtered.

'You fainted and Felix's father, the duke, has turned up.'

'Oh, dear,' said Dimity, accurately.

'Felix is well, thank you for asking, a scrape to the leg.'

'Oh, good.'

'But I think it is time we extracted ourselves.'

Dimity nodded. 'And?'

'I'm sending you back to the train, with the pretext that you aren't well. Tell Soap he needs to charge the dirigible.'

'What?'

'Oh, keep your voice down, do. They won't let us actually crash. That ship must be full of some very valuable equipment. Just tell him to head at it full throttle.'

Dimity nodded and stood shakily.

Sophronia helped her up, all solicitation. She took Bumbersnoot for herself. If the mechanimal was going to confer credence, she wanted to keep him with her.

Dimity began trudging back towards the locomotive.

The flywayman with the gun, Shaggy, his face welted from where Duke Golborne had struck him, was having none of it. 'Oh, no you don't, young master!'

Dimity froze, then turned slowly back.

'He needs to recuperate,' objected Sophronia. 'I suggested he return to the train for a snifter.'

'He can recuperate perfectly well right here,' answered the duke, turning back to Felix.

'Now what?' hissed Dimity.

Sophronia wasn't entirely certain Felix could get them out. Or even if he wanted to. And she was under no illusion that, if they were taken hostage by flywaymen *and* Picklemen, their female natures would remain hidden.

'We'll have to try something else. Invisible spiders?'

Dimity said, 'Sidheag's better at those than me.' She angled her back towards the duke and flywaymen so they couldn't see, and gestured to Sidheag. She pressed her wrists together and waggled her fingers in a fair imitation of a spider.

Sidheag gave her a funny look.

Sophronia followed up by giving Sidheag the code for creating a distraction, pressing the first two fingers of both hands together in a quick, bird-like movement.

Comprehension dawned. Sidheag gave an almost imperceptible nod and then began to gyrate about like a madwoman, waving her hands around her face.

'Bees,' she yelled, 'I hate bees!'

Dimity watched this for a moment before squeaking herself, adding to the distraction. 'Oooo, eeek! Get them off!'

Sophronia unstrapped her hurlie, remembering what Soap had said about its being her version of a *charge*. She fed it to Bumbersnoot – her wrist felt naked without it. The little mechanimal obligingly swallowed it into his storage compartment, where it clanked against the crystalline valve already nestled there. If he had possessed the capacity to belch, he would have. As it was, he looked vaguely too full for comfort, whistling steam out of his undercarriage in a stuttering way.

Sophronia set him down, pointing him in the direction of the train.

She whispered, 'High speed, Bumbersnoot, forward, march. Go on, find Soap. Go to the train.' She waggled her free arm in a pinwheel, disguising her ducking down as an effort to avoid the mythical bees.

One could never be certain, with Bumbersnoot, which instructions he actually understood. Or chose to follow. Sophronia had, after all, rather stolen him. He hadn't exactly come with a protocol proclamation leaflet. However, something she said must have clicked into his operation wheels, for he began skittering down the track on his stubby little legs in a rapid and direct approach to the locomotive. How he might get Soap's attention from the cab was a mystery, but his small metal form was stealthy enough to be ignored by the enemy. Either that or because he was a mechanimal, he was deemed non-threatening.

Sophronia began her own fit in earnest, waving off bees. The three girls used the distraction to back – or, more correctly, gyrate – away from the duke, Felix and the two confused flywaymen.

And then, delightful music to the ear, Sophronia heard the dulcet sounds of a locomotive cranking to life.

A ROUSING GAME OF MARBLES

The duke noticed that there was a train heading slowly but inexorably in their direction. 'What's going on, boys?' he shouted over the resulting hubbub.

Sophronia said, 'Sorry, Felix, but you're in safe hands now. I guessed you don't want to stay with us, at this point.'

'Mr Temminnick, what are you about?' Felix's voice was deeply suspicious. He leaned up on one elbow to see her. The three girls had managed to wiggle impressively far.

Sophronia thought he looked heart-wrenchingly vulnerable.

Then he turned to the duke. 'Father?'

Sophronia immediately regretted any sympathetic feelings.

The train moved relentlessly towards them, picking up speed. Felix lay across the tracks.

Sophronia said, 'Sir? You might want to move your son.' She paused, significantly. 'And your dirigible.'

'You wouldn't!' the duke protested. 'Stop this immediately! How on earth did you get a message to your driver? You've been here the whole time. What is going on?' He turned to glare at Felix. 'Son, order this little friend of yours to stop. What's he doing taking charge like this, anyway? You rank him!'

Sophronia, still backing away, made a deep – almost courtly – bow.

Felix said, 'Never doubt Mr Temminnick's word on the matter of immediate actions. Father, if you would be so kind, I think I ought to move off the rails now?'

The train kept on coming.

The duke said a rude word and bent to part lift, part drag his son up the berm on the side of the tracks.

Sophronia, Dimity and Sidheag moved to the other side, staying as close as safety might allow.

Shaggy shot his gun at the oncoming locomotive in a futile effort at stopping it. Then he and his companion raced for the airship.

The locomotive charged forward. The girls spaced themselves and braced to leap.

The engine was in front of them, and then the cab.

Dimity went first, grabbing the jamb of the open doorway on the driver's side and swinging herself in behind Soap.

Sidheag swung in right after. Sophronia barely made it, stumbling on her dismount. Falling forward, she crashed against Soap. She barked her chin on his shoulder, causing them both pain, but quickly tried to extract herself. Soap, having reflexively embraced her with one arm, refused to let go, as though reassuring himself that she was safely back with him. He wasn't even looking at her, his other arm and his attention focused on the work of crashing a train. Sophronia allowed the embrace; she was relieved, too. She even enjoyed that for the briefest of moments she could examine his adorable, familiar face, absorb his warm, firm presence, without fear of romantic repercussions.

He said, letting her go gently, still without looking away from the various levers, dials and gauges, 'Welcome back. Did I interpret Bumbersnoot's message correctly, Sophronia, or do I owe our fine friends here an apology?'

'No apology necessary.' Sophronia rubbed her chin.

'So you say, but you're not about to hit their dirigible with a ruddy great train.' Soap donned a slightly maniacal grin.

Sophronia stuck her head out, took a look and shared his glee.

Dimity ran to the other side of the cab to look out, around Monique. 'Lord Mersey is clear!'

'More's the pity,' muttered Soap.

'Now, now,' Sophronia reprimanded, 'he was unexpectedly connected, as it turned out. His father was on board that airship. Caused some useful confusion.'

Dimity said, 'There they go! Bye-bye, gentlemen.' She waved cheerfully at Felix and his father as they flashed by.

The dirigible was directly in front of them now and struggling to lift off in time to avoid being hit.

It wasn't going to make it; it was too slow. The train had got up speed faster than Sophronia thought possible. Clearly, she would have to learn more about trains.

'Brace yourselves!' yelled Soap. He didn't bother to brake.

Sidheag said, voice wobbly, worried about the train, 'Soap, you could slow down a little!' Her little pal, Dusty, was happily stoking the boiler up into the red; he didn't even register what they were up to.

The train wasn't going all *that* fast – a horse at full trot might have kept pace – but it still relentlessly ploughed into the dirigible. Sophronia held the doorway behind Soap, leaning out just enough to watch the carnage. She was reminded of the time, what seemed like an age ago, when she had tumbled out of a dumbwaiter and landed in a trifle.

The dirigible was designed to float easily and with minimal effort, not to withstand a train-sized battering ram. The gondola was only made of thin wood, and splintered around the locomotive much as the custard and strawberries had once done over Mrs Barnaclegoose's favourite bonnet.

They thrust easily through the one-room interior of the dirigible, leaving bits of propeller, small steam engine parts and wood scraps scattered behind. The train didn't even try to derail.

The balloon section, suddenly free of a deal of weight, bobbed upward, swaying wildly from side to side.

Dimity gasped. 'Would you look at that?'

Like some strange form of fruit from a floating trifle, the heart of the flywaymen's dirigible spilled forth vast numbers of crystalline valve frequensors. Hundreds of them scattered everywhere. They must have been all set up, below the airship deck, in hundreds of little cradles, all linked to one big aetherographic transmitter. It explained everything, including why the airship could only boast a skeletal crew – the weight alone!

The frequensors, which were like faceted milky glass, sparkled, rolling everywhere. Some fractured into thousands of pieces, some were smashed under the wheels of the train as it completed its destructive charge and emerged unscathed, leaving carnage in its wake. *Again*, thought Sophronia, *not unlike me and that trifle*.

The dirigible's balloon, along with the top portion of what remained of the gondola, bobbed higher. Sophronia and Dimity stuck their heads out of their respective doors; Dimity, pushing Monique carelessly aside as if she were a curtain, craned to look behind. Monique was still screaming, but that might be due to the indignity of being treated like drapery.

Dimity yelled, 'The duke has left Lord Mersey and is trying to collect prototypes – sorry – frequensors. Oh, dear, it's as if he's lost his marbles.'

Sophronia said, 'I wager the pickled duke is none too pleased and is going to demand an explanation from his son.'

Sidheag looked at her, face sombre. 'Will Felix rat us out?'

'I begged him not to.' It was the best answer Sophronia could give, because she didn't know. Would her Piston beau reveal who they were and where they came from?

Soap said, monotone, concentrating on the track in front of them, though it was clear now and not worthy of such focus, 'Don't have much faith in your sweetheart, there, do you?'

Sophronia said, 'I've no illusions as to my consequence. If forced to choose between me and family, I don't know if he has the backbone to go up against the duke. I hadn't the right to ask that of him. Why should he do that for me? We've no formal engagement. I tried to encourage change, but in the end a man can't be blamed for his nature.'

Soap still did not turn. 'Perhaps someday you will apply that same sentiment to me,' he murmured.

Sophronia was startled by the idea.

The train let out a puff of smoke and Soap tooted the horn merrily. They picked up more speed on a slight decline.

Sophronia added, 'Then again, he may surprise me.'

Into the resulting comparative silence Monique said, 'Well, that was an interesting manoeuvre.'

Sophronia replied, 'They were responsible for the mechanicals' malfunctioning. Each one of those prototypes responded to a crystalline valve installed in a nearby household mechanical. That's why so many were serviced recently.'

Monique said, 'Took you long enough to figure out.'

'It's going to take them a while to re-valve all mechanicals.'

'But when they do . . . ' Monique added, darkly. 'Can't you see the disaster in front of you? Or are you still blind? Let me down, I can help.'

'Why the vampire involvement? Why you? Why your hive?' demanded Dimity.

'You are *complete imbeciles*, all of you! What do you think has been happening all this time? Since I first tried to repurpose the prototype valve almost eighteen months ago. When you two plebeians stopped me with a cheese pie. You think this has all been a lark? You think the Picklemen are interested in anyone's welfare besides their own?'

Sophronia frowned. *What has welfare to do with it?* She

wanted to step in, but it was much smarter to let Monique run her mouth. If allowed to vent poisoned steam, she might reveal everything.

Sidheag, on the other hand, was red-faced and aggravated.

Sophronia caught her friend's yellow-eyed gaze and shook her head sharply.

Sidheag glared at her, expressing ire.

Sophronia mouthed, 'Let her talk.'

Sidheag sighed.

Monique continued her diatribe. Dangling from a train doorway apparently stretched the tongue as well as the shoulders. 'You think this prototype was designed to speed up floating? Oh, no, that was simply a decoy use. You think it's for point-to-point communication? Take over from the telegraph? That's only one application. No, the Picklemen have been intending *this* all along. Put one of their little toys inside each and every mechanical in England, and you know what the Picklemen have?'

Sophronia said, without inflection, 'A standing army located in every household, able to take direct commands from them at a whim.'

Monique nodded. 'A power currently limited only by the need to service every single mechanical in the realm. And transmission distance. They are moving fast to solve the first problem, and they have scientists trying to improve upon the second. There are some who think if they could only get close to the aetherosphere, they could transmit to most of the country. But all they need is London. London is what matters.'

Sophronia, being a country girl, took mild offence at that

but understood Monique's point. London was, after all, the seat of power. In addition, almost every good London family, progressive or conservative, employed mechanicals. Only the vampires and the werewolves abstained.

If she hadn't seen all those crystalline valves with her own eyes, she would have thought Monique's talk vampire propaganda. It all seemed so far-fetched. She couldn't deny the fact that the very idea that Monique had been in the right all along rubbed her the wrong way.

Sophronia turned away, uncomfortable. Bumbersnoot was sitting smugly by Soap's feet. He'd emitted the prototype and the hurlie. Sophronia retrieved both, stuffing them into pockets.

Dimity said to Monique, 'And why haven't the vampires brought this to the attention of the government?'

'The potentate knows. And the dewan, of course. But what can the Shadow Council do against such a manoeuvre? Parliament has a daylight hold on operations, and too many MPs are affiliated with Picklemen. Cultivator-rank minions are everywhere. If we made any overt move against them, they would simply deny everything. Intent to commit a crime is not a crime. Besides which, we don't know exactly what they propose to do with the power. Any public outcry would be greeted with grave suspicion as vampire hysteria. *Those supernaturals see plots everywhere, they always do.* Secrecy was our only option, and now you've botched that up, too. What a plague you are, Sophronia!'

Sophronia said, 'You started it.'

Monique rolled her eyes. 'You are a child.'

Sophronia asked, 'What's our school's position been in all this?'

'Is that your loyalty? Are you going to fight for a finishing school, Sophronia, for the rest of your career? It's not a very wealthy patron.'

'I have other options.' After the Pickleman revelation, Sophronia was looking favourably, once more, on Lord Akeldama. At least she knew he wasn't a Pickleman!

Monique scoffed. 'You are going to have to choose sides. We all do, in the end.'

Sophronia cocked her head. 'Are you trying to recruit me?'

'Cut me down and I'll consider putting in a good word with Countess Nadasdy.'

'Thank you for the thought, but I have a better vampire offer.' Sophronia was, however, in a quandary. What was she going to do now? Even if she told Lord Akeldama, would he put a stop to the Picklemen? The other vampires were doing a piss-poor job of it. Lord Akeldama didn't seem the type to involve himself directly, which left ... well ... her.

Monique, having spoken her piece, corked up.

Sidheag and Dimity joined Sophronia in a huddle close to Soap, so they could discuss without being overheard.

'Options?' said Sophronia.

Sidheag said, 'You know my wishes.'

'You can't flog Monique, it's not done at your age,' said Dimity, presuming as to Sidheag's feelings.

Sidheag said, 'No. Well, yes. A switch tickle would do her some good. But what I meant is that I want to continue on to

Scotland. My pack needs me; that is the reason we started this whole thing.'

Sophronia nodded. 'Soap, do you think you can make it all the way there on the back tracks without danger?'

'Birmingham and Leeds areas might give us stick. But if necessary we can stash the train and continue on in a more traditional manner.'

'Oh, yes, simply hide a whole train somewhere.' Even Sophronia was doubtful.

Soap smiled cheekily.

Dimity said, 'Monique said it's going to take the Picklemen a while to get all mechanicals installed with the crystalline valves. They must be ramping up valve production.'

Sophronia nodded. 'After we get her to Scotland, if we sourced the factory site, we might be able to cause a delay in manufacturing.'

Dimity said, 'We do need to get back to school eventually.'

'Can't do anything substantial from there,' objected Sophronia.

'Do we *have* to do something substantial? Is this really our problem? What does it matter if Picklemen control mechanicals?' Dimity had already been kidnapped by vampires in the interest of subverting Pickleman interests. She was tetchy on the subject and preferred to remain out of it.

Sophronia said, 'Just think, Dimity, what if they controlled the soldier mechanicals in our school? Mechanicals aren't only servants, they can also be weapons. This is not something we can simply float away from and go back to studying poisoned tea. This is important.'

Dimity sighed. 'But we do have time?'

Sophronia walked back to Monique. 'What's your best estimate on how long until the Picklemen control a usable majority of the nation's mechanicals, given valve production and distribution times?'

Monique glared at her.

'Tell me and I'll let you down.'

Monique narrowed her eyes. 'Six months, a year at the outside. Mine was supposed to be a covert operation tracking their activities, designed to discover just such useful information. You messed it up.'

'Covert? In a *train?*'

'They didn't realise, until you came on board.'

'That's debatable,' Sophronia said, but cut Monique down with her bladed fan.

The blonde girl lowered her arms slowly, wincing from the pain.

Sophronia left Monique's wrists bound together. Dimity took up a position, watchfully close. They couldn't let Monique get into anything. However, the girl seemed more concerned with getting her shoulders back in order and making snide remarks about Dimity's dreadful attire.

For the rest of the afternoon, Sophronia, Soap and Sidheag concentrated on stoking the boilers and making certain the train kept up a steady pace. There were no switches for a while, so they clipped along smoothly and in relative peace. Soon the full moon rose over the horizon and night descended.

Sophronia distracted herself from thoughts of Felix by wondering if crashing a train into the Picklemen's operation had managed to stall their dastardly plans all that much, or was it merely a minor inconvenience? Would more mechanicals be singing 'Rule, Britannia!' soon or would it be months from now?

Before they lost daylight, Sophronia spent time tinkering with Bumbersnoot. Vieve had taught her how to pop open his casing to clean and oil him properly. She hadn't noticed any changes after retrieving him from Madame Spetuna. But there was always the possibility that when he visited her and the flywaymen, they got hold of him and installed a tiny crystalline valve. Had he a voice box, Bumbersnoot could become their 'Rule, Britannia!' canary in the coal mine. Madame Spetuna had, after all, been infiltrating the Picklemen. But there was no evidence of tampering. Sophronia resolved to leave Bumbersnoot with Vieve for a proper check-up. In fact, she had a real need to consult with Vieve on much of what they had learned, and stolen, and crashed into.

'Getting on towards supper,' said Soap, catching her attention. He looked tired, his face drawn, his eyes only mildly twinkly.

Sophronia closed Bumbersnoot, set him to nibble at a bit of coal, and stood up.

'Food is all in the back.' Only then did she realise how hungry she was.

'We should stop for the night,' said Dimity, sounding unusually decided on the matter.

Sidheag wanted to press on, but Sophronia agreed with Dimity.

'It would be best to stop. It's full moon night, and the tracks could be crowded with private celebration trains now that the sun is down. It's not safe. Plus, we all need rest. It should be safe; timetables list this line as vacant all night long.'

'Picklemen might catch up to us,' objected Sidheag.

'I think they have other things to worry about. If Felix holds his tongue, they might continue to disregard us as a group of vagrant boys. Might even prefer us to the drones we stole the train from.'

'Except that we killed one of their dirigibles,' Sidheag answered.

And we're relying on Lord Mersey's discretion. Behind Soap's back Sophronia gestured, making a sad face. Sidheag sighed but agreed. She, too, cared about Soap, and he couldn't keep going indefinitely. They had to rest for his sake.

They rolled into a tiny station in a town so small they couldn't even determine its name. It was nothing more than a platform next to a switch. There was no porter. There wasn't even a ticket box.

Nevertheless, someone was paying attention, for a young lad with a cart pulled up next to the station shortly after they arrived. He hailed Soap from the roadway.

'Aye-up, circus in town?'

Soap looked startled, the gold Dimity dress streamers having slipped his mind.

Sophronia stuck her head around him and said cheerfully, a grin plastered to her face, 'Indeed it is!'

The carter looked at her suspiciously. 'You don't *seem* like a circus.'

'More a tumbling troupe, if you know the type.'

'Oh, indeed?'

Sophronia jumped down to the track and did a little somersault forward, bouncing out of it on to one knee with a flourish.

The lad did not look impressed.

Dimity came to her rescue, jumping down and then doing the same kind of tumble manoeuvre. She then climbed up on to Sophronia's shoulders. It was a move they'd practised in class, for reaching items stashed in high places, but weren't very good at. Sophronia stumbled to hold her footing. Dimity waggled her hands around madly.

'It's been a long day,' said Sophronia apologetically.

The carter's eyebrows were still suspicious, but he was clearly pleased by their friendly manner. He offered up some useful information: 'Hamlet probably not sized to do you any favours. Try up a few stops. There's a market, end of this week, be a good spot for a carnival.'

'Thank you kindly!' chirruped Sophronia. 'We may just do that.'

The lad doffed his hat and clicked his donkey into a lumbering walk.

Their inadvertent addition, Dusty the stoker, cleared his throat as the grumbling from the locomotive died down and the steam engine came to rest.

Sophronia looked at him, surprised into remembering that he was with them, not merely an extra feature of the stolen train.

Sidheag hadn't forgot him. 'Is something wrong, Dusty?'

'Mr Sid, sir, it's only that we're running low on coal. If you

lads want to keep going, you'll need to get fuel from some-
wheres, and this station's not big enough to have reserves.'

'I'd better check the tender.' Soap disappeared behind the
boiler. He came back a few minutes later, only to nod his
agreement with Dusty's assessment. Soap might be a novice
train driver, but he had an excellent working knowledge of
boilers and their coal consumption. He was also dragging a
very dirty Bumbersnoot in his wake.

'Guess who's eaten too much?'

Bumbersnoot was leaking steam out of his carapace and
steam out of his ears and had a definite bloated appearance.

'Oh, Bumbersnoot, have you been eating all our reserves?
Bad dog.'

Bumbersnoot's ears sagged, guilty.

'Not a whole lot we can do about it now,' said Sidheag, protecting the mechanimal from Sophronia's ire.

Sophronia sighed. 'I hope he hasn't damaged himself.' She
put Bumbersnoot in a corner and tied his reticule straps to a
nearby protrusion so he couldn't eat any *more* of their precious
coal. He did look unwell; it was troubling. 'I should probably
check his insides, but he's running too hot to touch. Who'd
like first watch?'

Soap said, 'I'll take it. What do you suggest, a regular
walkabout, plus roof and skyline? Say every quarter hour or
so?'

'If you're sure you're not too tired.' Sophronia really was
worried about him. He looked so exhausted.

'I'd rather a solid block of sleep later.'

Sophronia said, 'Very well, then, I'll take second.'

Sidheag agreed to third and Dimity fourth. Dusty said he'd take fifth, unfamiliar with the division of two-hour watches.

Sidheag said kindly, 'There is no fifth, but you've been doing all the stoking and aren't even part of our operation. You should sleep the full night.'

'We're most grateful for all your help, by the way, Mr Dusty,' added Sophronia.

'And I'll make it worth your while once we get to Scotland,' said Sidheag.

Dusty looked embarrassed as everyone turned appreciative attention upon him.

'What would you like?' continued Sidheag. 'Position at the castle?'

Dusty said, blushing, 'Oh, now, Mr Sid, I'm quite happy as a stoker.'

'Very well, then, we will try to arrange matters so our making off with this train doesn't affect your stoking career in any detrimental manner,' said Sophronia.

Dusty looked confused by the long words but disposed to be amenable.

Monique said, from the doorway where she sat hunkered under Dimity's watchful gaze, 'You won't be working for a vampire-run operation ever again, that's for certain.'

Dusty looked ashamed.

'Don't you worry,' said Sidheag, turning her nose up at Monique, 'I'll make certain the werewolves look after you.'

Dusty said, 'Never knew I'd end up mixed up with the supernatural simply because I got to stoking the wrong train at the wrong time.'

'Good stokers are hard to come by,' said Soap, 'valuable asset and don't you forget it.'

Sidheag agreed with him, slapping Dusty on the shoulder, causing a puff of black dust to rise into the air.

'Thanks, lads,' said Dusty, dipping his head to hide his pleasure.

After that, they let themselves down and trailed off to various coaches. Now that they had all six carriages to themselves, they considered each occupying a separate coach in a kind of private hotel scenario. But in the end, they decided it was better to stick together. While Soap sat first watch, Monique safely trussed up in the cab, Dusty and Sidheag slept in one coach with Dimity and Sophronia in the next one down. They chose the carriage closest to the locomotive so that they could hear Soap shout if anything untoward occurred. Bumbersnoot stayed in the cab, where Soap could keep an eye on him and his overindulgence.

Dimity might have protested that Sidheag should not be alone with Dusty, even if it was a first-class conveyance, but as far as they could tell, Dusty still had no idea they were girls. Should anyone hear any details of this escapade, Sidheag's reputation would be ruined, if being alone with Captain Niall hadn't already done the trick. Sophronia was eager for a moment alone with Sidheag to learn more on that particular situation, as Sidheag and the good captain seemed to have got close. Unfortunately, Sophronia suspected even she didn't have the necessary competence to extract information on Sidheag's finer feelings from Sidheag. The girl could be remarkably closed-lipped. Frustrating, as other people's finer feelings were fun to talk about.

After such an exciting day, Sophronia thought she would fall asleep easily, but her mind whirred like a mechanical. She stared up at the ceiling of the coach, thinking about the vampires, and Picklemen, and Felix, and Soap.

She thought Dimity was asleep already until her friend spoke into the silence. 'Will Felix come back to you, do you think?'

'Oh, Dimity, he won't do, not for me. I tried to make him over but he's a dress in the wrong size no matter what I do.'

'But, Sophronia, he's a duke's son.'

'He's a Pickleman's son.' *And I regret letting him get close. Why was I so taken by those blue eyes? I wonder if, all along, it was Felix who thought he could change me.*

'Not one for the Picklemen, then?'

'I simply feel that world domination is not my cup of tea. Is that short-sighted?'

'No. I thought you might decide against them.'

'You did, why?'

'They don't feel Sophronia-ish. Something about those green-banded top hats. I mean, how silly would you look in a green-banded top hat?'

'No one said I would have to wear one. They shouldn't have started with me right from the beginning, if they hadn't tried for the prototype ...'

'So are we going to work with the vampires in this? Join up with Monique?'

Sophronia shuddered. 'What an unpleasant thought.'

'You're not the one they kidnapped.'

'Exactly! It feels equally wrong to help them.'

'But we can't go up *against* everyone, either. We haven't even finished properly yet.' Dimity sounded small and pathetic.

'No, but we can manipulate them to annihilate one another. I'm not sure how quite yet, but I'll think on it. There's always my *vampire friend*.'

'Felix won't like it if you annihilate his father.'

'I told you it wasn't going to work. Can't base a marriage on annihilation, not even when one is an intelligencer and the other a Pickleman.'

'No' – Dimity was philosophical – 'I suppose you can't. It's too bad. I thought you rather liked him.'

It was such a simple, wistful statement, and yet, for some reason, it brought hot tears to Sophronia's normally dry eyes. 'I rather *did* like him.'

Dimity whispered, fully sympathetic, having had her heart broken by a Dingleproops only recently, 'Did you write him poetry?'

'No, luckily, I did not.'

'Well, then, less to recover from.'

'Good point.'

'Don't worry, we will find you someone.' Dimity was ever the optimist. 'Possibly not as handsome.'

Sophronia said, to lighten the mood, 'I wonder if Monique has a brother?'

'Oh, really, Sophronia. Be serious. You must have something you *want* in a beau?'

Sophronia thought of Felix's blue eyes and lazy ways. And then of Soap's dark, cheerful gaze and jocularity. She thought that she wanted Soap's gentle personality and Felix's focused attention. She wanted Felix's breezy, relaxed approach to high society and Soap's easy infiltration of the lower orders. She wanted humour, and kind hands, and sweet smiles, and genuine longing looks. She wanted that expression she had caught between Captain Niall and Sidheag. She wanted trust. *I'm going to spend most of my life pretending to be other people, hiding and skulking in shadows. I want someone who will remind me of who I am. Once I've worked that out.*

What she said was, 'I want a man who stays out of my way.'

'Oh my, well then,' said Dimity with utter confidence, 'you should marry my brother. You are still engaged, I believe.'

That caused both of them to laugh uproariously. The very idea of Pillover marrying anyone, let alone Sophronia! It took them a while to calm sufficiently to sleep after that. They would keep giggling. Things were always funnier when one was lying down.

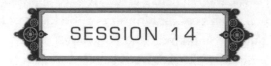

SESSION 14

Dirigibles Versus Trains

Soap was a silent figure sitting in the doorway of the cab as Sophronia approached, two hours later. He was smoking his awful cob pipe and staring into the moonlit night.

'My turn,' she said. 'How's everything been?'

'Quiet as a dry boiler.' Soap knocked out his pipe; he knew she disliked the habit.

'Bumbersnoot?'

'Sleeping it off.'

'Monique?' They turned to look at the blonde's slumbering form.

'That one. Why'd we not dump her from the train when we had the chance?'

'There's still time.'

Soap snorted. He jumped down from the cab. The crunch of his landing on the railway stones was awfully loud.

'Beautiful moon,' he said as it appeared from between rain clouds. 'Don't see much of it down in engineering on the airship.'

'Hope any local werewolves are locked away.' Sophronia was thinking of Captain Niall and the dewan. Where were the two werewolves holed up while they battled moon-madness? She fervently hoped it was secure and silver-coated. She'd encountered Captain Niall moon-mad once, and lost her best petticoat to salivating jaws. The dewan was stronger, bigger and angrier; she could only imagine what he'd be like. More would be lost than undergarments.

'Must be tough, being a werewolf. Never to see full moon.'

'Better than being a vampire, never to see the sun, miss,' replied the sootie, his tone a warning.

Sophronia then did something quite daring. She wasn't sure why. Perhaps she was emboldened by the quiet stillness. Perhaps it was the freedom inherent in her masculine garb. But she shifted close to Soap, side by side and companionable, staring at the moon. She was terribly tempted to put her head on his shoulder. It was exactly the correct height.

'So long as you are doing it for all the right reasons, I can't talk you out of it,' she said, realising she could no more change Soap's desires than she could Felix's allegiance.

'But you aren't going to help me make it happen, are you, miss?'

'No, I'm not.' Sophronia's face burned and she knew he was looking at her. In the silvery light her blush wouldn't show, thank heavens. She wanted to run from the inevitable conversation, from any confession of forbidden affection, from the mere possibility that she might have to break Soap's heart.

'You don't agree with Miss Sidheag, yet you are helping her.'

He had a point, so Sophronia held her tongue. She couldn't articulate why she felt differently about Soap, more proprietary. But she did.

'You could talk me out of it, Sophronia.' He said her name carefully, cautiously, experimenting with the sound of it on his tongue. She was always 'miss' to him. She was always his superior. Was he practising for a future when they might be equals? Without werewolf status he'd never be able to call her that, not in public, not in the social world she was training to inhabit, not even as friends.

Which was why she couldn't talk him out of it, not really. Sophronia wasn't going to make promises she couldn't keep, not to Soap.

She replied using his real name, saying only, 'Perhaps I could, Phineas. But it's not my place to do so. Any more than with Sidheag. You have as much a right as she to your own choices, even if I think you both foolish.'

She hoisted herself into the cab of the train without looking at him, remembering how warm and gentle his lips were against her own, and how the muscles in his arms felt wrapped about her. *I'm fickle*, she thought. *And I don't deserve to be tinkering with anyone's heart.*

Soap's hand caught her ankle. 'I want to be worthy.'

She could hardly believe he would dare touch her, on the leg! But she kind of liked it. So she crouched and covered his hand with hers. 'You already are, Soap.'

'Not in the eyes of the world.' His hand was as soft on the back as it was callused on the palm.

'And this is your best solution?'

'No. This is my only solution.'

Soap went to bed.

Sophronia's heart hurt and she had no idea why. She sat look-ing out of the cab windows, first one side, then the other. It was excessively dull. Lady Linette had warned them of this. 'Try not to think it glamorous, ladies. Intelligencer work is nine-tenths dis-contented ennui, and one-tenth abject terror. Rather like falling in love.' *So far*, thought Sophronia, *love has been more a series of crushing discomforts. Perhaps I'm going about it the wrong way?*

Monique shifted once or twice. She must be cold, for the cab was open to the night, and though the rain still wasn't in earnest it had settled into a consistent drizzle. Sophronia checked Monique's bonds, and the place where Dimity had lashed them to the train. *All secure.*

Sophronia wasn't so foolish as to think her enemy asleep. Still, when Monique spoke, it startled her.

'You're a queer one, Sophronia. You had Lord Mersey on your string and let him go. Regardless of his political connection, that marriage could have been lucrative. And imagine, if you man-aged to turn him, you would have gone down in the record books as one of the best Mademoiselle Geraldine ever produced.'

'And lose the love of my husband by driving away his family?'

Monique scoffed. 'Love, what has love to do with any of this? If you're throwing over a peer in favour of that simpering, soot-covered savage, you're more puerile than even I realised.'

Sophronia went hot about the ears. No one spoke about Soap that way, especially not Monique! Her temper got the better of her.

'How dare you say such a thing. You're not even fit to lick his boots!' Sophronia hissed, afraid of waking the others.

'Boots! He's too poor to have any. That boy wouldn't know how to clean boots, let alone wear them. You're barely class yourself, Sophronia. Who are your parents, after all? You can't afford to marry down, and *no one* can afford to marry a sootie!'

This made Sophronia all the more upset, because it was true. Had she been rejecting Soap all along not because he was ruining their friendship but because of his station in life? 'Clap your trap shut, Monique, or I'll fill it with something disagreeable.' She lashed out, angrier with herself than Monique, but taking it out on her regardless.

Monique snorted. 'I'm only offering you a bit of helpful advice.'

'Because we both know you've got my best interests at heart? You're nothing more than a failure, Monique. You couldn't finish properly, so you ride the coat-tails of a vampire hive because no decent family would take you for their son.'

Now it was Monique's turn to gasp in outrage. 'I *wanted* to become a drone! I'll have a chance at immortality. What are you going to do the rest of your life? Cosy up with a sootie and pop out half-breed babies to muck in the coal dust like their father?'

Sophronia considered all the various ways she had learned to kill someone. She catalogued them in her brain and spent a satisfying few moments applying each to Monique in order. Then she concentrated on her breathing, attempting to stopper up her anger and regain control of the situation. Then she stood and, casually, tore another strip off her much-abused shirt and gagged Monique with it. Tightly. Monique drooled a bit around the edges of the rag, which was satisfying to see.

The rest of the night was blissfully uneventful, outwardly at least. Sophronia was troubled by her own feelings of guilt. She was traumatised by the realisation that she had never given Soap a fair chance because she was afraid of his lowly position. She tortured herself with imagining what-ifs. What if Soap were not a sootie? What if Soap were the same class or race? Would she have closed herself off to his feelings so brutally? Had she been cruel as well as snobbish? The speculation kept her wide-eyed and staring out into the night the whole rest of her watch.

Everyone was awake at dawn. There was a sense of nervous urgency that drew them, uncomplaining, into the cab. They stoked the boiler, started the engine up and got the train moving northward with silent efficiency. No one commented on Monique's gag.

Sophronia felt awkward and uncomfortable around Soap. More aware of the way he stood, the set of his shoulders, the nuances of his expression. She tried to monitor her own reactions, to be friendly but not too friendly. She tried not to think about his affection for her, or their future apart.

They chugged along at a slow but steady pace. They learned more about the switches and how to operate them, neatly avoiding several collisions. They were getting cocky about the whole proceeding. They were also running dangerously low on coal, not to mention food.

They stopped for lunch, ate the last of their reserves, and had to un-gag Monique to feed her. Which meant they had to listen to her. Which meant they had to gag her again right quick.

'She's only a drone,' sneered Sidheag. 'And she lost the operation, so Countess Nadasdy will not be happy with her. I say we dispose of her.'

'She is trained. If we let her go, she's not without resources,' cautioned Dimity.

'She's a rotten egg waiting to explode,' said Sophronia.

Soap said, 'I'd rather we don't actually kill her, I'd as soon not go down for murder.'

Dusty only looked embarrassed by the whole conversation.

In the end, they elected to push Monique out of the door as the train crossed a small bridge over a goose pond. The water looked particularly dirty. Soap slowed the train while Dimity untied Monique's wrists. The girl made a delightful squawking noise around the gag as she fell. She also made a decidedly satisfying splash. Hopefully, there wouldn't be another train along for ages.

With Monique gone the mood lifted. They began to plan how to acquire more coal and food.

Then Dimity gave a holler. She'd spent most of the afternoon hanging by one arm out of the doorway, while Sophronia took the same position behind Soap. This left room in the middle for Sidheag and Dusty to stoke.

Dimity explained her holler. 'I see a dirigible on the horizon.'

'Flywaymen?'

'Hard to tell, they're far off.'

Sophronia came over, shading her eyes. 'I don't *think* it's the one we crashed into, how could they repair it that fast? Besides, this one looks armoured.'

'Wonderful, does it have a cannon mount and recoil guard?' Sidheag asked.

'Looks like.'

'I guess the Picklemen decided we know too much,' said Dimity. *Rather calm*, Sophronia thought proudly, *under the circumstances*.

'Or your darling Lord Mersey ratted us out,' said Sidheag.

'Not my darling anything, Sidheag.' Sophronia was abruptly tired of that game. And she didn't like the way Soap's shoulders hunched at Sidheag's words.

'If they know we're Mademoiselle Geraldine's girls and not Bunson's boys ...' Sidheag stressed her point. Bunson's boys on the loose larking up to Scotland were one thing. Bunson's boys were dangerous with exotic inventions but could be depended upon to come round to the Pickleman agenda eventually. Mademoiselle Geraldine's girls, on the other hand, were dangerous with information and couldn't be depended upon by anyone but their patrons.

That was the moment when Sophronia realised their safest course of action would have been to return to school. The Picklemen would never make a direct move against Mademoiselle Geraldine's, for that would only get intelligencers investigating. Plus, they couldn't afford to make an outright enemy of Lady Linette.

The dirigible following them had a propeller spinning at high speed. It had also caught a stiff breeze and was gaining on them.

Nevertheless, a train was faster than most dirigibles, except those new high-flyers out of France. They could tell even at a distance that this was an older model, of the kind Queen

Victoria once employed in the Royal Float Force, heavy and heavily armed.

They had only one choice.

'I guess we try to outrun it,' said Soap. 'All hands to the boilers!'

By this point in the journey, most of the girls had given Dusty a hand with the boilers, breaking whenever he needed a rest. As a result, they had all developed some rudimentary shovelling savvy. They also had arms screaming from the unexpected activity. Sophronia had thought, before this journey, that she was rather fit. She was, after all, prone to climbing around airships and swinging from hurlies. But stoking was a whole different beast. It was awfully hard work, and explained Soap's delightful muscles. There were only two shovels on the train, so they took turns going as fast as they could, working their way through what coal was left in the tender at an alarming rate. One girl, inside the tender, scooped it forward into range, then the stoker shoved it as fast as possible into the boiler.

The train screamed at the top of its pitch, engine taxed almost beyond capacity.

'Any more and we won't make those turns,' Dusty cautioned Soap, who nodded his agreement.

The girls kept shovelling.

'We don't want to blow her, and we don't want to lose the rails!' yelled Soap.

So they had to relax their efforts, even though Dimity reported that the dirigible, while not gaining on them, was keeping pace.

It was a challenging afternoon. Mademoiselle Geraldine's pre-

pared its young ladies for unusual situations, but it did not pre-
pare them for heavy labour. The very *idea*! Even as intelligencers,
actually *working* was not expected of women of standing. Now
that Sophronia, Dimity and Sidheag were acting drudges, they
didn't even have time to stop for tea. Not that there was any tea.

As the sun began to set and the moon rose, now on the
waning side of full, they realised the tender was empty.

It wasn't a surprise, they knew it was coming, but now they
had to face reality.

They fed the boiler more slowly, eking out the last of the
reserves that Bumbersnoot hadn't consumed, drawing out the
inevitable.

'The flywaymen are gaining on us,' reported Dimity.

An hour or so later, 'They're on our tail now.'

Half an hour after that, 'Cannons are up.'

And then, 'Can't see them any more, they must be right on
top of us.'

A boom sounded.

'They're firing!' said Dimity.

'Yes, dear. We can hear that,' said Sophronia.

Nothing happened; the train continued to clatter along.
The cannonball must have missed. There was a long pause
while the dirigible reloaded. Soap gave the engine all the
throttle they had, but the boiler was cooling regardless.

Another boom sounded.

This time Dimity didn't report the occurrence. But the train
did shake dramatically. It shuddered and then began to squeal
as if the brake were being applied.

Soap said, 'We're dragging something against the line. One

of the back carriages might be off the tracks. It could derail the rest of us if we aren't careful.' He let the train slow further.

Sophronia said, 'We'll have to decouple them. Only solution. Should have thought of it sooner; dragging less weight, we would have used less coal.'

'Too late now,' said Soap.

'Never!' said Sophronia, readying her hurlie.

'You can't go out there,' objected Dimity. 'They're shooting cannons at us!'

'One cannon, and it takes them time to reload, not to mention recover the height of the airship and reseat the recoil guard. I have ten minutes.' Before she'd finished her explanation, Sophronia leapt and grabbed the top of the doorframe, swinging to climb up on to the cab roof. She might have been more graceful had they not been moving fast. As it was, she bumped her shin.

'Sophronia,' reprimanded Dimity at the top of her voice, 'you're too impetuous. You'll get yourself killed!'

It was a lot easier to run along the top of the carriages and jump from one to the next when she was moving in the opposite direction to the train. As soon as she'd crossed the freight carriages, she saw the problem. The second-to-last carriage, the one in front of the coach that held the air dinghy, had detached partly from the transmitter's carriage. The air dinghy was tilted oddly, because half of the coach below had been blown away.

Sophronia crouched on the roof of the transmitter to evaluate the situation. Then, trying not to worry over the danger, she hooked the grapple part of her hurlie into the top edge of the freight carriage and lowered herself down the side. Partly standing on the coupler base, and partly dangling from one arm, she examined the coupler at her feet. Bent double, she was grateful she'd chosen to leave off her stays.

One of the holding pegs had fallen out, and its broken chain was dragging on the track. The coupler was linked only halfway as a result. The drag on the line that Soap had described must be coming from further back, probably that last coach.

Sophronia worked to free the second peg, to lose the dead weight of those last two passenger carriages. It was wedged tight as a new glove. It didn't help that she had only one hand to apply to the task, her other being occupied holding her steady, dangling from the hurlie. She also had no way to brace herself. She banged at the peg with the heel of her hand. Nothing.

She pulled out a vial of perfume oil and tried adding that, to grease it loose.

Still nothing, and now her hand was slippery.

She swung about and kicked at the peg hard. All that seemed to do was bruise her foot. Her various weapons weren't going to work. She needed brute force and she hadn't anything about her person.

It wasn't in her nature to give up. She climbed up the freight carriage and ran as quickly as she could back along the top of the train.

Time had run out.

Behind her came cannon fire. She flattened herself to the top of the carriage.

The train shook and she heard the ghastly noise of metal and wood rending asunder. The train slowed to a crawl.

Sophronia looked behind and saw that the last carriage was now a mess of wood and plush interiors dragging behind. Their poor little air dinghy, which had served them so well and proudly, was part of the wreckage.

Queen Victoria's old military floaters were able to take the weight of only four cannonballs. It was one of the reasons they'd been discontinued. That meant the flywaymen behind them only had one more shot.

Sophronia had just enough time while they reloaded to do what needed to be done.

She jumped to her feet and dashed on, ending on the roof of the cab.

She stuck her head down over the edge into the engine room.

'Soap, I need you!'

'I'm a little busy right now, miss.'

'Miss?' said Dusty, confused by the gender switch.

'I'll explain later,' reassured Sidheag.

'Let Sidheag drive,' said Sophronia to Soap.

'I'm helping Dusty!' protested Sidheag.

'Then let Dimity drive. This will only take a moment.'

Dimity's face went owl-like in awe at her new responsibility. Nevertheless, she gamely stepped forward. Soap reluctantly relinquished his position.

'Just keep this gauge here at that mark, see? And this one between those two lines? Got it, miss?'

'I think so, Mr Soap.'

'Another *miss*?' objected Dusty.

'You can't tell me that one surprises you?' protested Sidheag.

'Are you a *miss*, too?' Dusty was still gamely shovelling.

But Soap had swung himself out and climbed up on the roof next to Sophronia. They had other things to repair than Dusty's sensibilities.

'This better be important, miss.'

'Come on! They only have one more shot.'

'How do you know?'

'With airships, weight is weight, they can't have redesigned it that much. That's an old model. It can only carry as much as it did in the old days.'

'If you say so.'

Sophronia was already running, crouched low, along the roofs of the carriages back towards the problem coupler. Soap followed gamely. They reached the edge of the freight carriage unscathed. Soap was not quite so sure-footed as Sophronia, but then she was beginning to feel that this was her native environment, running over the roofs of a moving train.

She pointed to the problem below. 'There, can you work that last peg loose?'

Soap hung over the edge. 'I'll do my best.'

Sophronia handed him the hurlie and he lowered himself down.

He dropped further than she had, bracing one foot precariously against each of the tiny bars at the ends of the carriages, straddling the coupler. It was a good thing they were moving slowly. He wrapped both hands about the peg and tried to shift it, twisting back and forth, tugging. The muscles of his back and shoulders strained. It was a dangerous position. If he was successful and the back carriage separated, he would fall off the end.

The peg wouldn't budge, so he shifted to bang at it with his feet, just as Sophronia had done. Then he grabbed and wiggled it.

Cannon fire sounded. Sophronia, crouching on top, flattened herself to the roof once more.

Soap returned to pulling just as a massive jolt hit the train, jerking the coupler.

He tugged, everything jumped and the peg worked free all at once. Now lacking the safety peg, and with the back carriages dragging against the tracks, the train decoupled. The front part of the train drew away.

Soap was forced into an uncomfortable contortion. He shifted his weight and pinwheeled forward, into the emptiness where the train had been. Sophronia lurched for the hurlie rope, grabbing on to it just in time. Her arms wrenched and she almost slid over the side, for Soap was no lightweight. She gritted her teeth and braced her chest against the transmitter edge. Front padding had some uses but it wasn't comfortable.

Soap swung and slammed against the back of the freight carriage. But they weren't dragging him along the track, which was something. Sophronia strained, holding him up by pure force of will, for he really was too heavy for her.

Soap was a dead weight. Sophronia's arms began to shake and she wasn't going to be able to hold him for long.

Then his head lifted and he twisted, scrambling for some kind of purchase on the train. His feet found the remaining half of the coupler. With Sophronia's added weight on the hurlie, he managed to stand, leaning against the back of the freight carriage.

'Soap! Soap, are you hurt?' Sophronia's voice sounded overly breathless and winded to her own ears.

'Just stunned and a little bruised, miss. Don't you worry about me.'

'If you're able, can I let go of the hurlie? Then you can crank it in yourself?'

'Ready, miss.'

Sophronia let go. Soap managed to pull in on the hurlie rope so it was once more taut to the grapple over the top rail. He used the tension to climb up to the roof.

Sophronia pounced upon him. She was not so brave as to hug him, but her hands were quick to stroke over his head, checking for injury. He'd lost his cap, and the texture of his tight, curly hair was reassuring. She could feel no stickiness of blood, although he would have a bumper of an egg on the back left side.

'How do you feel? Are you dizzy? Did you rattle your brain?' She could not stop petting him.

Soap submitted meekly to her ministrations. 'I'm fine, miss. Not much brain to rattle. You know me, same colour and toughness as old boot leather.'

Sophronia sighed and forced herself to stop touching him.

He caught one of her hands as she lowered them.

'Though I do like your concern, miss.' He was looking at her with those serious dark eyes. The ones that switched twinkle for intent.

The horror of almost losing him curdled her stomach and she felt quite ill. Sophronia also wished she could see into his eyes clearly, check the state of his pupils. Sister Mattie had warned them about derangement of the brain due to physical force.

The train gave a start, as though sensing its newfound freedom, and picked up speed.

Sophronia braced Soap solicitously.

He let her, because he knew she needed it.

The moment Sophronia realised this, she knew she was in trouble. Because it had always been that way between her and Soap. And it *was* more than friendship. And she was an idiot not to have realised it sooner. What was it she had told Dimity? *I want a man who stays out of my way.* Soap wouldn't ever get in her way.

'Miss, are you well?'

'Soap, I . . .'

They heard shouting above them and looked up to see the underside of the flywaymen's dirigible, managing to keep pace.

Several men were leaning over the edge, their faces pale in the dim light of evening. One of those faces was Felix's and another was that of his father.

The Duke of Golborne was pointing a very wicked-looking pistol at them.

'You know what,' said Sophronia to Soap, 'I think I have rather decided to hate guns.'

'Interesting decision in your line of work,' replied Soap conversationally, letting her go and slowly turning to face this new threat.

The duke yelled down, 'Stay where you are, young lady!'

So Felix has told him who I am. Or what I am, at the very least. Sophronia ignored the duke and stared at her erstwhile beau. Felix Mersey had the grace to look ashamed. Sophronia ought to have felt betrayed, but mostly she simply felt disappointed.

Sophronia yelled up at the duke, 'I can't very well obey you, sir, even if I wanted to. In case it has slipped your notice, I'm not the one driving this train.'

'Oh, I noticed. And here's what we are going to do about it. You leave the darkie here and I'll keep a careful eye on him while you go order the driver to stop. If you manage that in the space of ten minutes, then you will return to find him still alive. How's that for a fair bargain?'

He gestured casually with the pistol as he talked.

Soap said, calm and mild-mannered, 'I take your point about guns, miss.'

Sophronia said up to the airship, 'I'm disappointed, Your Grace. I thought you hired others to do your dirty work.'

The duke was not to be distracted by taunting. 'Sometimes if you want something done properly, you had best organise it yourself. You can't distract me, young lady; my son here has told me all about your wiles and ways. I fail to see the appeal, but he assures me of your many stealthy means of attraction. I've loosed your coils about him and I assure you they will have no effect on me.'

Sophronia was slightly revolted at the idea that she would use any wiles whatsoever on someone the duke's age. She was also angry that Felix had attributed their nascent romance to her training. Although, of course, he might be blaming her to get out of trouble with his father. But she was also a little flattered that the duke thought she was that good.

Nevertheless, there was a gun to think about. It was now pointing, despite the dirigible bobbing and the train swaying, with a remarkably steady hand, directly at Soap's chest.

Sophronia looked into Soap's face. 'I'll be quick as I can.'

He whispered, unheard by the men floating above them, 'Just make a break for it, miss. Now that we dropped the dead weight, I'm certain the train can outrun them with the last of the coal. I'll be fine.'

Sophronia looked over his shoulder, out into the country-side rushing past, stalling for time. She caught sight of *something* moving at speed across the open fields towards them. Probably attracted by the cannon fire.

Two somethings.

One of which had a top hat tied to his furry, lupine head.

'Now, Miss Temminnick!' insisted the duke, pistol cocked. *So he knows my name as well as my gender. Fantastic.*

Sophronia leaned in to Soap, who still wore the hurlie, which was still hooked to the top railing of the freight carriage.

She fell against him as though to embrace him goodbye in an excess of emotion. 'They only have one ship,' she whispered into his ear.

Soap was confused but willing to participate even under the threat of an anxious gun. 'Yes, miss.'

'And there are four of us, four people who know too much.'

'Yes, miss.'

'If we separate, they can't chase all of us.'

'Ah,' said Soap, following her reasoning, testing the tension in the hurlie. 'Yes, I see.'

Soap understood her. Soap would always understand.

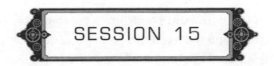

SESSION 15

DEWAN EX MACHINA

S oap was still shaky from his head bang, but he was stronger than Sophronia, and they hadn't time to switch anyway. Thus, for purely practical reasons, he had to hold the hurlie.

Sophronia turned to say to the duke, lips trembling with simulated emotions, 'I'll do anything you say, Your Grace, only please don't hurt him.'

The duke looked utterly disgusted by this. Whether it was the idea that he would waste a bullet on a sootie, or the idea that Sophronia might harbour real feelings for an underling, it was difficult to tell which.

Then Sophronia threw herself at Soap, wrapping her arms and legs about him in the apparent throes of some passionate fit. It was the final embrace of lovers about to be parted for ever, worthy of Romeo and Juliet.

In the same movement, like a dance, Soap sank them to

their knees. Then he leaned backward and with a shift of weight slid them both off the side of the moving train.

Though the hurlie did enough to slow their fall, it played out too swiftly, and the train had picked up enough speed that they tumbled hard to the track below. The moment they hit the ground Sophronia had out her bladed fan and cut them free of the hurlie. Soap curled himself protectively about her, because he was prone to being stupidly careful with her welfare, so that he took most of the fall – *and that on top of his crash earlier*.

They ended with Sophronia sprawled indelicately on top of him. She unwound herself, heart beating double, because Soap was lying so very still.

'Soap! Soap?'

'Just give me a moment, miss, gathering my wits back about me. Not every day a lad intentionally throws himself from a train. Not every day I get you on top of me, neither, could be the shock of both at once.'

Sophronia ran her hands over him for the second time in so many minutes, checking for injuries. Not that she was a trained surgeon, to know when a bone was out, but she could at least determine if he had any open wounds.

He shifted uncomfortably under her touch. 'Whoa there, miss,' he almost squeaked, 'that's enough of that!'

'Oh, dear me, are you hurt? Have I hurt you more?' She'd never forgive herself if she damaged him further.

'I think most of me's fine, miss. Just, please, leave off the touching.'

'I do apologise.' Sophronia was mortified. Of course, Soap's dignity! He'd hardly want her pawing at him. 'I was only checking.'

'Whoa, now. Not that I didn't like it, miss. You can check me much as you like, only later. I think right now we needs must focus on those friendly fellows. They've chosen to stay with us and let the train go.'

Sophronia rolled off Soap and on to her back, looking into the sky.

The flywaymen and their military dirigible were sinking down to the berm at the side of the track.

The train was out of sight – Sidheag, Dimity, Dusty and Bumbersnoot with it.

Sophronia stood and brushed herself off.

Soap unfolded himself slowly. He was shaken by the fall, bruised and scraped quite a bit.

At her solicitous look, he said, 'I think it's all working, but, miss, knowing you sure isn't kind to a body.' He turned to the open field, clearly thinking about the duke and his gun. 'Should we make a run for it?'

'Ah,' said Sophronia, 'I believe we have reinforcements.'

So it proved to be, for, as the duke disembarked from his new dirigible, two werewolves came dashing up.

Sophronia stood and, dragging a reluctant Soap behind her, went to join this new gathering.

The werewolves chose to face the flywaymen and the duke, rather than the girl and the sootie. Probably wise.

While Sophronia and Soap walked towards them, the wolves, disregarding all sense of propriety, shifted form right there, in front of the whole dirigible crew in the middle of an open field. They had their backs to Sophronia, but she nevertheless took in the sight with no little embarrassment.

Soap said, 'I do believe they think you are a lad.'

'Or this is too important to care about my moral standing.' The dewan was speaking as they ambled closer.

'. . . and firing on a train, Your Grace! I mean to say, this can't be authorised by the queen, I should have known about it. And you know you can't use cannon fire in a private matter on home soil. What were you thinking? The entire countryside reverberated with the sound. People will think we are at war!'

Duke Golborne said, 'My dear dewan, there is no one around to hear. Had I known you were running nearby, I might have employed a quieter projectile. Only creatures with such well-developed hearing as yourselves would know to come investigate. I assure you, I was being quite circumspect.'

He had not, of course, answered the dewan's accusations.

'What on earth possessed you?' the dewan demanded.

'It was necessary. That train was carrying something valuable of mine. I wished it returned.'

'And may I ask what?'

'You may *ask*, of course.'

Sophronia and Soap pitched up.

'Good evening, my lords, Your Grace,' said Sophronia.

All eyes turned to her. It was uncomfortable. Sophronia was suited to life as an intelligencer because the one thing she really didn't like was everyone's attention on her. That, plus fullfrontal werewolf, was challenging even for a girl of her acumen.

Captain Niall, standing a little to one side of the dewan, but equally unclothed, swore softly and said, 'Miss Temminnick, what on earth?' He grabbed the top hat from his head and held it to cover his privates, mortified that a pupil should see him in such a state.

The dewan had no such scruples. Even knowing this odd-looking young lad was a girl did not deter him from his annoyance at the whole situation. He was not a man who tolerated being waylaid on a trip.

He frowned at Sophronia. 'You again! We are due up north now, and yet you, young lady, seem bent on interfering with everything. What is it this time?'

Sophronia debated how much information to reveal and to what end. Her primary goal still had to be getting Sidheag home, and then getting herself and her companions safely back to Mademoiselle Geraldine's and out of Pickleman clutches. Best, she thought, to throw herself on his mercy.

'Oh, my lord,' she said, eyelashes fluttering, 'I am so grateful you have come! What would we have done without you? This duke has been so wicked. First he tried to steal this train, so we had to keep it away from him, and then he fired his big gun at us. It was very scary.'

'Oh, yes? And why do you think he wants the train?' The dewan was only partly taken in.

'I believe it has something that belongs to the vampires.'

'Oh ho, does it indeed? You mean besides those gold streamers? And which vampires would that be?'

'Westminster Hive.'

'And you can prove it how?'

Curses, we shouldn't have pushed Monique overboard. 'Oh, well, we accidentally tossed the evidence. But I can assure you it *does not* belong to this man.' Sophronia gave the dewan her steady gaze of pure honesty.

The duke said, 'This is preposterous. You can't possibly take her word against mine!'

'Can't I?'

'It hardly matters, the train is gone now,' pointed out Captain Niall.

'True, but we could catch it easily enough,' answered the dewan, speaking of their supernatural speed.

Sophronia brightened. 'Oh, could you? Good. Lady Kingair is on board.'

'What!' Neither the dewan nor Captain Niall was pleased to hear that.

Sophronia said, 'Why do you think we sneaked on in the first place? The train was headed north and she wanted to go home. I know she isn't furry, my lord, but she considers herself a werewolf. That's her family you're going up to reprimand, and she wants to be with them. You can't blame us for trying to get her there.'

Captain Niall recovered from his embarrassment and actually chuckled at that statement. 'I did warn you, sir. They aren't ordinary girls. Unless you lock Lady Kingair up, she'll keep trying.'

The dewan looked enquiringly at Sophronia.

Sophronia nodded. 'And we'll keep helping her.'

'Why?' demanded the dewan.

'Because she's our friend.'

The dewan was frustrated with the whole mess. He looked at Soap. 'And what have you to do with any of this?'

'Oh,' mumbled Soap, embarrassed under the direct glare of such a rich and powerful man, 'I'm only a sootie.'

Sophronia said, stalwart, 'Who else do you suggest we get to drive the train?'

'This is all quite ridiculous!' stated the duke. 'They're feckless mischief-makers. You must see that.'

Captain Niall, although much lower in rank, took offence at that accusation. 'Your Grace, Mademoiselle Geraldine might train her girls to no good, but mischief for mischief's sake is strictly forbidden. They are not evil geniuses, after all, that's Bunson's sphere.'

The dewan looked back and forth between Sophronia and the duke. 'I am tempted to agree with the captain. These two have a satisfactory explanation as to why they are involved with a train. On the other hand, if there was something valuable of yours on that train, Your Grace, why were you firing a cannon at it? Your explanation seems a little wanting. Either you want the train destroyed because of what it contains, or you are after these two. And since you let the train go and stayed with these scamps, I must suppose it is them. Why?'

Because I know too much, thought Sophronia.

The duke still had his gun and was staring hard at Sophronia. She had not revealed his plot to the werewolves. She had mentioned nothing about mechanicals or crystalline valves. She had held her peace regarding his evil plans, whatever those plans were. Did he trust her to keep them hidden? Or did he realise that she was not talking because the whole thing sounded preposterous? She was trained to know that the best explanation was always the simplest. They both knew that the childish whims of a group of girls, worried about their unhappy friend, made a plausible excuse. A countrywide Pickleman plot for mechanical uprising did not.

But what could the duke say to counter her, without revealing that plot himself?

Sophronia was betting on the duke's not being as quick as she.

The duke glared. 'My boy should have warned me about you sooner.'

Captain Niall said, 'Now, now, Your Grace, Miss Temminnick is a little precocious. There's no cause to insult the lady.'

'Lady?' snorted the duke.

There was a scuffle from behind him, on board the dirigible. It looked as if Felix was taking some exception to his father's tone. But Felix had a bullet wound to the leg, and several large flywaymen appeared to be dragging him back from the railing. Obviously, they had been instructed not to let him join the conversation.

'Unhand me, you brutes!' he yelled, batting at grasping hands. And then, 'Sophronia! Sophronia, there are more—' He was cut off by a massive hand.

In the interim, the duke decided on a new tactic. 'Please excuse my son, he is overwrought. Well, my dear dewan, if you remand the young lady here into my custody, I will see that she gets safely back to school. I'm heading in that direction myself, I must take my boy back to Bunson's, after all.'

The dewan looked as if he might jump on this plan, just to relieve himself of the responsibility of determining what was going on. A matter that, no doubt, seemed petty when compared with an entire Scottish werewolf pack running amok without an Alpha.

Captain Niall, however, was still thinking like Sophronia's teacher. 'I don't know, Your Grace. You did fire a cannon at her.'

'At her train,' corrected the duke.

'So you acknowledge it was *her* train?' said Soap.

Everyone stared at him as if they had forgot he existed, which they probably had.

'Who cares for your opinion, sootie?' demanded the duke.

The discussion might have gone on for a good long while, except that behind them came a deal of hollering and yelling, and over a small hill marched Sidheag, Dimity and Bumbersnoot, armed with coal shovels and determined to come to the rescue.

Sophronia said to Soap, 'They probably ran out of fuel just the other side, then found us gone. They should have stayed out of this.'

Soap said, stalwart friend to the end, 'They didn't know what we were up to – taking the tumble intentionally. They're only doing what you would do in their position.'

Sophronia nodded. 'True.'

The dewan said, 'Is that Lady Kingair? Oh, good, she can help sort this out. Sensible female, for a mortal girl.'

No one had noticed, but the duke was backing towards his dirigible. A dirigible that was casting off, preparing to float away.

No one except Soap. 'Uh, sirs?'

'Now!' yelled the duke, his gun swinging to point at Soap.

Only then did Sophronia realise that Duke Golborne wasn't the only one with a gun. Perhaps Felix had been trying to warn her about that, not protect her honour.

Three of the flywaymen and the duke all shot at the assembled party.

Captain Niall, acting on supernatural teacher instinct, leapt to protect Sophronia. A bullet hit him broadside and the force of it thrust him over so that he landed fully on top of her.

The dewan moved equally fast. Disregarding the guns, which the men reloaded, he charged for the airship. It was already a few feet off the ground. It was military issue, after all, designed for this kind of manoeuvreing.

The duke tumbled over the edge of the gondola and back inside, displaying the fact that he favoured yellow hose – *I knew there was something funny about that man!*

The dewan made a gigantic leap to grab the side of the dirigible, but even supernatural strength wasn't enough. His grip slipped and he fell back to earth with a thud. Had he been in wolf form, he might have made it, but then what? Werewolves weren't able to float.

He landed, swearing a blue streak.

Two flywaymen leaned over the edge and fired down on him.

He merely tilted his head back and bared his teeth.

Sophronia worked to lever herself out from under Captain Niall. He was bleeding from a shot to the shoulder, which seemed to have passed through and out of his back.

'Captain Niall?'

'It's not silver, Miss Temminnick. I'm in for a bit of a rough few hours but should be shipshape in no time.' He sounded more annoyed than hurt.

The dewan walked back towards them, looking very put-upon . . . and very hairy and, well, dangly. Oh, dear, and Dimity was running over to them. How on earth was Dimity going to react to dangly bits? *Will she faint? She'll probably faint.*

Sophronia righted herself and looked over Captain Niall's equally naked body. 'Captain, would you mind shifting a little to the . . . ' She went perfectly still; horror hit so hard it felt as if her skin would crawl off her flesh.

Soap?

Soap was lying, fallen and still, a surprised look on his face, clutching at the side of his chest, where a great deal of blood was pouring out of him and on to the grass. A *very* great deal indeed.

Strangely, Sophronia's mind kept on with her previous thought. *Oh, dear, that amount of blood will certainly make Dimity faint.*

She let out a raw scream, like that of an animal at the slaughter. It was coming out of her own mouth, but she couldn't control it. And then she was moving, shoving away poor Captain Niall, her arms no longer weak from shovelling coal. She threw herself across the distance separating her from Soap and knelt next to him.

'Miss, what a noise,' reprimanded Soap, his voice a whisper.

Sophronia stopped screaming. 'Soap,' she said hoarsely, 'I forbid you to die.'

'Now, miss, that's not fair. You know I always try to do as

you ask. This time it might not be up to me, and I hate to disappoint you.'

Sophronia placed both her hands over his, pressing against the wound. But there was so much blood. It was a litany in her head, *so much blood.* She couldn't do anything. For the first time in her life there wasn't a single action Sophronia could take, no information to discover, no trick to pull, no climbing to do, no action to turn about and bend to her ends.

Captain Niall came over. Captain Niall could save Soap. He was trained on the battlefield, accustomed to bullet wounds.

'Let me see, child,' he said, not unkindly. He pulled away her blood-covered hands.

Soap looked pale. Sophronia hadn't thought that possible. Normally her Soap was dark as Christmas cake and just as full of nutty goodness. He seemed flat and empty now.

The dewan was there, standing a little back. 'Goodness' sake, what's wrong *now?*' He was not intentionally unkind; at the sight of Soap's wound his gruffness turned soft. 'Ah, dear me.'

Soap's eyes were emptying. There was no twinkle there any more.

I'll take serious and longing over empty. 'Oh, please, Soap, please don't die. What'll I do without you? Who'll keep me grounded?'

'Now, now, miss, don't be silly, I never was all that ...' His voice faded off. Then he said, as if surprised, 'Burns a bit, that does.'

Captain Niall looked up from his examination. 'No good,

I'm afraid. Even if we had a surgeon to hand, looks like it's gone through to the gut, nothing fixes that. I'm so very sorry.'

Sophronia barely registered that Dimity and Sidheag had joined them. Her mind had no thought in it but blood.

Sidheag knelt next to her. Reserved, austere Sidheag was weeping openly. Tears carved rivulets down her soot-covered face. Dimity stood back, her hand covering her mouth, her eyes wide in horror.

'You're not fainting?' Sophronia enquired, dumbly. Her voice sounded as if it came out of a mechanical – tinny, distanced, unemotional.

'This is too serious for fainting,' replied Dimity. And then, because they'd been friends for so long, 'What are we going to do?'

Sophronia felt her face tingle. *I'm supposed to be able to fix things*. She wanted to scream again, and vomit, and cry all at once. It felt as if the skin around her eyes would split open under the strain. And there was so much blood, and nothing she could do. There was *nothing* she could do.

'Well,' said the dewan, 'at least it's not someone important.'

Sophronia rounded on him. 'You!' There was no *my lord*. She pointed a finger into his chest. She was about two heads shorter and half his weight.

He didn't know how to respond. 'Yes, little miss?'

'You're an Alpha, aren't you?'

'Of course, miss.'

'True Alpha?'

'Of course, miss!'

'Bite him.'

'What!'

'Go on, bite him!'

The dewan looked utterly confused at being ordered around by a small bundle of girl who was apparently quite insane.

But Lady Kingair added her insistence to the demand. 'I think you should, my lord. He'd make a fine werewolf. He's a good lad, strong and fit, nice age for it. Healthy, apart from the bullet wound.'

'But he's' – the dewan struggled – 'he's not *one of us!*'

Sophronia said, 'You take lower class for clavigers all the time. In fact, we were taught that you prefer them, unlike the vampires. What's wrong with Soap?'

'He isn't a claviger! He hasn't been prepared. He hasn't been trained in what to expect. He's not ready. He's not petitioned. He's not paid his dues in service. It's against the supernatural order.' The dewan protested. 'He's not from England!'

'He most certainly is! He's from Tooting Beck!' protested Sophronia.

The dewan said, 'I mean, his skin colour!'

'It's a perfectly lovely colour!' protested Dimity. *Dimity, of all people.*

'He said he'd consider it. He was talking like he'd try, just the other night,' insisted Sophronia.

Soap blinked at the argument going on around him. 'Yes,' he croaked.

'See that! Go on, then, you bite him, my lord, prove you're the superior Alpha.'

The dewan threw his hands up. 'That is *not* how it works.'

Sophronia scrabbled for something to threaten him with. She hadn't a sundowner weapon. She hadn't even a silver knife. The dewan was too strong for her to attack him outright, anyway; he'd simply brush her aside.

She had nothing but bargaining left. And she could think of only one thing the dewan might want. She bartered herself. 'Do this and when I'm trained I'll indenture to you as an intelligencer. I'm good, you ask Captain Niall. And when I'm done, I'll be even better. I'll be the best there is, just so you won't regret it.'

Captain Niall said, 'Miss Temminnick, is this wise?'

The dewan seemed even more startled by this attempt at bribery, but he did pause. He looked down at Soap and then up at Captain Niall. 'Is she *that* good?'

'One of the best Mademoiselle Geraldine's has had in a long while. She will be an asset to whoever holds her contract in whatever form.'

Competitive instinct. Werewolves had a strong competitive instinct; Sophronia played on that. 'Mrs Barnaclegoose wants me.'

'Mrs who?'

She tried another one. 'Lord Akeldama has already given me patron gifts.'

'Has he, indeed?'

That was a name he knew.

The dewan appeared to be considering everything that had happened recently – the fact that Sophronia had kidnapped a train and scared off a duke. But he was no fool. Only a cautious werewolf could have survived so long a loner and sit in the queen's shadow. 'It's a fair offer. But you understand our deal will stand whether my bite is successful or not?'

Hope sprang in Sophronia's chest. Hope and fear and horror, but mostly hope. 'I understand Soap's survival is not a matter of your ability. It is a matter of his soul.'

'Or lack thereof. And you are willing to risk his life and your future on such a small chance?'

Soap was limp and silent now, his eyes heavy lidded. They were running out of time.

Sophronia took a breath, face still tingling with the strain. 'I am.'

The dewan nodded, decided. 'Very well, then, I will try. It would be better, ladies, if you were not present. This is not a pretty undertaking. Captain, if you would?'

Captain Niall limped around and forcibly picked Sophronia and Sidheag up, one under each arm, and carried them away. Meekly, Dimity followed, carrying Bumbersnoot under her own arm in a similar manner.

Captain Niall deposited them down near the track, far enough away so they could not turn to see what happened, but not so far that they could not hear.

It was not a pleasant symphony. There were slavering growls and groans, crunches and slurps, moans and cracks. Soap made barely any noise, too weak. There was no doubt he would have screamed if he could. Sophronia knew it was painful. Captain Niall said it hurt every time but it was worse at the beginning. It was an awful way to die, trying for immortality, and most people did die.

Sidheag was sick all over the rail. This was a little startling, because she was the only one to have seen or heard such a thing before. Captain Niall held her steady and soothed her softly. Perhaps that was the problem, perhaps she knew too much of what was happening. And Soap was her friend, too. Sophronia tried not to think about it.

Sophronia only sat, shaking. Had she damned Soap to a gruesome death, alone at the jaws of a beast? Had she made everything worse? Had she the right to make such a choice for him at all? Even if he had claimed that this was what he wanted. She had sworn she wouldn't help, and now she'd made it happen. *My word is worth nothing.* Dimity huddled next to her, patting her futilely on one shoulder, telling her over and over again that it would be all right. Everything would turn out for the best, in the end.

Eventually, the sounds stopped and the quiet of night descended and there was nothing but stillness.

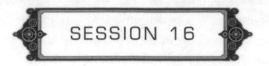

The Parting of the Ways

'He will have to stay with me.' The dewan spoke softly over Soap's sleeping form.

There was blood smeared about the dewan's mouth and down into the hair of his chest. He was trying futilely to wipe it off with a rag. It helped to think that he was a very sloppy eater and they had just finished a tomato soup course. Sophronia suppressed a hysterical thought – *a Soap course!*

She was sitting with Soap's head in her lap. It might have been awkward or embarrassing, particularly in public – although after everything that had happened, what did Sophronia care two figs for that any more? – except that Soap's head was that of a wolf. So was the rest of him. His fur was very thick and coarse and pitch black, like the coal for his beloved boilers. *He'll never float again*, thought Sophronia. He lay in the deep sleep of an exhausted puppy, but his wounds were heal-

ing. Right before Sophronia's eyes the bullet wound was closing and new fur growing over it. And his savaged neck, a gift
from the dewan, was knitting back together like cloth under
the invisible hand of an expert seamstress. The dewan had
explained that newly made werewolves stayed in wolf form for
the entirety of their first night. Soap had better do so, anyway,
to accelerate his healing.

'Stay with you? While you deal with the Kingair pack?'

'No, Miss Temminnick, I don't believe you take my meaning. He'll have to stay with me for a long time. I'm a loner, I
have no pack, neither does he, but as I've shifted him' – there
was pride in the dewan's voice; to metamorphose a new werewolf successfully was rare – 'he must stay with me to learn
control. It's my responsibility to teach him.'

'How long will it take?' Sophronia was simply glad Soap
wasn't dead. Separation seemed a paltry price to pay.

'Years, even decades.'

That is a long time.

'It depends on who he is.'

That part, Sophronia could answer. 'He's a good man, my
lord. You'll like him. Smart and capable and hardworking and
funny and fun and a leader, in his way, and . . .'

'I understand, Miss Temminnick,' and he sounded as if he
understood more than he let on, more than just her words, 'but
sometimes men are different as wolves.'

'Not my Soap.'

'We shall see.' The dewan finished with the rag and tossed
it aside. If the cold night air gave him any trouble, he didn't
show it. 'I might have to keep him a secret, for a while.' He

didn't explain the statement, but Sophronia smelled werewolf politics all over it. 'I trust you and your friends will be discreet?'

Sophronia arched a brow at him. 'Intelligencer trained, my lord.'

He chuckled as if at a joke, then sobered. 'I won't hold you to our bargain. A new werewolf is gift enough. It happens so rarely.'

Sophronia was honestly surprised and even a little touched. 'I keep my word, my lord. In this, if nothing else. If you'll only allow me to finish my schooling first?' *Plus, I have Picklemen to thwart.* Like it or not, with one bullet Duke Golborne had decided Sophronia's position. Every part of her was now bent on undermining his plans. She no longer cared what the Picklemen intended, she was going to stop them. No one shot her Soap!

Captain Niall said, from where he was sitting with Sidheag nearby, 'I'd take her up on it, my lord. You'll be a good fit, all three of you.'

The dewan nodded. 'Very well. Patronage it is. And don't think I've forgot your commitment, Captain. We need to get back on the run as soon as this new pup has mastered his paws.'

Sophronia asked, too casually, 'Why *do* you need Captain Niall, sir?'

'No hidden agenda there, little spy. He's to take over as Alpha of Kingair. Always was the intent. I can't leave them leaderless, not as I'm shipping them out with the Coldsteam Guards in a month. Exile as punishment for attempted treason. India is the best place for them, fighting on the front. Keep them distracted from their little plots. Keep them away from Lord Maccon.'

Sophronia was confused. 'But much as I respect the captain, he told us he isn't a real Alpha.' He'd said as much to the pupils on several occasions, without any shame. Some werewolves were Alphas, some weren't. *Only Alphas think it matters. Frankly, I prefer not*, he'd said. *Alphas tend not to live all that long.*

'No, but he's the best loner I've got in England right now. And he is a passing good military captain.'

'Oh, thank you kindly, dewan.' Captain Niall did not look particularly upset by the insult. Perhaps it wasn't an insult.

As the dewan was to be her patron, Sophronia decided he might as well get accustomed to her questioning him, so she said, 'But Captain Niall didn't do anything wrong! It isn't fair that he be punished with them.'

'All too often, being a werewolf isn't fair. Your friend there will have to learn that soon, too.'

Sophronia reflected on her own reaction to Soap's affections. 'I think that's one thing he's accustomed to already, my lord.'

The dewan said, 'I think we can move him now.'

'I have a suggestion,' said Sophronia. 'If we could find some coal and get that train up and running – why not just take it north, as we intended? You can travel during the day and night that way, and won't lose time tonight while Soap sleeps. You'll have to take Sidheag with you, of course. She knows how to drive the train.'

The dewan was intrigued despite himself. 'I could declare the train property of the Crown. Vampires stashed some fancy tech on it, you say? Well, if the Picklemen want it, might be a good idea to hide it away in Scotland.'

Sophronia heartily agreed. 'Give the transmitter to Kingair. It'll be safe in werewolf hands. It'll be a little while before the pack leaves, correct? By then they will have made it impossible for the Picklemen or the vampires to retrieve it.'

The dewan was looking at Sophronia with new eyes. 'I see what you mean, Captain.'

Sophronia continued to stroke Soap's fur, unconcerned by this scrutiny.

The dewan surprised her, though. 'While you have been plotting, little miss, so have I.' He turned to look at Sidheag, who was sitting only slightly too close to Captain Niall.

'It seems all this bother is because I ignored your request to join the pack, Lady Kingair. I realise now that even if I order you back to that school, you'll keep running away. Send the pack off to India and next thing I know, you'll stow away on a steamer.'

Sidheag gave him an enigmatic look.

Sophronia watched this exchange from under lowered lids.

'You're a little young for marriage,' said the dewan. His eyes were speculative.

Sidheag looked startled at that.

'But I think a long engagement would cover all but the sternest of societal sticklers. If you're in foreign climes, no one will notice how long you take, and if you're married by the time you get back, no one will be the wiser. Overseas campaigns can take decades.'

Everyone was looking confused.

Sidheag said, 'I don't follow, my lord.'

'I'll send the announcement to the *Chirrup*,' said the dewan to Captain Niall.

Captain Niall nodded. He didn't look upset, only resigned.

Sidheag cottoned on at last. 'Oh, dear me no! I mean, I couldn't. I mean, I couldn't force him into anything. What an awful thing to do!'

'Enough. You cannot object to an arranged marriage. You, a single young lady, wish to take up residence with a pack of werewolves. Lord Maccon is gone, and in the absence of blood relations, you at least must be engaged!' The dewan was not to be argued with. Not again in the same night.

Dimity piped up with, 'He's right, you know, Sidheag. And you could always cry off later, I mean overseas, if you really wanted to.'

Sidheag looked sideways at the handsome werewolf captain. 'You don't object?'

Captain Niall said, face impassive, 'It's a fair arrangement, and Miss Plumleigh-Teignmott is correct. It would help to cement my claim to the Kingair pack leadership, if I were engaged to the Lady of Kingair.'

'That sounds sensible enough,' replied Sidheag, sounding a little disappointed.

Then the werewolf smiled at her, shyly. 'You're far too young for me, of course. But with a long engagement, perhaps I might be given the chance to earn your affection?'

Sidheag ducked her head, self-conscious. 'I'd like that.'

The dewan looked self-satisfied, as if he'd suspected this result.

Dimity sighed at the romance of it all. 'Imagine, a long overseas engagement, how marvellous!'

Sophronia's heart sank a little. First Soap and now Sidheag. Life was going to be lonely at Mademoiselle Geraldine's. But she was excited for her friend; after all, this was what Sidheag wanted – to be with her pack.

The dewan slapped his hands together and rubbed them, the clapping sound jarring in the damp night. 'Good, that's settled, then. Now I'm going to go and see about some coal for this train of yours. Captain, if you'll get the party there and settled? Ladies' – he looked severely at Dimity and Sophronia – 'I'll buy you two first-class tickets back to Wootton Bassett at the next station. And some proper attire.'

Considering the fact that he was still naked, both girls giggled.

The dewan trudged off into the night, to change shape behind a bush somewhere.

Captain Niall stood and, like a proper suitor, kept his top hat held in the defensive position. He turned to offer Sidheag his free hand. 'My lady?'

Sidheag took it, graciously. Her long, angular face wore an expression of wonder that made it almost handsome. *Whatever this relationship she develops with Captain Niall becomes, it will alter her for ever.* It wasn't so awful a thing that Sidheag would not be returning to Mademoiselle Geraldine's. *She doesn't need finishing school any more, anyway.*

Dimity bumped against Sophronia. 'Don't be sad, you still have me and Bumbersnoot.'

Captain Niall let go of Sidheag's hand and scooped up

Soap's limp wolf body with one arm. He'd recovered entirely from his own bullet wound. Even though Sophronia knew from experience that Soap was no lightweight, Captain Niall made it look easy. Soon Soap, too, would boast that casual werewolf strength. Soon Soap, too, would have that controlled, powerful way of moving. Will he tie a top hat to his head? Sophronia wondered.

She and Sidheag and Dimity trailed behind the captain back to the train.

'An arranged marriage. Sidheag, are you certain you don't mind?' asked Sophronia.

'Who else would have me?' joked Sidheag.

Dimity said, 'You have excellent standing!'

'And that's about all I have.'

'Do stop being silly,' reprimanded Sophronia, perhaps too sharply. She was exhausted by the physical and emotional trials of the last few days.

Sidheag replied, startled into honesty. 'He understands me, I understand him. Good marriages have been built on less.'

'Why, Sidheag, could it be you are a little enamoured with the good captain already?' Dimity's eyes shone.

Sidheag said, gruff and sharp, 'Of course I am. Who at the school isn't?'

Sophronia understood that it wasn't her own feelings that worried Sidheag. 'He will learn to love you. You're quite worthy of it.'

'The way he cared for you after the masquerade, I rather think he fancies you already.' Dimity was disposed to be less practical on the matter.

Sidheag nodded, looking optimistic. 'We will learn to love each other; it will all work out in the end.' This was remarkably prosaic, even for her. 'And I get to be with my pack, and I get to travel. That'll be fun.'

Dimity clasped her hands. 'The grand tour!'

'I hardly think fighting in the front lines of the British Army is a tour,' corrected Sophronia.

Dimity sighed. 'Why must you always crush my fantasies?'

'Sorry, Dimity, forget I said anything. Well, Sidheag, I, for one, will miss you terribly. How am I going to take down all the Picklemen in England without you?'

Sidheag laughed. 'Oh, you'll manage.'

'I'll help,' said Dimity. 'And there's always Bumbersnoot.' She patted the little mechanimal cheerfully.

Sophronia grinned. 'Quite right, we can't forget Bumbersnoot.'